Handmaiden of Palmyra

The moment the centurion Marcus's body was aligned with hers, Samoya became a woman possessed. She no longer had control over her movements or her emotions. She swayed, undulating like a dancer, her hips going one way and her breasts the other – but with every inch of her body touching his.

And then she let her hands wander down. Marcus was quite naked under his uniform. She had to feel his cock; to take it in her hands; to see it. She couldn't hold back another moment. So she looked at it and gasped; it was as magnificent as she had hoped.

Other books by the author

Odalisque
The House in New Orleans

Handmaiden of Palmyra
Fleur Reynolds

BLACK LACE

Black Lace books contain sexual fantasies.
In real life, always practise safe sex.

This edition published in 2002 by
Black Lace
Thames Wharf Studios
Rainville Road
London W6 9HA

Originally published 1994

Printed and bound by Mackays of Chatham PLC

ISBN 0 352 32919 X

Acknowledgments

Every name has its own story and for their love and support, past and present, I thank the following women: Beryl, Christine, Margaret Mary, Fiona, Sarah, Mireille, Ruth, Jane, Lisa-Anne, Sonja, Rosie, Reiko, Mariejanig, Francine, Sabah, Mozhan, Myrtle, Maggie, Ine, Suzette, Badiene, Frances, Roxanna, Peigi and Heather.

The following people really did exist and I have attributed to them characteristics they are known to have had. The major actions in their lives, as illustrated in this story, are as true as I believe them to be:

Queen Zenobia
King Odainat
Paul of Samosata
Cassius Longinus
Firmus the Egyptian
Prince Maaen
King Hairan
Lucius Aurelian
Timogenes

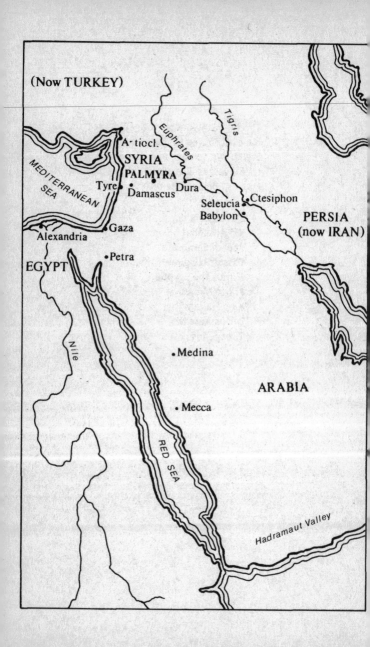

Syria 260 AD

Chapter One

'It had been very exciting,' thought the young Lady Samoya, rolling over, pressing her taut, bare belly against the rush matting on the marble temple floor, hearing the priestess's voice but not her words. Lady Samoya was not concentrating. Her mind had drifted back to her visit to the palace where she had seen explicitly erotic murals of the gods copulating with the mortals.

Though familiar with her own body and those of her female slaves, she had never seen a man naked. The size, length and shape of the gods' sexual equipment had amazed her. Why hadn't she noticed the equivalent bulge on the men she knew? Or was it only male gods who had such huge members hanging between their legs? And was this why there was a look of such ecstasy on the mortals' faces?

Samoya remembered how she had eyed up Anthony, the handsome, young, Roman cleric, and had wondered if, under his severe black robe, he possessed an instrument to rival that of the gods. She had felt an immediate desire to find out. The combination of that thought, his presence and the explicit murals had caused a sudden tingling deep inside her.

3

Anthony had been asked by his employer, Paul of Samosata, the Bishop of Antioch, to take his client's daughter on a tour of his palace and he had unwillingly agreed. His unwillingness had increased at the sight of Samoya. She was enticingly beautiful and her erotic beauty had disturbed him. She had a straight nose and a mouth that was ruby red, very full, and pouted. She also had a long mane of bound and braided red-gold hair. The criss-crossings of her hair ribbons were echoed in her leather thonged sandals as they wound up her long legs. Anthony vaguely wondered if it was that tightness, that sense of confinement that excited him. He would love to see the whole of her naked body bound with strips of leather. Anthony gave a shudder of desire as her pale oval-shaped face, with its violet-blue eyes fringed with long black lashes, haughtily inspected him. He found the forthrightness of her stare completely bewitching. And softly sexual. He had an incredible desire to touch her, to feel her breasts, her neat bottom, her sex. But she was out of bounds. He knew that. Anthony moved further away from her, so that he wasn't tempted, and nodded and smiled at her big blonde female slave.

Samoya had wondered how she could manage to touch Anthony's penis; he was purposefully standing to one side and avoiding her eyes. Normally, when she wanted to do something that her widowed father would not have approved of, she colluded with her favourite slave, the tall blonde, Nordic Irene. But there was no time for that now; besides, Samoya could see that Irene also found him interesting. She was giving him come-hither glances. That had annoyed Samoya, even more so when she noticed Anthony give Irene a slight nod and a sly smile. There had been talk of Irene's mother being a Christian. She wondered if Irene had given him a secret signal. Well, whether it was true or not Samoya didn't know, and didn't care. She had to work out what to do and do it quickly, before the tour was over.

Samoya looked at Anthony out of the corner of her eyes. He was handsome but not particularly tall, just a good height. He had light brown hair, hazel eyes, a long thin nose with slightly flared nostrils and a wide sensuous mouth. But what struck her most was the beauty of his long tapering hands. Then she had wondered if certain other parts of him were long and tapering too, and if he was wearing anything under his robe. She gambled that he wasn't. Even Christians wouldn't take their bizarre ideas to such lengths as to punish themselves by wearing underclothes when it was so incredibly hot.

Supposedly looking at the wall paintings, Samoya contemplated the problem. How could she unobtrusively put her hand beneath Anthony's cassock and feel his manhood? She decided that if she was to move back suddenly and deliberately stumble, she could put out a hand to stop herself from falling and allow that hand to race up Anthony's thighs and touch his penis. Having worked out what to do Samoya then had to manœuvre herself into a position to do it.

'And this is Leda and the Swan,' Anthony's voice broke into her reverie.

'Oh yes, Leda,' said Samoya, knowingly, 'wife of Tyndareus and mother of Clytemnestra. The swan is really Zeus ravishing her.'

Samoya didn't find that painting as interesting as the previous ones. It was not as graphic. She gave a hint of a smile and walked in front of Anthony so that he was made even more aware of the slimness of her waist and the swell and sway of her hips.

Samoya had asked to go with her father to the Christian bishop's palace and it was not at all what she had been expecting. It was luxurious in the extreme and the bishop kept an army of chefs who served food constantly and he made sure there was a liberal flow of the best wines from the Lebanon and Italy. Also the whole place was furnished with the best furniture and the finest silken wall hangings. And, although the bishop and his secretary were dressed in plain black robes, his beautiful and voluptuous female slaves were clothed in flimsy transparent silk showing off their alluring young bodies to great advantage. Samoya thought they looked more like women of sensual indulgence than poor downtrodden slaves of harsh, penitent Christians. Which belied the general rumour that Christians denied themselves the pleasures of the flesh. Which they called bad, wicked, a sin. That didn't seem to be the case with the bishop. Perhaps, Samoya thought, that was why he was having trouble with his community; some of them wanted his palace shut down and him thrown out, to be replaced by a severe mystic from Alexandria.

Samoya had moved closer to Anthony, away from her chaperoning slaves and, in a sensual whisper, had asked him about his life at the palace. Anthony had balked at answering. He had gazed at her lovely, pure young face unable to tell her of the Bacchanalian orgies that took place most evenings. Instead he had suggested that they return to the garden where the bishop and her father were wine-tasting. And that had been the moment Samoya had chosen to move back on him and fall swooning to the floor. Anthony, rushing to her aid, had knelt down beside her. As he did so Samoya had quickly slid her hands up his legs. Before her slaves had surrounded her, picked her up and carried her away, Samoya had managed to touch his hidden and bare length.

At the moment of impact, when her fingertips met his skin, Anthony had given a gasp of pleasure and surprise. As her fingers deftly surrounded his member a myriad of highly charged and sexual visions assaulted him, swirled around, and burst from him in a loud gasp. Now, more than ever he wanted to grab her, lay her on the floor, penetrate her, take her into ecstasy. With speed her hand had stroked the length of his thick and stiffening member. He had groaned with frustration and excitement.

Samoya had felt the softness of Anthony's testicles and the instant hardening of his penis and found it exhilarating. She had immediately appreciated that it had been her groping fingers that had made his manhood grow. Now she knew how men packaged their sex. It was kept tiny and concertinaed until aroused. Then it sprang into action. Samoya found that discovery thrilling. It gave her a sense of power and it was a revelation she would never forget.

Excited by the memory of her hands fondling Anthony's phallus, Samoya realised she was now wet between her legs. Unwittingly, she let out a long sensuous sigh.

'Samoya!' said the priestess, sharply, angrily. 'You are not concentrating. Get up and do the whole of that dance again. And you'll continue to do it until you get it right. Ever since your father took you to that wretched Christian's palace your mind's been anywhere except where it should be.'

The priestess was furious with her brother, Pernel, for taking his daughter to meet the Christian. It was not so much the licentious man himself she objected to. She could cope with him. It was his religion. And as far as the Priestess Verenia was concerned the newly founded sect was pernicious, destructive and, for women, both highly dangerous and highly derogatory. Verenia did not want her niece to be influenced by it in any way.

'I forbid you to go there again,' Verenia had said to Pernel and Samoya after they had let slip where they'd been. 'We do not associate with Christians.'

'Why?' Samoya had asked.

'Because they have some very strange ideas. You are young and could become contaminated by them. They do not allow priestesses in their religion. And their priests' main objective seems to be to deny women, their functions and their contributions to life and this will lead to a terrible lack of balance in the world.'

Samoya had protested that she had seen no evidence of this at the palace. Samoya's defence of the Christians had immediately alarmed Verenia. Her worst fears were being realised. They were trying to convert her. She had quizzed Samoya in depth about her visit and, not being entirely satisfied with her 'untruthful' answers, had brought forward the date for her initiation. This in turn had worried Samoya. She knew that as soon as her initiation ceremony was over her father would begin to organise her marriage. But marriage was not part of her plan. She wanted to go to Athens and study to become a doctor. She had learnt about herbs and their various properties, which ones were good and which ones were poisonous. She needed the priestess on her side. Her whole future was at stake, she had to get her own way with her father and stop any marriage plans he might have. The one person who could help was Verenia. Her word was law.

'Samoya,' said the priestess wearily. 'Stop day dreaming and do those steps properly.'

'I'm sorry, Aunt Verenia,' said Samoya, meekly and contritely. After the eighth time Samoya executed her dance perfectly.

'Now you may go,' said the priestess smiling at Samoya.

'Aunt,' replied Samoya, feeling the warmth of Verenia's smile and deciding it was the moment to chance her luck. 'Please, Aunt, would you ask my father if I can go to Athens and become a doctor?'

'I will,' said Verenia, and Samoya's heart gave an upward lurch of happiness only to sink quickly as the priestess continued, 'but not for a couple of days. There's too much to do here. Now, dress and go quickly to the gymnasium or you'll be late for your weapon training.' Verenia bent down and gave Samoya a quick kiss. Samoya knew it was true and not an excuse and she thanked the gods Verenia wasn't still annoyed with her.

After putting on her multi-coloured, geometrically designed, pure silk skirt together with its matching bodice, Samoya collected up her slaves who were patiently waiting behind a huge curtain at the back of the temple. They were not allowed to see the sacred dance Samoya had been practising.

The three girls were more or less her own age. They had lived with Samoya since birth. They were the daughters of other slaves and born in Pernel's household. Except Irene. Pernel had bought her, a five-year-old orphan from one of the Germanic tribes from a garrison town on the Black Sea. Pernel had been much taken with the paleness of her and her sweet temperament. He kept her as a rarity but insisted her mass of thick blonde hair was always tied up and covered. He didn't want her stolen.

Irene was Samoya's daily confidante and at night they slept together. She had always slept in Samoya's room but recently Samoya had invited her into her bed. No one knew they gently stroked each other to sleep.

Samoya linked arms with Irene as they made their way quickly through the suburban streets to the gymnasium. She was looking forward to her lessons and to a good gossip with her friend Zenobia.

When Samoya arrived at the large building on the outskirts of the city she found the doors were locked, the lessons were over and everyone had gone except one slave.

'The Lady Zenobia told me to tell you that she's gone to practise outside the city.'

'She could have waited,' said Samoya, huffily.

'And she's taken your equipment with her,' said the girl.

'All of it?' asked Samoya. 'The bows and arrows and the javelins?' There were times when Samoya wished Zenobia wasn't quite so independent and headstrong.

9

'Yes,' replied the slave. 'And I know exactly where she'll be so I'm to guide you.'

Samoya found the slim figure of Zenobia who was practising javelin throwing on an incline overlooking the city. She sat down when Samoya appeared.

'It's too hot to do any more today,' said Zenobia. 'Anyhow, what kept you so long? I've been here for ages.'

'The priestess. She kept making me do that dance again and again. She said I wasn't concentrating . . .'

'Were you?'

'Not really.'

'Were you thinking about that man, Anthony?'

'Yes.'

'Don't. A Christian bishop's secretary is no match for you.'

'Who said anything about a match and marriage! Anyway don't you ever think of men?' replied Samoya, peevishly.

'No, not men, only princes,' replied Zenobia.

Suddenly the distant sound of marching feet hit their ears. The two beautiful young women shielded their eyes from the sun as they looked away from the city of Antioch, down the other side of the hill. Soldiers in neat formation were heading straight for them.

'Persians,' screamed the horrified slaves, wanting to run.

'Don't be ridiculous,' said Zenobia sternly. 'They're Romans. Look at the uniforms and the standard.'

'What shall we do?' asked Samoya.

'Do? That's a silly question. The Romans are our allies,' replied Zenobia.

'I meant,' countered Samoya, 'do we sit down here and wait for them to pass or do we run ahead of them?'

'Why should we run anywhere? We're going to walk sedately into Antioch. And, if the Romans catch up with us, so be it. Mmm, I wonder if our war with the Persians is over.'

They were half a mile from the city gates when Zenobia jumped across a log blocking their path and fell, badly twisting her ankle. She gave a sharp yell and sat down by the roadside.

'Look how it's swelling,' cried Zenobia, staring at her feet.

Samoya immediately knelt beside her friend and felt the offending ankle.

'It's all right. Nothing's broken, it's only a sprain.'

Then Samoya tore a strip of clothing from the hem of the nearest slave's dress and wound it loosely around Zenobia's foot, not as a bandage but as a sling, and gave Zenobia the two ends to hold on to.

'Hop and hold on to me. I want you down by the water's edge,' said Samoya.

'Why?' asked Zenobia.

'Because I'm going to dip your foot in the cool water. If you put it in and take it out then put it in again it will take the swelling down.'

Samoya and the slaves helped manœuvre Zenobia past the reeds so that she could put her foot into the water.

'Oh!' Zenobia exclaimed. 'That's cold.'

'It's meant to be. It wouldn't do you any good if it wasn't.'

'That's very clever of you,' said Zenobia.

'I told you I want to be a doctor,' replied Samoya.

'Do you think you'll be able to?'

'No reason why not,' said Samoya, her eyes shining at the thought. 'I've asked Priestess Verenia to have a word with my father.'

'So?'

'He has a great respect for her and for the Goddess,' Samoya stopped short seeing the expression of doubt on Zenobia's face. 'You've forgotten she's my father's sister. And if she's on my side . . .'

'The training's expensive.'

'So what, my father's rich. He can afford it.'

11

'Yes, but with your brothers away fighting the Persians doesn't he rely on you to help with the business?'

'Yes.'

'And if they should be killed and anything happens to him well . . . Aren't you his heir?'

'Yes. Look, why are you making difficulties where they don't exist?'

'I don't know, I just can't see it happening,' said Zenobia, suddenly very serious.

'What do you mean you can't see it happening? Now you're being ridiculous. Look, if the priestess says I'll make a good doctor, my father will agree.'

'When I'm queen I'll build schools of medicine here in Syria,' said Zenobia, dreamily.

'When you're queen!' exclaimed Samoya.

'Yes,' replied Zenobia. 'A fortune-teller told me I'd be a queen and loved by two emperors.'

'Oh!' said Samoya, a note of disbelief in her voice. She stared at her friend. She was very attractive but she was skinny and that was not fashionable. Samoya's father told her every man preferred big voluptuous women. They wanted someone rounded with rolls of flesh they could get hold of, cuddle up to and find comfort in. Samoya smiled to herself remembering how her father was always trying to fatten her up with delectable pastries and delicious sweets. Perhaps Zenobia was going to become fat but there was no sign of that yet. Also, although she was very beautiful and had a good mind, which some men did like, Zenobia was very argumentative. Which, her father said, most men didn't like. So how was she going to manage to make not one but two emperors fall in love with her? Of course Zenobia's father was rich. Richer than her father. Perhaps he was going to buy her an emperor.

Zenobia, trailing her foot in the water, caught the tone of disbelief in her friend's voice.

'That's what I asked,' said Zenobia.

'What?' exclaimed Samoya.

'If my father was going to buy me an emperor.'

'How did you know what I was thinking?' asked Samoya.

'It was obvious.'

'And what else did this fortune-teller say?'

'She said, "When I say love, I mean love". So that put me in my place,' said Zenobia laughing, then adding, 'but she also told me that I would reign until the sun went from west to east.'

'But it can't.'

'Exactly. So I'm going to reign forever.'

'Did you pay this fortune-teller good money?' asked Samoya sceptically.

'No.'

'But you believed her!'

'Why shouldn't I?'

'Perhaps she tells every girl she'll be a queen.'

'No. I don't think so.'

'Mmm, and when did this fortune-teller tell you this?' asked Samoya.

'Here, whilst I was waiting for you. She appeared out of nowhere, grasped my hand and told me. She said she had wanted to do it the other day when I was shopping in the market-place.'

'Are you still allowed to go to the market-place?' Samoya interrupted with astonishment.

'Yes, of course.'

'My father won't let me go there.'

'Why not?'

'He says it's a place of insurrection, and dangerous.'

'I had a couple of eunuchs protecting me.'

'My father won't even let me go with them. He says there are too many brawls there these days and he says it's all the fault of those Christians. Anyway where is this fortune-teller now? Perhaps she could tell my fortune.'

'She went towards Antioch,' said Zenobia.

'What did she look like?' asked Samoya.

13

'Ancient, toothless, with masses of gold bangles on her arms and long ear-rings and she walked with a stick and had a bright red mark in the middle of her forehead.'

The two friends were so busy talking that they failed to realise the soldiers were approaching until their slaves began to get very fidgety and some of them started to cry.

'What's the matter now?' Zenobia asked angrily.

'The soldiers, m'lady,' they cried.

Samoya started to her feet as the standard-bearer came into view. Zenobia tried to do the same but found she couldn't stand, and she couldn't walk as her foot throbbed too much.

'But I'm not staying here looking like a washerwoman in front of those Romans,' said Zenobia.

Then Samoya ordered a number of slaves to carry her friend on their shoulders. It was uncomfortable, awkward and slow, but Zenobia preferred it. And nobody was going to argue with her.

Lucius Aurelian was a man lost in thought. He had managed to come through the war unscathed and he put it down to his belief in his sun god, Elagabalus. Every time he went into battle he prayed for himself and his men. He also prayed that he be allowed to see the green mountains of his homeland again, that beautiful country that faced Italy across the blue Adriatic. He was tired of land-locked deserts, harsh, arid mountains and peoples with ways he didn't understand. Lucius Aurelian was a handsome, stocky, sturdy peasant and he was a man in a hurry. He wanted to get to Rome. He wanted to be the first commander to tell the Emperor Gallienus that the Persians were thoroughly beaten and it would take two generations before there were enough men in Persia old enough to form another army. He smiled to himself as he reflected they had given the Persians an extra difficulty. He, and his ally,

Odainat the Prince of Palmyra, had made certain there were no generals left alive to teach them war games. The Persian Army was utterly decimated. Lucius Aurelian's one regret was not taking the Persian king captive. That wily, wicked old monarch had fled to the furthest, most easterly part of his kingdom. Lucius's thoughts were interrupted by his second-in-command riding up beside him.

'Nice, sir,' said Marcus Protarchus.

'What?' asked Lucius Aurelian.

'Peace,' his young officer replied. And pointed to the gentle river flowing through the fertile plain and women happily washing their clothes whilst their children played jumping up and down and splashing in the water.

'Yes. *Pax Romana*, and long may it last,' agreed the commander, thinking it hadn't always been like that.

Some years before, the Persians had got as far as Antioch, sacked the city and massacred everyone on the plain. Lucius had seen the result and that was anything but pleasant. But now there was peace. There were still pockets of Persians, soldiers turned bandits, needing to be rounded up. They were causing trouble in the scrublands and in the desert but generally there was peace. He began to think of the pleasures of peacetime. Of good food, wine and women. He hadn't had much of any of these things for some time.

The straight, wide road, built centuries before by previous marching armies, suddenly came to an end and they were on the outskirts of the city. The river was less wild, more domestic and houses were dotted about on its banks. Lucius Aurelian looked about him at the magnificent villas of the rich merchants and wondered which one he would choose as his billet. There was no point in rising from the ranks if one didn't take the perks that went with the position. His men would stay at the garrison but he would have some comfort. He might even take young Marcus with him. The Roman

15

commander took a paternal interest in Marcus. He was from Ethiopia and Lucius had found him as a young orphan wandering the streets of Alexandria. He was beautiful, with a fine muscular body and Lucius had immediately taken him into the army. He would rather he was killed as a soldier than live misused in the male brothels of the city.

Marcus had proved a good, loyal soldier but Lucius Aurelian recognised a young man straining at the bit. He might find peace too overwhelming and take his pleasures too seriously. Or fall in love, or worse, fall in lust. Aurelian decided Marcus was far too good-looking to be left to the tender mercies of the Harpies in the taverns of Antioch.

'Marcus.'

'Yes, sir.'

'See that villa over there.' Lucius Aurelian gestured away from the road to a mansion on an incline surrounded by orange trees.

'Yes, sir.'

'Ride over and inform the owner that he will have the honour of putting up his Imperial Majesty's representative for the next couple of days. I will ride on to the garrison.'

'Yes, sir.'

'And Marcus . . .'

'Yes sir?'

'Tell them his second-in-command will be with him.'

'Oh! Thank you, sir,' said Marcus, and cantered off towards the villa.

Lucius Aurelian gave a wry grin at the next, and curious, sight that greeted him. A group of young women, carrying bows and arrows and javelins were endeavouring to walk with one girl slung between them as if she was dead. But it was quite obvious from the squeals of merriment that she was very much alive. Although he did make out the odd moan of anguish coming from her.

Lucius Aurelian halted his procession and rode over to see what had happened. Samoya saw him first.

'Whatever you do don't drop Lady Zenobia,' she said sharply to the slaves, 'but a Roman is riding towards us.'

'Then put me down immediately,' ordered Zenobia. There was no way a Roman, whoever he was, was going to speak to her when she was at a disadvantage.

Gently, the slaves lowered Zenobia so that she stood on one foot leaning heavily on Samoya.

'You look to be in trouble,' said Lucius Aurelian, staring down on them from the height of his well-bred Arabic horse.

The slaves huddled together warily but Zenobia and Samoya gazed straight at him thinking how manly and magnificent he looked in his uniform.

'Yes. I've hurt my ankle,' announced Zenobia, surprised to find a Roman speaking Latin with a foreign peasant's accent. But his bearing was so obviously one of authority she decided he was no ordinary soldier but must be the commander. Also there was something about him, in his carriage, in the twinkle in his hard blue eyes, in his masculinity and muscularity that she found inexplicably attractive. He was interesting. Zenobia found this exciting, possibly dangerous. To her amazement she realised she wanted him to touch her. The sturdy hand now gripping his sword she wanted to be gripping her. She tossed her head and admonished herself. The thought was absurd. The man was a jumped-up peasant in Roman uniform. Nevertheless, he was in the position of power and could give her what she wanted. Zenobia decided to try her luck. She gave him her most dazzling smile.

'I don't suppose you have a spare stretcher so that I could be carried home properly,' she said.

Samoya stood open-mouthed at her friend's audacity. Lucius Aurelian burst out laughing. He had grown so used to the cowed women of the east bowing and scraping to their men that he found her barefaced effrontery utterly refreshing. He looked at her carefully. Slim and dark with flashing green-brown eyes. She had a fire in her that stirred his war-worn bones.

'Stay where you are and I'll see what I can do,' he said, and galloped back to his men.

'Zenobia, how could you!' exclaimed Samoya, when the Roman was out of earshot.

'Easily,' she replied. 'I was fed up being carried like that and my foot's really hurting. I lay up there on those girls' shoulders and I visualised being gently borne along in a litter. And suddenly . . .'

'What do you mean visualised?'

'Imagined,' said Zenobia, with studied patience.

'Oh! Do you often visualise things?' asked Samoya.

'Yes. If I want something I imagine it and then it comes to me. Of course it's not always completely as I imagined it. A makeshift stretcher's not a litter but it is closer than those slaves' shoulders.'

Moments later Lucius Aurelian returned with four foot-soldiers. He had a roll of canvas slung across his saddle. They were carrying very long poles. Lucius threw down the canvas, they unravelled it, then slotted the poles through its long-sided loops. Lucius Aurelian dismounted and bowed to Zenobia.

'Allow me,' he said and lightly picked her up.

It was at that moment of contact, when his strong arms embraced her tiny body, that their very essences were united. It was a moment so powerful that neither of them would ever forget it. And it was so unexpected and sudden that it took them both by surprise. It was almost as if their touching flesh fused and became one forever. Zenobia felt her blood coursing through her veins at a rate that made her giddy. She was feeling an excitement, mixed with apprehension, that she had not experienced before. It was like having pins and needles from the top of her head to her feet, only it was pleasant, very pleasant and she wanted more. She felt

18

as if she was burning, her very essence being consumed by his touch. She could hear her heartbeat. Hear it throbbing. But the painful pulsations in her injured foot seemed to have miraculously disappeared. She wanted him to hold her tighter, to caress her, stroke her arms, her legs, her breasts. She gave a brief glance up at his lips. What would those lips taste like? How would they feel on her chaste mouth? Zenobia closed her eyes. She dared not look at the Roman in case he guessed the turmoil inside her. Then she leant into him to smell his body.

Lucius Aurelian glanced down at the pure, young but determined face that lay against his chest and was perplexed by his own emotions. He'd had many women in his time but none had aroused the fire in his loins that the young woman he was now cradling had managed to produce. The sweet smell of her drifted into his nostrils. He found it intoxicating. He wanted to stroke her, to kiss her, to protect her, to take away the pain in her foot. He wanted to make gentle love to her and never stop loving her. Something in her response, in the language of her delicate body as she nestled into him told him that the sensations he was experiencing were not one-sided. This heightened his feelings. From a gentle loving he wanted to crush her under him, to make passionate love to her. The feel of her had ignited a sensitivity within him that in all his thirty-odd years he'd had no idea existed.

The two of them were suspended in space, unaware of anything or anyone except themselves and their own brief rapturous moment. It was a second of time that lasted an eternity. Lucius held Zenobia fractionally tighter then laid her down on the canvas.

'A stretcher fit for a queen,' he said, his voice trembling slightly as he said it. 'Now, all you have to do is tell my men where you live and they will deliver you to your home.'

They stared at one another, his blue eyes boring into

19

her green-brown ones. Something incredible had happened between them but neither gave the other the slightest indication that they knew. But they did. Every pore, every nerve ending knew the truth.

Zenobia whispered her address to the soldiers.

'Safe journey,' said Lucius Aurelian, giving her a quick salute, then he rode back to his legion.

Samoya, aware that something odd had occurred between Zenobia and the Roman, changed from one foot to the other feeling uncomfortable. She could not put her finger on it but there was a strange tension in the atmosphere. And it made her feel superfluous, unnecessary. She glanced at the disappearing figure of the soldier and then at her friend lying on the stretcher.

'Zenobia, are you all right?' she asked.

'Wonderful . . . I mean, much better,' said Zenobia with a look of warning that shouted 'don't push it Samoya, the soldiers might hear' and Samoya understood. 'Why don't you come and visit me this evening and I'll tell you then.'

'I can't,' wailed Samoya.

'Why not?' her friend snapped back as the soldiers raised her high.

'It's my last rehearsal at the temple. Have you forgotten it's my initiation tonight.'

'Yes,' said Zenobia truthfully. 'I had forgotten.'

She was one year older than Samoya and had been initiated into the mysteries of the Great Goddess the previous year.

'Then tomorrow,' she called, 'come early tomorrow and tell me everything that happens tonight and I will tell you everything, too.'

Samoya watched her friend being taken at a fast trot towards the city gate. She rounded up the slaves and they ambled slowly in the same direction. Samoya knew that whatever had happened to Zenobia it was something she could not mention in front of the soldiers. Perhaps she could get away after rehearsals, nip in and

20

see her friend before the ceremony. Then she would find out. Samoya was pondering on this and just about to enter the city gates when her attention was taken by an old crone sitting under an olive tree. She was making a gummy slurping sound with her mouth as she tried to chew bits of dried bread. She looked up as Samoya passed. Samoya noticed the red mark on her forehead and stopped. The old woman raised a crooked finger and beckoned her and Irene to sit beside her. She took hold of Samoya's hand, stared at it hard, closed her eyes then chanted:

> 'To travel to a distant place
> Of great riches and extreme bad taste
> To be a wife but love another
> However, one day you will run for cover.
> Then fortune smiles
> But you will be a widow twice
> Before you are a mother.'

Samoya, intrigued, was unable to ask the gnarled old woman a single question because she quickly dropped Samoya's hand to gaze intently into Irene's eyes. Then, almost in a trance she intoned the words:

> 'A soldier not a slave I see
> A war for you but not for me.
> Across the empire you will roam
> By three rivers, N, E, T.
> Thereby lies your destiny
> One you win, two you lose
> Three is ever more your home.'

The old woman closed her eyes and turned her back on Samoya and her slave.

'But . . .' said Samoya.

'Leave me,' said the ancient, sternly. 'I have nothing more to say.'

'Payment,' said Samoya. 'How do we pay you?'

The old woman moved her head slightly, enough to notice that Samoya was wearing gymnasium clothes and no jewellery.

'Give a gold coin to the first beggar you see,' said the crone shuffling away. The rest of Samoya's slaves who had been standing, waiting, drooping in the heat, now asked what the old soothsayer had said.

'I'm going to be a widow twice before I'm a mother,' said Samoya, 'and Irene's going to be a soldier.'

'A soldier!' they exclaimed, 'that's a laugh. She can't throw a ball straight let alone a bow or a javelin. And she's a slave and a woman so how's she going to be a soldier?'

'We don't know,' said Samoya, suddenly remembering the woman had said she'd go to a distant place but said nothing about doctoring. One a queen, one a widow and the other a soldier, though Samoya as she trudged the last half mile to her home, unusually quiet. Those were very odd predictions.

Zenobia was lying as still as she could as the soldiers carried her through the gates and into city streets. She closed her eyes to shut out the glare of the sun and her surroundings. She wanted to spend time trying to recapture the sensation that had engulfed her body when the Roman commander had carried her in his arms. It was a moment she had not wanted to stop. She had wanted him to kiss her but if he had brought his lips down on hers and kissed her, what would she have done? She had felt her lips swell with longing, an almost unendurable longing, together with an irresistible desire to be crushed beneath the weight of his body and have his hands roam over her breasts and between her legs . . .

'You feeling better, Lady?' said one of the soldiers.

'Oh yes, thank you,' she replied, feigning sleepiness.

'Thought you were, you were almost smiling,' he said.

Zenobia frowned. She must be careful not to let her feelings show. The soldiers must not guess she was having fantasies about their commander.

'How much further now?' another soldier asked.

Zenobia propped herself up on her elbows and looked about her. She was being carried down the main colonnaded street of the city. And people were staring at her. She felt confused and vulnerable.

'Turn second right and then left, it's the first house you come to,' she said, closing her eyes again in an effort to retrieve her delicious day-dream. But the magic was gone. She couldn't bring it back.

A sadness flooded over her as she realised she might never see the man again. And why should she? He was only a Roman soldier. She was going to be a queen. But the sensation was something to be remembered. When she read the great poets, when they wrote about love, now she would know what they meant. Love? It was the first time that the word and the thought had ever crossed Zenobia's mind. Love. Was that what she had felt in that instant? If it was then she realised it was an uncontrollable emotion. Not something she approved of. Love, she decided, would be banished from her repertoire of feelings. Especially love for a lowly Roman. Zenobia was interested in emperors. At the very least, princes.

Then another thought struck her. If the war with the Persians was finished then the Prince of Palmyra would be returning home. Perhaps she could make her father leave Antioch for Palmyra and concentrate his business in the capital. It was after all the oasis in the heart of the Syrian desert, and the crossroads of the East and the West. With his wealth she'd soon be accepted into society. And maybe, just maybe Odainat, Prince of Palmyra would fall in love with her. He wasn't an emperor but he was the King's brother. And he was a brilliant soldier. The King certainly wasn't. The King thought about nothing but debauchery. Perhaps the King could be made to stand down in favour of his brother? Perhaps the King's brother needed a wife to help the King stand down?

'Is this it?' asked the soldier, breaking into her ambitious reverie. 'For if it is it looks more like a palace than a house.'

'Yes,' replied Zenobia, simply. 'This is my home.'

And the soldiers carried her up the marble steps of her father's magnificent mansion.

Chapter Two

'You must submit willingly,' said the voluptuous Princess Bernice, who, enveloped in a golden cape, was sucking on a juicy quince.

'Yes, Your Highness,' replied Samoya, instinctively keeping her beautiful face bland, not allowing her true thoughts to be betrayed by the slightest flicker of emotion.

Samoya, like everyone else in Antioch, knew Princess Bernice was procuress for her decadent brother, King Hairan.

It was two hours before dawn and the darkest part of the night. The great bedroom, held up by pillars and decorated with murals, was lit by candles. Samoya was feeling put out. Too late to visit Zenobia she had come back from rehearsals at the temple and found Princess Bernice and her entourage waiting for her. And the only thing Samoya was really interested in doing was taking a nap before her initiation ceremony. With the unexpected, and unwanted, arrival of the Palmyrene princess this was denied her.

Samoya was furious the Palmyrene was in her house. There was nothing she could do about it, except be polite and hope the Princess would go away convinced that Samoya was unsuitable for any role at court. For, before the day was out, one of the fathers in the city would lose a daughter. Of course that father would be told it was an honour; that his daughter had been chosen for her beauty, elegance and good breeding and that he and his family would be serving the Palmyrene Empire. But every father knew it wasn't just the Empire his daughter would be serving.

Samoya wondered who had told the Princess about her. Perhaps it was one of her father's business rivals not wanting one of his own daughters to be picked. Samoya desperately hoped she would not be chosen. That would throw her plans for her future in complete disarray. Nevertheless, Samoya had to play hostess and etiquette demanded that she had to comply with the Princess's requests.

'Loosen her hair.' Princess Bernice commanded a buxom bare-breasted female slave, who immediatley set to work to release Lady Samoya's luscious red-gold tresses from their tight silken bindings, allowing her crowning glory to cascade sensually over her shoulders.

'That's much better,' said Bernice, dismissing the female slave.

'Do you know why I'm here?' asked Bernice imperiously.

The King's sister was sitting on an ornately carved, sweet-smelling cedar wood chair and staring lasciviously at the lithe, barefoot, young woman in front of her who was clothed in a creamy-white linen shift, encircled at the waist with a belt of plaited gold.

'No, your Highness,' lied Lady Samoya as she watched the Palmyrene princess begin to strip herself of her ornaments.

She slid gold bracelets down her full rounded arms, took off her gold anklets and her many necklaces which were made from a variety of precious stones interlaced with gold. Bernice tossed them carelessly into her jewel-box then she clapped her hands. From a far corner of the room two huge Nubians, wearing the briefest of tunics, stepped forward. One was carrying an alabaster bowl, the other a pitcher.

'Undress me,' commanded the Princess.

She held out her arms so that the slaves could remove her golden cape, her translucent purple silk ankle-length robe, her long black silk drawers and leave her naked.

Samoya felt a wisp of envy as, mentally, she measured her own small rose-bud breasts against the ample fullness of the Princess's. She gave a deep sigh. For the first time in her life Samoya wished she looked like someone else. Which was surprising because, whatever quirks of character Samoya possessed, vanity was not one of them. But, because she did not have the standard and 'in vogue' beauty, she did not know she was beautiful and would have been genuinely amazed had anybody told her she was. Samoya thought that if she was a candidate for marriage it was due to her father's fortune not to her own physical assets.

There was no doubt about it, thought Samoya, the Palmyrene princess was stunning. She was also very sexual. Her large, round, deep brown eyes, enhanced by black kohl, were set in a large round face. Her unmarked, dark olive skin was highlighted with soft red on her cheeks, her thick sensuous lips were painted a much brighter red. Her whole body, her large breasts, her rounded arms and stomach, her curvaceous thighs and legs, oozed sexuality.

Samoya felt uncomfortable. Even in the half-light she could feel the other woman giving her an odd stare.

Bernice was sizing up Samoya. The more Bernice looked at her, the more she thought that she was the one who seemed to have the right possibilities. However, Bernice knew she had to tread carefully. The girl's father was a problem. He had told her that unless his daughter was willing to be married and go to Palmyra he would not give his permission. His lack of desire to see his daughter married increased Bernice's determination to see that she was. And to her kinsman, Prince Alif. It was Bernice's job to make sure the girl agreed to her proposal.

'Now take off my hair clips,' ordered Bernice.

The handsome young Nubians obediently began the intricate task of extricating Princess Bernice's delicate pure gold decorations from her mass of softly waving black hair.

'So, you don't know why I'm here?'

'No, Your Highness, I don't,' replied Lady Samoya.

'I will tell you,' said Bernice, as the slaves finished brushing her hair. Bernice rose up from her chair and walked naked and with the liquid grace of a large, sensual feline towards a mountain of fabulously embroidered silk cushions. She lay down on them like a panther waiting to strike at its prey. She sighed provocatively then spread her legs wide and stuck her feet out towards her slaves.

Samoya's eyes followed her every movement. She wondered why the slaves should have left the strange long thin leather belt tied around the Princess's waist. Samoya gazed at it carefully. It did not end with the usual floppy flat tassels, instead it had been thickened, moulded and stiffened. It seemed to her as if the Palmyrene princess had two huge leather truncheons dangling between her legs.

Bowing low the two Nubians set the bowl on the floor in front of the King's sister. They poured soothing, warmed, aromatic oils from the pitcher into the bowl. Then each slave took one of their mistress's feet, lowered it into the bowl and slowly and rhythmically began to massage Bernice's ankles moving along her calves and up her thighs.

'Our kinsman, Prince Alif needs a wife,' Princess Bernice stated baldly. 'And one family in Antioch will be honoured by my choice. Now, what do you think of that?'

'I think it is no business of mine for it is too great an honour for our simple family,' whispered Samoya, sweetly, with downcast eyes. The fragility of the girl excited Bernice.

She felt a rush of licentiousness. She wanted to touch Samoya, feel her soft, pale skin, her legs, her breasts, her lips. She wouldn't do it yet. There was pleasure in waiting. She would enjoy the sensation of anticipation. To assuage her immediate desire Bernice began to run her hands sexily along the thick well-muscled legs of her two black slaves.

Enjoying the feel of their skin, Bernice looked up slyly at Samoya. The girl's figure was almost boyish, her small breasts did not have the full bloom of womanhood. Her violet blue, slightly almond-shaped eyes, would make a pleasant change from the endless brown and black ones usually seen at court. Her short, straight typically Palmyrene nose and her red-blonde hair meant she was of good old stock. Although Samoya and her father lived in Antioch, they both had the shapes and colouring that were special to Palmyra and that part of Syria. Bernice liked what she saw and, fully aware of his inclinations, she knew her brother would, too. In that instant she decided she would take the Lady Samoya to court. Bernice had no doubt whatsoever that the King and Prince Alif would be very pleased with her choice.

Samoya stood silently by, watching the Princess's slaves perform their duties. Nobody would have guessed that she was intensely wary of the older woman and that she realised she was in a difficult situation. She did not want to be married. But if Princess Bernice chose her as Prince Alif's wife what could she do? How could she refuse?

Samoya reasoned that to be turned down by the Royal household would do little for her future marriage prospects, and that did have to be taken into consideration. But to be chosen meant living a life of virtual prostitution. At least, that was the rumour in parochial Antioch where scurrilous stories of life at court in Palmyra were a constant source of gossip for its inhabitants. Samoya suddenly realised how she could escape from her predicament. The demands of the Great Goddess took precedence over those of the King. She would ask Priestess Verenia to take her as a novitiate into the temple. Samoya tried not to look crestfallen as she remembered she would be unable to talk to the priestess that night. The King's sister was exercising her Royal prerogative to attend the special initiation rite at dawn. And the next few days would be filled with various temple ceremonies, Verenia would have no time to see her. Samoya mentally stamped her foot with impatience. Instinctively she knew that time was of the essence. A wave of irritation flooded through her, knowing she had no alternative but to wait.

Samoya looked towards the two huge black slaves who were bending over their mistress massaging oils into every part of her body. Samoya felt a tingling in her body and her face suffuse with blushes. The tingling was familiar. Samoya remembered how recently she had gone to bed and had let her hands glide down her lithe body, exciting herself. As her fingers had roamed, exploring past her fair red-gold mound to the fleshy lips beyond, her hidden sex had grown softer, more pliant and wetter with her every languid stroke. She had fantasised about ordering Irene to put her head between her outstretched legs and lick her hidden opening. But she hadn't done it. Instead her slave, lying beside her, had realised what she had wanted and had stretched out her hand. She had gently stroked Samoya's buttocks then pushed her fingers round finding Samoya's wet sex and had rubbed gently on her virgin lips. She had continued to play with her until an exquisite sensation had forced its way down and out through her body in a great shudder. She had been left with a feeling of contentment and had slept a deep, deep sleep.

Samoya watched the Princess roll over squirming as the slaves' big hands fondled her full breasts, stroked the black curly mound between her legs and her big fleshy bottom.

'A moist, tingling pussy is one of life's greatest pleasures,' said Bernice, 'and I have one now. You two know what to do.'

Samoya was mesmerised by the woman's words. She felt a thrill pass through her body as one of the men nestled between Bernice's thighs and let his tongue travel between his mistress's legs, pushing slowly at her secret lips until his tongue was darting at her clitoris. Bernice began to sway and moan and lift her hips. The other slave stayed caressing her breasts. 'Deeper. Go deeper,' commanded Bernice hoarsely as she writhed with pleasure. 'Do as I say or I'll have you whipped.' The slave buried his tongue deeper and moved it faster inside the Princess's sex.

Samoya was quite amazed. She was a mass of contradictory emotions. She was repelled and excited. It seemed to Samoya as if she was opening and swelling. She felt a tremendous desire to be touched. She forced her hands to stay by her side, although, almost of their own accord, they kept wandering over her thighs. She found her mouth had gone dry. Her throat was constricting. She licked her lips and swallowed hard trying to increase her own saliva. Her breasts were aching. She tensed the muscles in her buttocks.

As she watched the huge black slaves obey their mistress and fondle and suck Bernice, Samoya gave tiny wiggles of her hips and clenched her fists in an effort to stop herself lifting her dress and touching herself.

Watching the Palmyrene princess gliding on the silken cushions, moving with her eyes closed as the men continued to caress every part of her full, rounded nakedness, Samoya thought perhaps she would be able to inch her way from the other woman's presence without Bernice being aware of her departure.

'Stay exactly where you are,' commanded Bernice to Samoya. 'I might need you.'

As she said that the Princess untied her belt and handed one of the thick phallus shaped ends to the slave who was sucking her.

'Be a man,' she ordered. Only then did Samoya realise that the slave was a eunuch. The slave positioned his knees between Bernice's thighs, tied the belt around his waist, held the object poised at the entrance to Bernice's sex and waited.

'Now, enter me,' said Bernice, seconds later.

Samoya watched transfixed as the slave gradually pushed the thick long leather truncheon into Bernice's wet sex. He moved his body backwards and forwards as if the object was attached to him and let it plunge deeper into Bernice's warm swollen pussy. Before she realised what she was doing, Samoya found herself moving her hips in rhythm to the slave's thrusting. Tensing and untensing her buttocks, her breath, like Bernice's, issued in short sharp bursts.

'Are you wet between your legs?' Bernice asked.

'I don't know,' replied Samoya haltingly.

'You don't know!' said Bernice between gasps as the slave continued to penetrate her. 'Then stand beside me. I will feel you and I will tell you if you are.'

Trembling, Samoya slowly walked over to where Princess Bernice was lying. Bernice reached out a hand and gently began to stroke Samoya's ankles. Samoya's whole body shook at the woman's touch. Bernice's hands went higher and higher under the creamy white linen robe. Samoya held her breath as the Princess's fingers started to caress the soft fleshy lips at the top of her thighs. Samoya could feel her wetness exuding and her nipples had hardened. Samoya wanted them touched.

'Do you like that?' asked Bernice, softly rubbing Samoya's juicy, wet and open sex.

'Yes,' replied Samoya, hoarsely. The touch of Bernice's finger gliding backwards and forwards was making waves of the delicious tingling flow through her body, from her throat and neck to her breasts, to her belly and her womb then down; down to change from a sensation that she could barely hold to a lubrication that she could feel. And with that feeling the whole cycle was reproduced again but taking her higher and higher as the wetter she became the more Bernice's fingers were able to invade her, push upwards and stimulate her. As she watched the slave eunuch pretending to be a man and piercing Bernice with the leather dildo and the other fondling her breasts, squeezing their large brown nipples between his fingers, Samoya wanted to feel more hands straying onto her body. Bernice suddenly stopped stroking Samoya's sex, and hauled her down on the cushions beside her. Still jerking to the slave's rhythm, Bernice pulled up Samoya's robe, encircled her rose-bud breasts and teased her erect, dark pink nipples.

'Remove your robe,' commanded Bernice.

Samoya obeyed. 'Now, give me your mouth and open your legs wide.'

Samoya turned her full pouting mouth towards the Princess who began to trace its outline with her tongue before bringing her lips down hard on Samoya's.

Samoya closed her eyes and gave herself up to the touch of Bernice's mouth on her mouth, tongue on her tongue and her plump exploring hands on her breasts. Samoya began to writhe.

Moments later Samoya felt another body over hers and then a newer, stranger, more wonderful diversion as something small and warm, wet and thick began to trace the edges of her swollen labia. She opened her eyes to find that the huge black eunuch who had been caressing Bernice's breasts was now upturned beside her. He had his head between her legs. It was his thick tongue which was searching out, exciting and thrilling Samoya's open wet sex. Then he touched her clitoris.

That touch was so potent, so enthralling that Samoya instantly let out a great gasp of pleasure and rolled and writhed and swayed. And she continued to do this until every ounce of energy inside her contracted to her belly. With her body rigid and arched she suddenly shook with the delirium of ecstasy. Then a great rush of fervour balled up inside her and was expelled in a massive explosion.

Samoya lay back exhausted and overwhelmed by varying emotions. She glanced at Bernice whose thighs were quivering as the slave with the phallus shape continued to pound into her. She was rolling and moaning then she arched, went rigid and with a long shriek of gratification suddenly collapsed and fell back on the cushions. Bernice took Samoya gently in her arms and kissed her cheek.

'My dear you enjoyed that, didn't you?' said Princess Bernice.

'Yes,' replied Samoya in a whisper.

'Would you like it to happen again?' asked the seductive older woman, softly caressing Samoya's breasts and nibbling her ear.

'Yes.'

'And you can, if you agree to marry Prince Alif. You see the Prince has some very interesting habits and desires,' said Bernice, smiling cat-like as she remembered some of his more perverted antics. 'And one of them is that he enjoys watching women make love. He would love to see you with your legs stretched far apart and me fingering your lovely sweet little virginal delights. And I would suck you and I would teach you to suck me. After all, you enjoyed that slave putting his tongue between your legs, didn't you?'

'Oh yes,' Samoya replied enthusiastically.

'I will get him to show you how it's done,' said Bernice, picking up her truncheons. 'And these.'

Bernice began to run them along Samoya's thighs,

'Feel the softness of the leather, open your legs a moment.'

Samoya did as she was told and Bernice began to trail the thick object along the girl's sex, and despite her recent orgasm Samoya reacted by opening her legs further.

'Ah, so you'd like to have it stuck in you would you? You'd like to be penetrated by my handsome treasure. Well, you will, but not now. Another day I will show you how to get pleasure whenever you want it. I will have one made especially for you. Now all you have to do is say you'll come to Palmyra and marry Prince Alif. Will you do that?'

Bernice kissed Samoya's soft yielding lips and caressed her breasts whilst leaving the dildo poking very slightly at the girl's entrance.

'Yes. Oh yes,' said Samoya. The awakening had begun. She had discovered her body and its potential for pleasure.

'Good. Then that is settled and I will talk to your father. Now we must hurry,' said Bernice. 'The Goddess waits.'

Bernice turned to her slaves and told them to dress her and then dress Samoya. Whilst the purple silk robe was once more wrapped around her ample form, the leather thong belt re-tied around her waist and the fine spun gold cape was draped over her shoulders Bernice gazed at the girl lying on the cushions. She was perfect. A beautiful face, a superb body and from the intensity of her reactions obviously very highly sexed. Bernice had confirmed her original estimate. Samoya was the choice and the King would be thrilled. She had a lot to learn but, Princess Bernice licked her lips at the thought, she would be easy to teach. And Prince Alif would have a most submissive wife.

The two slaves gently roused Samoya from the sleep she had drifted into. They rubbed her body with fresh aromatic oils, paying special attention to her nipples and between her legs. Samoya had thought that after the violent explosion she would never want to be touched down there again. Much to her surprise she discovered that far from not wanting it she had been sensitised. Her whole body was alive, her secret opening was still open, pulsating and enjoying their soft caressing hands. She wanted more. Lazily and sensuously she writhed backwards and forwards, up and down as the two eunuchs coated every inch of her so that she was again sexually heightened and glistening. Then the two Nubians covered Samoya's body with her fine linen robe.

'We'll do it again soon,' said Princess Bernice, gently touching the girl's hard nipples, then running her hands up her legs and giving Samoya's sex a final thrust with her fingers. 'That's to remember me by. Oh and Samoya . . .'

'Yes, Your Highness?' said Samoya trembling at the woman's expert touch.

'I suggest you do some practising on your slaves. Line them up, make them open their legs, suck them, find out which ones you like best, who responds and opens fastest to your tongue. Then open your legs, make them bury their heads between your legs and suck you. You've been felt by experts, you know now what you should feel, so tell them exactly what you want, make them do it. But don't allow yourself the real thing. That pleasure is for another time and place. And my dear, after you've tested them, bring the best, the sexiest ones with you to Palmyra.'

Listening silently to their mistress with a secret smile upon their faces, the two Nubians tied the gold belt around Samoya's waist, put a garland of bay and asparagus leaves on her head, gave her her empty clay cup and her ceremonial flute. There was still an hour before dawn but Samoya was ready for the Goddess with Many Names.

Princess Bernice clapped her hands and the doors of

the great bedroom opened into the black night and the courtyard. Irene and the other female slaves appeared with candles. Slowly, they walked in procession out of Pernel's mansion and into the dark freshly swept streets. As they wound their way towards the temple other friends and acquaintances joined them. Everyone walked barefoot except Princess Bernice who was borne along in a litter. Normally her eunuchs would have carried her but no male was allowed anywhere near the temple at the time of the rite, especially the important rite of initiation.

It was as Samoya put her foot on the first step leading up to the great gaping stone vulva that was the entrance to the temple that a shiver of fear blew over Samoya's body. In the heat of extreme sexual excitement she had agreed to marry the Palmyrene Prince Alif. Somehow the marriage had to be stopped. But who would help her? With each step she took Samoya prayed fervently to the Goddess to send her a saviour.

Chapter Three

Over the next few weeks very few of Samoya's arrangements went according to plan.

Princess Bernice stayed on at the mansion making it impossible for Samoya to get away and see Zenobia. She had wanted to tell her friend about her meeting with the old crone at the city gates and what she had said about her and Irene's futures.

She had also wanted to tell her about Princess Bernice. How that decadent woman had spread her own legs wide, allowed her slaves to part the lips of her sex, and thrust their fingers and their tongue into her hidden place and how watching this had excited Samoya. And seeing this had sent a raging hunger storming through her body so that when the debauched Princess had told her to stand beside her and had stroked her thighs and found Samoya's sex, it had opened willingly to her touch. She wanted to tell Zenobia how unexpected and thrilling it was to feel the other woman's fingers exploring her. How her inner parts seemed to be made purely for pleasure and Princess Bernice had shown her how those parts could be aroused. She wanted to tell her friend how the insistent moving of the Princess's fingers inside her sex, stimulating the walls and membrane of her excited vulva had made her wet, juicy and craving for more. How the lower portion of her body had reacted to the other woman's touch as if she were a musical instrument and suddenly a beautiful tune was being played on a part of her that she had never thought about or considered. She also wanted to tell her friend how one of Bernice's beautiful black eunuchs had put his body over hers, his head between her legs and had sucked at her open wanton place flooding it with desire. And how he had found a spot, a point within her, that when touched by his tongue covered her in waves of licentiousness that were so delicious that she had writhed and squirmed, never wanting it to stop. And how she had been overwhelmed by erotic dreams of total abandonment.

And that, whilst her body was being subjected to such pleasures, she had imagined men putting their sex into her mouth. Ordering her to suck it, lick it, tease it with her tongue until the sap was released. And then she had imagined being bound hand and foot and gagged. And other men crawling up between her thighs, their members feeling their way along her legs, parting her exposed self and thrusting into her, taking her, whilst an unknown hand continued to play with the tiny point increasing her feeling of ravenous desire. She wanted to tell Zenobia all these things and also how under the influence of extreme sexual pleasure she had agreed to marry Prince Alif.

Samoya was unable to do it because Bernice seldom let her out of her sight. She felt she was watched and spied upon all the time. And much to her chagrin her father ordered Irene to sleep with the rest of the slaves. She was unable to confide in her and had to sleep alone. When the Princess wasn't beside her, her eunuchs were dogging her footsteps. Even when Bernice was actively bargaining with Pernel over the size of Samoya's dowry she kept Samoya by her side. Bernice played with her like a cat with a mouse. This annoyed Samoya on many levels. Uppermost because she was in a permanent state of sexual arousal and frustration. She wanted to be touched by the Princess again. Wanted her eunuchs to stroke their hands over her body. She was denied this at every juncture. She kept hoping the Princess would call her into her bedroom, but she did not. Samoya had then decided she would play sex games with Irene but her father's dictum made sure she couldn't do that either.

Late one morning, a week after her induction, Samoya managed to evade everybody, her father, her slaves, even Irene, but most of all she managed to get away from the oppressively sexual presence of Princess Bernice and her mainly male entourage.

In a quiet corner of the large and carefully designed courtyard, surrounded by tamarind and fig trees, Samoya sat by herself. She gave a sigh of relief, adjusted the many layers of her long, blue, floral patterned silk robes and stared contentedly at the fountains and the flowers, the myrtle hedges and the birds. The garden always soothed her. When she was agitated it calmed her. When she was moody and melancholy its symmetry of line, its combination of metals and stone, its colours: the cool blue and green tiles in the covered walkways and the vibrancy of the reds and yellows in the flowerbeds, the honeysuckle, jasmine and roses, and the brightly coloured flitting butterflies, made her spirits rise, gave her peace of mind and left her serene. She closed her eyes and sat quite still, unaware of anything except the sweet smell of roses and the buzzing of the bees.

'Stand.' The suddenness of Princess Bernice's order broke through her contentment.

Without thinking, Samoya stood to attention. Bernice lifted the back of Samoya's skirts revealing her neat bare buttocks.

'Hold that up,' said the voluptuous Princess.

Bernice was carrying a small cushion on a long golden

cord. She placed it on the cedar bench where Samoya's buttocks had been moments before. Then she put her hand, palm uppermost and her fingers sticking towards the bright blue sky on the cushion and told Samoya to sit down again, making sure her sex was arranged so that Bernice's fingers had instant access to her.

'Tell me, which season do you like best?' Bernice asked, as she eased her fingers along Samoya's hovering labia.

'Spring,' Samoya replied, and the touch of Bernice's cool fingertips on her soft warm sex caused her juices to flow. Samoya rolled her hips and took more and more of Bernice's invading fingers.

'You must not squirm,' Bernice hissed. 'You must not let anyone guess what I am doing to you. You must learn to enjoy this without betraying pleasure. And you must learn to use your muscles. They must grip my fingers.'

'My muscles!' exclaimed Samoya, bemused.

'Your love-muscles. Squeeze my fingers with your love-muscles. Now do it,' she ordered. 'Grip and talk to me as if nothing was happening. We don't want your father realising his sweet virginal little daughter is having her very wet pussy played with.'

Bernice's words made Samoya wetter. She tensed her buttocks then flexed her inner muscles and gripped Bernice's fingers.

'Good,' said Bernice with approval. 'Continue to do that whilst pointing out to me the flowers in the garden. That way your father can know what you are saying but will have no idea what I am doing. He will think you are teaching me the joys of gardening; we will know I am teaching you the joys of sex.'

Samoya sat beside Bernice, her back upright, her nipples stiff and poking hard against the soft silk of her bodice and told Bernice which plants were what. Whilst Samoya spoke in a loud voice and loosed and unloosed her inner muscles around Bernice's ever thrusting fingers, Bernice continued to play with her and whisper in her ear.

'Your nipples are stiff. Would you like me to touch them. Don't stop talking, just nod your head.' Samoya nodded her head. 'Tonight I will have dinner in my bedroom and I want you as my guest. Do you understand . . .?'

'But my father . . .'

'I will tell your father I have to teach you court etiquette, which of course I do – and I am. I want you to come to my bedroom, but before you do I want you to cut a hole in this bodice so that those delightful nipples of yours are exposed and touchable and I want you to slit all your skirts from waist to floor. From now on you are to be accessible at all times.'

'At all times!' exclaimed Samoya.

'Yes, from now on at all times you are to be accessible to me and anybody else that I say may have access to you. Is that understood? Carry on talking, just nod your head.'

Samoya, excited by Bernice's suggestion, nodded her head vigorously. There was something so blatantly sexual in the thought that Bernice or one of her slaves could bend her over and stroke her whenever they pleased. In anticipation and muted excitement Samoya squeezed her muscles harder around Bernice's fingers.

'All your trousseau will be made in this way. I will leave you two of my slaves. They are fine dressmakers. They will help yours to make everything according to my instructions.'

'Who?' asked Samoya.

'Two girls, Phyllis and Hermione. They are excellent. Their needlework is the finest. Oh and tonight, Samoya, I want you blindfolded.'

'Blindfolded! Why?' asked Samoya.

'For my pleasure. You have to understand, Samoya, everything is done for my pleasure. Even teaching you is done for my pleasure,' said Bernice, withdrawing her fingers from Samoya's sex. 'I want you to go now. I want you to rest, sleep. It will be a long night tonight. Besides it's almost noon and it's getting too hot even for playing.'

Samoya left the Princess and went to her cool marble-floored room to obey her commands. She was thoroughly aroused, her sex was open, full, swollen and frustrated. She wanted and needed it touched and stroked. It was only noon. How could she last until the evening in her heightened state of sexual awareness? She undressed and sitting on a number of silk cushions arranged against the marble wall, slit her skirts from top to bottom. Samoya was sitting naked, cutting small holes in her bodice when Irene came in unannounced. Since Princess Bernice's arrival she had seen very little of Samoya and had been acutely jealous. Her lips pouted sexily as she looked at her mistress.

'Why are you cutting up your beautiful clothes?' Irene asked.

Samoya looked up at her blonde slave. She wondered whether to tell her the truth or not. She stared at Irene's wide lips, her large breasts, their prominent nipples skimpily covered by a thin strip of black silk, and her long thighs loosely encased in black diaphanous silk and thought how she would miss her if she went to Palmyra without her. Then she remembered Princess Bernice's instruction before her initiation. Test your slaves. Find out which are sexually interesting. Perhaps this was the time to see if she would take Irene to Palmyra with her.

'You ask too many questions,' said Samoya witheringly, adding, 'sit down on my bed.'

Irene was bemused by Samoya's tone. She had never talked to her like a slave. She had always been a friend. She didn't understand this new person who was going to marry a prince of the Royal household. Irene bowed and sat on Samoya's large bed.

Having cut two perfect holes Samoya put the pale

green bodice back on, making sure the nipples stuck through enticingly. She chose a couple of her newly-slit fine transparent skirts, one in fiery red, the other in muted yellow and put them on over her bare skin. She tied a long thin leather cord many times around her waist and left her feet without slippers. She twirled around the room noticing how the skirts flared wide showing off her buttocks and her neat red-gold mound. And Irene sat watching her, excited, desperately wanting to touch Samoya's protruding nipples and the secret place at the top of her thighs. The place that was hers whenever they slept together. Samoya danced over to where Irene was sitting and bent her body offering her breasts to her slave.

'This is why I cut my bodice,' she said boldly. Irene did not touch Samoya, but stayed still, her eyes downcast. She didn't know what to do, what was expected of her.

'Touch my nipples,' Samoya ordered.

Tentatively Irene put out a hand and took the tiny red buds between her fingers and squeezed.

'Kiss them, suck them,' commanded Samoya. Irene did as she was told, then suddenly Samoya pushed her slave back on to the bed so that she lay flat. Then Samoya knelt, her knees either side of her slave's head, her sex hovering over Irene's mouth.

'I want you to put your tongue here,' commanded Samoya holding her secret lips apart so that her slave could see every hidden curl and crevice within. 'I want you to kiss me and lick me and find my special spot.'

Irene was shaking. For weeks she had wanted to bury her head between her mistress's thighs and now, in an unemotional, unloving way she was being ordered to do it. She wondered why. What had changed Samoya? When they slept together there had been a sweetness between them, when they had stroked one another there had been a gentleness, a lovingness. But now she was being commanded to do it and she didn't want to.

Irene turned her head away. Samoya was furious. All her pent up frustration spilled out in a spoilt child's rage.

'You're being disobedient,' she roared. 'I will whip you for that. You're a slave, only a slave, my slave. Remember that and bend over.' Swiftly Samoya untied the leather around her waist, tore Irene's skirt from her body and made her part her legs. She stroked and teased her slave's bare buttocks with the thin leather strip, dragging it backwards and forwards over Irene's full rounded pink skin. Then she stepped back and the leather whistled through the air and landed on Irene's flesh with a sizzle. The girl jumped with the pain. Samoya did it again and again, finding increasing sexual excitement with each stroke and at the sight of the livid marks on her slave's pale flanks. Irene was hers. To do with as she wanted and the power she felt as she whipped the prostrate girl overwhelmed her, adding further impetus to her desires. Irene's body jumped and curled, writhed and hurled as the leather flashed down on her naked buttocks. Samoya began to stroke herself between each lash. Her sex had opened wider with the thrill, her juices were oozing out of her and she needed Irene's tongue to start licking her.

'Now you will suck me,' said Samoya, 'but first you will thank me for whipping you.'

'Thank you, mistress,' said Irene, sliding off the bed and kneeling before Samoya in a state of supplication. Her buttocks were burning deliciously from the searing stripes, her nipples were hard and her sex, too, was open, wet and juicy. The beating she had received had excited her. She wanted to taste Samoya. She wanted to feel the softness of her mistress's sex unfurling beneath her tongue.

Samoya lifted the girl's head up by her hair and, parting her own legs and jutting her hips forward, thrust her slave's face into her pubis.

'Suck me. Put your tongue there and find my special

spot. If you don't I'll whip you again. And say thank you mistress, thank you for being allowed to touch me.'

'Thank you, mistress, thank you for allowing me to touch you,' said Irene.

Her tongue pushed its way past her mistress's tiny red-gold curls and sought out the furls and furrows that lay hidden beyond in the pink throbbing squashiness that was Samoya's hidden life. Irene trailed her tongue down, then up. Samoya jerked. Irene had found her small protruding morsel of hard flesh. Her tiny imitation penis had grown and grew more inflamed as it was flicked by Irene's tongue. Samoya braced herself, steadying her body by gripping Irene's shoulders as her slave's slurping tongue produced in her the most erotic visions. She began to sway. She began to shake and tremble. Something else she wanted. Something deeper, further inside her.

Samoya slid to the floor and lay with her legs spread out, her hips braced upwards. Irene knelt before her mistress, her arms outstretched, her hands enclosing Samoya's breasts. Playing with her nipples, her head down between Samoya's legs slurping, sucking, Irene began to enjoy the taste and feel of the wet softness of Samoya's sex. Irene's bare criss-crossed marked buttocks were raised showing her second opening and the open pinkness of her own sex displayed beyond her pale down.

'Put your fingers inside me,' ordered Samoya.

Irene loosened her grip on one of Samoya's breasts and let her hand wander down past her belly, past her own flicking tongue and slowly began to push through deeper and deeper into Samoya's swollen sex. She began to thrust harder and harder. Samoya closed her eyes and raised her hips higher and higher to take that thrusting deeper. And she squeezed her muscles around Irene's fingers.

'Are you practising my dear?' the Princess's voice drifted over them.

Samoya's eyes shot open. Princess Bernice was standing in the doorway, her two black eunuchs beside her.

'Then you must allow us to help you.' Princess Bernice sauntered into the room followed by the two slaves. As she moved, Bernice swished her skirts and Samoya noticed that her skirts were also slit from top to bottom. Her sex was inviting and available and she was wearing her belt with the truncheons attached. Bernice stood beside Irene and touched the pale skin of the slave's bare buttocks.

'Who has had her bottom whipped?' she asked, rhetorically, stroking the marks. 'Did you do that, Samoya?'

'Yes, Your Highness,' replied Samoya from the floor, beginning to raise herself on her elbows.

'Oh don't get up my dear,' said the Princess. 'It is a very pretty sight. One we have all been enjoying. Tell me, is your slave used to being whipped. Have you done it regularly?'

'No, Your Highness.'

'Then I must congratulate you. For a novice you've done extremely well. You obviously have great potential.'

Bernice slowly began to unwind her belt; when it was completely undone she unknotted the middle giving half to one Nubian and half to the other.

'I see you are an obedient girl,' said the Princess and flicked her fingers over Samoya's nipples peeping through the holes in her bodice. 'And for that you deserve a present. You two,' Bernice beckoned to the two eunuchs, 'kiss her nipples.'

With one eunuch on either side of her the two men leant over Samoya and clasped their mouths over Samoya's rosy projecting nipples and teased them more erect with a combination of tiny bites and flicking tongues. Samoya raised her hips higher and Irene went deeper in between her thighs.

Bernice picked up a couple of cushions and shoved

47

them beneath Samoya's buttocks. Then she spread her skirts and placed her feet either side of Samoya's head and squatted over her face, her open ripe sex hovering above Samoya's mouth.

'Now, my dear, whilst your slave sucks your pussy you are going to suck mine. That neat little tongue of yours is going to pleasure me. And whilst you are doing that I am going to order one of my slaves to violate your slave with my little treasure.'

Princess Bernice pointed to the larger man of the two and commanded him to strap on the leather dildo.

'Now take her,' she said, watching the big Nubian crawl between Irene's legs, stretch her sex wider and then invade the kneeling slave's sex. As he thrust into her, Irene gave a howl of pleasure and jerked forward, her teeth nibbling on Samoya's clitoris. Samoya's head jumped up as Princess Bernice clamped her sex onto Samoya's mouth. Her tongue slid up into the dark wetness of the wet folds of the Princess's sex. And the salty taste of her eased out over Samoya's lips. Samoya brought up her hands and opened Bernice wider so that her mouth and tongue could bury deeper, take more of her. Bernice's open swollen wetness slid easily across Samoya's mouth and she gasped with delight. But Samoya had not discovered Bernice's hidden point. She was so intent on going in she had not allowed her tongue to travel up. Bernice desperately wanted that distended, hardened, and now quite large and very excited tip caressed.

Bernice changed her position. She lay on her side beside Samoya so that her sex was level with her mouth but not touching it. Bernice raised one leg high in the air.

'Bring me my other treasure.' Bernice ordered the eunuch still teasing Samoya's nipples with his mouth. She opened her sex wide with her hands. The eunuch knelt against the Princess's buttocks, the large dildo in his hands, ready and waiting for her next command.

'Let it enter me,' she said.

Bernice put her raised foot on the Nubian's shoulder and he brought his hand holding the leather truncheon round under one leg and slowly, almost tenderly, drove the instrument into her wantonness. Bernice sighed and rolled her hips echoing the sighing and rolling of the slave whose head was still nestling between Samoya's legs and sucking her whilst she was being penetrated by the other eunuch with the dildo.

'Samoya,' said Princess Bernice between gasps as the slave performed his duty. 'Turn your head and watch.'

Samoya turned her head and watched the great leather truncheon going in and out, in and out of the Princess's sex and she pressed her own love-muscles on Irene's fingers and squeezed. She wanted the leather truncheon too. She wanted a man. Samoya wanted to feel a phallus going up inside her.

'You want it too, don't you?' said Bernice, with relish. 'But you can't, not yet. You'll have a man before you have this. And I will be there to watch. I want to see you take a big thick shaft, perhaps even more than one. I want to see a man, a real man on top of you, sticking his cock deep into you and watch you squirm, my dear. Watch you wanting it, getting it and squirming. That'll be my treat. But that's not for today. Now you are going to put your head back between my legs and that beautiful, strong tongue of yours is going to find my clitoris and it is going to lick it, nibble it, suck it. And if you don't do it properly this time it will be you who is whipped. Do you understand? I told you before, my pleasure is paramount. So find my clitoris and lick it.'

Samoya felt a sudden strange thrill at the thought of being whipped. The lash cutting across her flesh, marking her. The mixture of pleasure and pain. Bernice was groaning beneath the insistent thrustings of the eunuch and the leather truncheon. Irene was moving faster and faster as the other eunuch pounded into her, her mouth still slurping at Samoya's sex. Samoya was overwhelmed by a series of sensations and she stretched her legs wider, her nipples were stiffer and aching again to be stroked or sucked or bitten. She stuck out her tongue and it immediately found Bernice's large, hard engorged point. She felt it rise under her and she nibbled at it mercilessly. She bit it and rubbed the outer rim of Bernice's labia as the leather dildo travelled backwards and forwards inside her sex. Bernice's foot stopped resting on the eunuch's shoulder. It rose high in the air and stayed there rigid, but shaking. All of Bernice was shaking. Then she came. With one tremendous scream she roared out her orgasm and then ordered the eunuch to remove the truncheon from her and the other from Irene. But Irene hadn't come and Samoya realised and asked that her slave complete her orgasm.

'Not now,' said Bernice sternly. 'Bring her with you tonight. And Samoya, don't play with her again. Neither must she play with you. And that is an order.'

Princess Bernice then stood up, readjusted her clothing and she and her slaves left the room. Samoya and Irene stared at one another.

'She'll never know,' said Samoya grabbing Irene's hand and pushing her onto the bed. 'Let's lie head to tail.'

She slid her hands down over Irene's body and clasped her breasts then slowly flattened herself and moved further down so that her slave's pale fringed sex was exposed. Samoya placed a finger at its tip and gently began to caress it. Irene opened beneath her fingers and her breath came in quick-fire gasps. The two of them moved sideways together and laid their mouths and tongues upon each other's sex working fast upon one other until their juices spread out over their legs, their bellies tightened into a ball and they came in tandem. The two young women lay beside each other, their bodies exhausted, their minds beyond sex and erotic visions. They forgot about fingers and mouths and false cocks and imaginary phalluses.

'I want you with me in Palmyra,' said Samoya, kissing her slave's neck as they lay satiated and happy. And Irene was only too pleased to be asked. They fell asleep in one another's arms.

But when Princess Bernice had departed she had not closed the door. She had stood in the doorway watching Samoya and Irene play with one another's bodies and she had smiled a smile of licentiousness and contentment. She was going to enjoy her dinner and her dessert. She ordered the eunuchs to prepare some of her special playthings and then she went to bed and to sleep. She knew, more than the disobedient girls, that it was going to be a very long night.

In the cool of the early evening Samoya's father called for her to join him in a game of backgammon in the main reception hall. He said he was waiting for clients and needed some recreation.

'You are looking exceptionally pretty,' he said as he gave his daughter an affectionate peck on her cheek.

Samoya had made her face up with great care. As commanded by the Princess she was wearing her skirts that were now slit from top to bottom. She had draped a flowing shawl over her bodice to hide her protruding nipples from her father but at the same time obeying Bernice's instructions. As she sat down on the cushions her skirts billowed out and her naked buttocks resting on the slightly stubbly fabric of their covering, excited her.

They were in the middle of their game when Bishop Paul and his secretary Anthony arrived. Samoya's father immediately took the bishop into an ante-room to conclude some business telling Anthony to finish the game with his daughter. Anthony stood in front of Samoya watching the retreating figures of his employer and Samoya's father. They were deep in discussion. The tone of their voices suggested serious haggling.

Samoya looked around the great room. All the slaves were standing to attention at the far side of the room. She called to Irene and told her to bring a higher table, and some peppermint tea for Anthony. Irene smiled a conspiratorial smile. She knew that Samoya had falsely swooned during their visit to the bishop's palace in order to be able to grab hold of the young man's cock. She wondered what her mistress planned to do now. Irene walked away and Samoya let her shawl droop slightly so that the young man had a brief glimpse of her rosy nipples sticking out through her bodice.

The young man swallowed hard. He broke out in a sweat. He seemed all too vulnerable in his loose, flowing black robe. He felt his penis gain a life of its own and surge into action. Samoya watched the sudden bulge appear from his loins and looking at him straight in his eyes she licked her lips. Anthony began to shake. Irene returned with a larger, higher table and the peppermint tea. Samoya stood up so that Irene could place everything properly. As she did so Samoya swirled her skirts. And Anthony had an instant vision of Samoya's neat buttocks and the tiny red-gold triangle at the top of her silky thighs. Samoya rearranged herself on the cushions. Her skirts were spread out, hiding her limbs from view but still enabling her to feel the roughness of the cushions on her bare bottom and on the soft folds of her opening sex. Irene carefully picked up the backgammon board and set it to one side. Then she bent down and put the new table in front of Samoya. In bending, Irene's diaphanous black skirt was stretched over her large buttocks and Anthony was able to see clearly the criss-cross marks left over from Samoya's whipping. His cock gave a further lurch at the sight and he wondered who had done it and where. He looked at the tall blonde slave-girl with renewed interest but his glance was cut short by Samoya's voice.

'You may sit down now,' said Samoya politely to Anthony, pointing to the pile of cushions opposite, recently vacated by her father. Irene poured out the very hot peppermint tea and handed it to Anthony.

As he raised the steaming brew to his lips, Samoya slid down her pile of cushions so that her feet stuck out under the table. She wiggled her feet under his robe and slid them up and further up until her toes were touching his testes. And there was nothing he could do. He was shaking too much to do anything except sit imprisoned by her toes whilst his hands held the bowl of hot tea. Samoya looked at him innocently and juggled his large, soft sac between her feet and then moved one foot upwards and began to glide up and down on his thick erect penis. He gasped.

'It's your move, I think,' she said, stretching backwards on the cushions, bracing herself, giving herself more leverage to rub his engorged cock with her feet. 'But perhaps Irene should make it for you. She can play too,' Samoya nodded to her slave.

Irene picked a couple of ivory counters off the board and was about to move them when Samoya jostled her hand and she dropped them.

'Oh dear!' exclaimed Samoya. 'They've gone under the table. Irene, that's very naughty.' Samoya gave Irene a loud resounding slap on her bottom. 'You'd better find them. We can't continue otherwise. Go under the table . . .'

Irene, with her bottom smarting from the recent slap, bent down. Samoya leant forward and whispered in her ear.

'Put his cock in your mouth.'

Irene slid on the marble floor and wiggled her way under the table. Samoya quickly withdrew her feet and pulling her skirts apart, crossed her legs and sat in the lotus position showing her sex and its pink openness to Anthony. Before Anthony had time to recover from the lewdness of Samoya's movements, Irene had raised his robe and her fingers, ice-cold from the marble floor, encircled his warm tool. The joining of heat and cold on his sensitive skin sent a riot of tingling up from his balls and down through his belly and his penis grew stiffer, longer. Then Irene fixed her large wide mouth over his long hard cock and sucked.

'I think it's my move now,' said Samoya, letting her shawl drop completely so that Anthony was able to see her nipples sticking out through the holes in her bodice. Picking up a counter she began to encircle them, pleasuring herself with the feel of ivory against her stiff, dark rosiness. 'But I think I've a better idea.' And Samoya traced the counter down over her breasts and her belly until it was resting on her clitoris. Then very slowly and lightly she began to rub her small erect protuberance.

'And now it's your move again,' said Samoya, opening and closing her legs slightly as she rubbed herself.

There was nothing he could do. His hands were too far from the table to touch a counter. Irene was sucking his cock until it was so thick that he felt he could almost take no more, was teetering on the verge of orgasm, and afraid he would soon topple into that abyss of pleasure. He was trembling. He wanted to take the beautiful innocent-faced licentious young woman sitting opposite him playing with her sex. He wanted to penetrate her slave, Irene, whose mouth was taking more and more of his shaft whilst holding his sac. His very essence was gurgling up within him. His stomach had tightened into a ball of longing. He couldn't hold it any more. With a long loud cry he came, spurting into her mouth.

In the distance Samoya was suddenly aware of voices. Her father and the bishop were returning. She covered herself decorously and put the counter back on the board. Irene sidled out from beneath the table. Anthony sat red-faced and confused. Samoya thought her father would ask questions about the game. Seeing him approaching she stood up quickly, deliberately upsetting the entire board. She looked at Anthony.

'Oh dear! Never mind. I think you won!' she said.

Her father hurried into the room closely followed by the bishop. Pernel seemed agitated.

'Where's the Princess?' he asked.

'In her room,' replied Samoya.

'We've just had a messenger from Palmyra. She's wanted back there immediately,' said Pernel, noticing Irene on the floor beside his daughter. 'You, go and tell Her Royal Highness.'

Within minutes Pernel's mansion was in a state of uproar. The Christian bishop and his secretary made a hurried departure. For very different reasons, both of them looking pleased with themselves. The bishop as he had obtained an exceptional vintage of wine at a very reasonable cost and Anthony because Irene's mouth had given him an excellent orgasm. He was quite amazed by the dexterity of her tongue and Samoya's aptitude for blatant sexual games had caught him unawares. He had thought the previous time, when she had fainted and grabbed his cock, that it was an accident. Now he realised she had engineered it. He made a note to visit Pernel's home again – soon. And perhaps he'd get the big blonde slave to go down on him once more. He walked in silence beside the bishop thinking perhaps her precocious mistress might devise some other but equally exciting games.

Unfortunately, Anthony's erotic fantasies were in vain. The news had not yet been announced that Samoya was to marry Prince Alif. When he found out he would console himself with the slaves at the bishop's palace. And hope that the time would come again when he would meet the violet-eyed beguiling daughter of Eve and her enchanting Nordic slave, Irene. And then he would screw the living daylights out of both of them for teasing him so well.

When Irene arrived in the opulent room and gave Princess Bernice the message that she was urgently needed back in Palmyra the Princess immediately threw herself into a simmering rage. Bernice had been looking forward to an evening and night of debauchery. She had planned a variety of lessons for Samoya and her slave. And punishments.

Bernice watched her two eunuchs pack away her special playthings and sighed with anger. A great opportunity had been lost. There were times when she regarded her brother the King as a nuisance. But his word was law. She had to obey and return immediately. A pity. Those two young women had deserved their punishment. Bernice looked across at Irene who was standing still and silently waiting to be dismissed. Well she would have to defer Samoya's lessons in obedience until she arrived in Palmyra but she could punish the two of them in a minor way now. She would take Irene with her.

Samoya was devastated when Princess Bernice announced her intention. By the time she stood on the steps of her father's mansion to wave them goodbye Samoya was a ball of pent up fury. She kissed Irene with tears streaming down her face. But it was all she could do to say a civil word to the Princess.

Before climbing onto her seated camel Bernice beckoned Samoya over. She parted her cloak and tweaked her nipples, reiterating her command that every bodice must have holes for her nipples, every skirt slit from top to toe and that she was to wear these things at all times. If decorum was needed she could cover up with a black or a white flowing robe. But no matter what, she must remain accessible. Bernice then gave orders for Samoya's arrival in Palmyra. She was to wear white and gold. She must be perfumed and oiled and arrive completely shaved.

'Prince Alif likes a naked mound,' she said. Then the camel driver hauled the camel up and Bernice rode leisurely away.

Samoya was standing by herself when she felt eyes boring into her. She turned to see the Princess's two enormous black charioteers leering at her. Samoya stared back at them. There was something about them that made her shiver. They approached her menacingly. Samoya refused to budge. She was not going to back down or show fear, especially on the steps of her own home. They put their hands under their tunics, and brought out their massive cocks. Samoya held her breath.

'One day, Lady,' they said, 'one day we're going to have you.'

'Never,' she said and spat at them.

'Oh we will and we'll make you pay for that.'

'Amos, Aaaron,' called the Princess Bernice. The two charioteers dropped their tunics hiding their huge members. They bowed insolently to Samoya, turned on their heels and joined their mistress. And then the Princess, her caravan and Irene were gone.

Samoya was left with her father and the preparations for their journey to Palmyra. For weeks everyone ran about hither and thither preparing Samoya's trousseau, especially her clothes; the finest cottons and silks were pleated and embroidered and sewn with gems. According to Princess Bernice's instructions, and with help from the two slaves she had left behind, Samoya ordered her dressmakers to make holes in all her bodices for her nipples and she had the holes edged with fine leather, so that they were secure and did not tear. And the slashes in her clothes were hemmed and edged properly so that they became part of the design. Under the watchful eye of Princess Bernice's two slaves, Phyllis and Hermione, the dressmakers did as they were told. But it did not stop them gossiping and the rumours in Antioch grew about the licentiousness of the Palmyrene court and how could Pernel allow his daughter to go to Palmyra.

Pernel ordered the jewellers to turn the most beautiful, flashing precious stones into diadems and bracelets, necklaces and anklets. And told the best wood-carvers to design and make stools and chairs and tables to go with his daughter to Palmyra. He bargained with the carpet merchants who came with samples from all over the world so that Samoya could take the finest merchandise with her. And Pernel and Samoya organised the caravan, the camels, the attendants and the route.

After some weeks Samoya managed to get away to see her friend Zenobia, but when she arrived at her opulent mansion it was in the process of being boarded up. Numerous camels were standing heavily laden in the street and Zenobia was instructing various camel drivers where to load her most precious belongings.

'We're leaving now for Palmyra,' Zenobia told her friend the moment she saw her puzzled face. 'We would have left by now if the Christian bishop hadn't arrived and started discussing theology with me. My father was furious but I can't resist a good debate.'

'How boring,' said Samoya, thinking there was the Great Goddess and that was that. 'Was his secretary with him?' she added.

'Oh the good-looking Anthony! No he wasn't. He's been sent to Alexandria for some reason or another.'

'But why are you going to Palmyra?' asked Samoya completely perplexed. Zenobia had given no indication that she was planning to leave Antioch. In fact, now Samoya thought about it, Zenobia had been most mysterious. She had not visited her at all in the previous weeks. She had been so busy preparing for her own journey it hadn't worried her but now she felt upset that her oldest, closest friend could have made such a decision and was leaving without saying goodbye.

'My father thinks we can do better business there now the war with the Persians is over,' Zenobia replied; deliberately omitting to tell Samoya that she had spent hours convincing her father that her prospects for a really good marriage would be considerably improved if they were in the Syrian capital.

'But . . .' wailed Samoya, 'I have so much to tell you.'

'Tell me now, quickly.'

'I can't.'

'Yes you can. Give me the gist,' said Zenobia sharply.

'Well, it looks as if I'll be going to Palmyra too,' said Samoya.

'What happened to Athens?'

'I can't go because I've agreed to marry Prince Alif.'

'Oh! I didn't think you wanted to marry,' said Zenobia.

'I didn't,' said Samoya.

'Well, what made you change your mind?'

'Princess Bernice,' said Samoya, enigmatically. Now was not the time for confidences. With slaves and camel drivers all around them she couldn't tell Zenobia any more. Neither could she ask her the questions she had wanted to ask about the Roman commander.

'Well Samoya, good luck and I'll see you in Palmyra,' said Zenobia, covering her tiny body and its beautiful coloured robes with her black desert cloak. The two friends kissed and Zenobia was helped up onto her camel and rode imperiously out of Antioch. Samoya gathered up her own slaves and trailed home aimlessly through the streets intensely disappointed and feeling alone and friendless.

She walked slowly with a sullen gait. Because she was feeling aggrieved, Samoya decided on impulse to defy her father's strictest orders and return to their mansion the long way round, via the market-place. Samoya told herself he had said that before her initiation, before she was officially a woman. Now she could do whatever she wanted.

A couple of her slaves demurred, pointing out that she was not suitably dressed for such an escapade. Samoya glanced down at her long finely pleated pale pink robe edged with gold that carefully hid the slashes that left her sex on display and the green bodice with her rosy nipples peeping through that also showed off the curve of her young breasts and her pale skin. She pulled her fine creamy-white silk cloak that enhanced her red-gold hair closer to her body. Secretly she agreed with them but she would not admit it.

'Stay close to me,' she said, 'we might find something nice, some pottery or a new trader with different carpets.'

But a couple of them who had felt Pernel's whip in the past for disobedience tried to argue with Samoya. This annoyed Samoya intensely. She slapped them hard, quickly silencing further protests by telling them they would be relegated to the kitchens if they disobeyed her.

The slaves gathered round protecting her from the stares of the shopkeepers and customers as they wound their way up and down the sun-bright cobbled streets. The closer they got to their destination the more wares were laid out on stalls in front of people's higgledy-piggledy homes. People were coming and going, arguing, buying and selling along a narrow channel in the centre of the street. Samoya found her illicit visit exciting and stopped and started amongst the stalls without fear, forgetting to keep close to her slaves. When she saw a beggar, remembering the old crone's words, she quickly slipped a gold coin into his hand.

Suddenly there was a roar and a commotion. Samoya found herself pressed against the wall as men in black cassocks went charging by, shouting and screaming, flailing their arms and throwing stones, and overturning barrows and trampling on the market-sellers' wares.

'What's happening, what's happening?' Samoya called out.

'Get back, stand back,' was the only response.

'They're arguing over the merits of the different gods,' cried somebody. And before anybody knew why there was a full-scale riot in progress. Everybody had joined in. The men in their black robes were fighting temple priests, market-sellers were hitting and punching one another. And everybody seemed to be sliding on fruit and slipping on vegetables. Terrified, Samoya looked around in desperation for her slaves. Some of them were lying injured on the ground, others had been caught up in the fighting and were being used as missiles and thrown across the stalls. The noise of the shouting and screaming and stands collapsing muffled the sound of horses' hoofs approaching. The first thing Samoya knew about them was when she was whisked into the air by a strong coal-black arm and dumped unceremoniously over the rider's lap. Rider and horse then galloped through the mêlée. People scattered before the oncoming stallion.

Once they were past the rioting crowd and the horse was moving at a sedate trot, Samoya, fed up with staring at coal-black muscular thighs, wriggled so that she could look up into the face of her rescuer. And fell instantly and wholeheartedly in love.

Her heart gave a leap as she gazed into the face of the most beautiful man she had ever seen. He was wearing Roman uniform, but she didn't know enough about Roman insignia to recognise his rank. But his bearing, the breadth of his shoulders, his stance in the saddle, everything about him was commanding. And sexy, very sexy. He drew on the rein and his pitch-black eyes stared down into hers.

'Where do you live?' he asked. His liquid brown honey tones washed over Samoya and she felt a fluttering in the pit of her stomach. 'And don't tell me near the market, because I'll know you're lying.'

Samoya hadn't even thought of telling a lie and gave her father's address straight away.

'Did he know where you were?'

'No,' she said and shivered at the thought of her father's anger. 'Oh my slaves, my poor slaves.'

'Don't worry about them,' said the Roman soldier, 'I had a platoon behind me, we saw what was going on, they had orders to pick everyone up.'

'But where will they take them?' asked Samoya worried. 'To the garrison?'

'Not everyone. They'll take your slaves to your home,' he said. 'Now, young lady, what's your name?'

'Samoya Cato,' she replied. 'And what's yours?'

'Marcus Protarchus, and I think you ought to ride in a more dignified position,' he said, helping Samoya to sit up and then held her steady in his arms.

Samoya's creamy-white cloak had kept her body completely covered. She was grateful for the protection it had provided but now she realised how much the slit skirt would be to her advantage. She spread her legs wide across his saddle so that the fold of her skirt fell neatly either side of her legs leaving her sex and buttocks bare. She leant her back against the Roman's leather breast-plate and manœuvred her bottom so that it nestled neatly between his thighs.

They trotted like that for some time until Samoya moved slightly. As she did so his penis began to move and grow. She felt it stiffening. She enjoyed the feeling and exaggerated the up/down movement of the horse so that she could enjoy it some more. His growing continued. His extension, his muscle with a life of its own was pushing its way between her bare buttocks and her sex. She tensed her labia muscles. She wanted him to think it was the movement of the horse that kept her jerking back on to his ever-enlarging phallus. And it was in part, but each time she landed on his manhood she squeezed her muscles and in return felt an answering tremor run through him.

Samoya edged herself forwards giving herself extra leverage. Then she moved back again onto what was now a long, thick, hard rod throbbing along the lips of her sex. This, she decided, was not only the best ride she had ever had but his member seemed to be equal to that of the gods in the bishop's murals.

They rode on in silence. She could feel her nipples hardening and turned from the waist, letting the cloak

62

covering them droop so that one of her nipples grazed his biceps. Marcus's arms held her closer. The whole of his body stiffening on this contact. Samoya spread her legs wider. She could feel a primeval wetness flowing from her innermost depths lubricating her movements. She was gliding on him, backwards and forwards. To onlookers they were riders in perfect harmony with the horse. Only they knew they were copulating.

Samoya's throat was parched. Her whole body was shaking as she kept up the rhythm. Every inch of her was screaming take me, take me. Then she felt his breath against her neck. Her scalp prickled. She swallowed hard. Her stomach had tightened into an excited knot. She moved her head to one side. His lips trailed over her hair and caught at her ear-lobe. Her sex expanded, opened, moved, under his erect penis.

'I want you,' he said, and flicked the reins so that the horse immediately set off at a gallop.

'Where are you taking me?' Samoya asked hoarsely.

'Somewhere I can fuck you,' he replied, and pointed the horse towards the city gates.

'Where's that?' she whispered.

'Wait and see,' he said, thrusting his hard member against her.

Marcus had decided that he would take her to the house where he and his commander were billeted. He would carry her upstairs to his room. He would hold her tight, he would kiss her lips, and slide his hands up her legs and his fingers would play with her secret hidden place. He knew she was wet and ready for him. He would caress her exposed nipples, tear away her bodice, fondle her lovely breasts. Then he would throw her back on his bed, part her legs wide, come up between her thighs and gently penetrate her open, wet wantonness.

Similar visions were taking place in Samoya's mind. But he had the advantage of knowing where he was going to do it. She had to set their love-making in a void. All she could see were his hands roaming over her pale body, touching her, exciting her, the feel of his fingertips on her nipples, his chest on her breasts, his lips on her lips, his tongue in her mouth. Samoya's mind was a whirl of anticipation. She didn't know which part of his body to concentrate on. His mouth coming down on hers, forcing her lips apart, pushing in with his tongue. His hands raising her robe, stroking her thighs and then touching her secret place, that would open for him. That was already tingling for him.

Her visions intensified. They took on an essence of reality. She would let her hands glide over his silken, glistening, coal-black muscular thighs. Samoya drew in a sharp breath as she thought of the moment she would hold his shaft. It would be stiff as a ramrod and she would lift his uniform and there it would be as massive as Jupiter's but black and throbbing with energy. Ready to plunge into her. Her hands would encircle it and feel its pulsating rhythm and desire. Samoya found she was holding onto his arm and rubbing it up and down as if it were his penis. He must have realised what she was thinking; between her legs the rod she was sitting on moved again and she wiggled in her wetness and in response.

Marcus clutched her tightly as they rode through the city gates. Samoya continued day-dreaming. First he would kiss her then he would lift her up and she would lock her legs around his waist and he would lower her onto the tip of his cock. She would be able to feel herself stretching as that magnificent member opened her and her sex took every last inch of him inside her.

Marcus placed her hand behind her back so that she could feel his shaft. The touch was electrifying. Her whole body shook with anticipation. She wanted to feel him on top of her, feel his body possessing her. Half a mile outside the city walls there was a large house standing on its own grounds. Marcus rode up to it, brought the horse to a sudden halt, called to a slave standing by the portico and threw him the horse's reins.

'Take him to the stables,' Marcus commanded, dismounting, then carried Samoya into the cool darkness of the house, sped up the stairs with her, and kicked open his bedroom door.

'My commander, Lucius Aurelian and I are billeted here.' He stood her on her feet them clamped his mouth on hers.

And the moment his body was aligned with hers Samoya became like a woman possessed. She no longer had command over her movements, her muscles, or her emotions. She swayed, undulating like a dancer, her hips went one way her breasts another, but with every inch of her body touching his. And then she let her hands wander down. She had to feel his penis. She had to take it in her hands. She also had to see it.

Marcus was quite naked beneath his uniform and as her hand reached for his cock and held it a great thrill rushed through her body. She looked at it and gasped. It was magnificent. She squirmed and parted her legs so that he could easily run his hands up and over her thighs. Automatically, she began to stroke his massive length. Up then down, up then down. He let out a great sigh as her cool hands held him and he took off his breast-plate revealing his broad hairless chest.

Samoya tingled from her throat to her belly as his fingers began gradually penetrating her open, moist willingness. Keeping his fingers inside her he lifted her up and carried her over to a large trestle-bed covered with cushions. He threw her down, pulled up her dress, spread her legs wide, put his mouth on her mouth and his cock at her hidden wet entrance.

Samoya wound her arms around his neck and raised her legs, wound them around his waist, and crossed her ankles over his back.

'Yes,' she whispered. 'Yes, take me now.'

Marcus needed no further bidding. Slowly, with great

care, he slid into her. Little by little he penetrated until she had opened completely and took the whole of him. They rolled and swayed and raised and lowered their bodies in unison. She stroked his back and held her hips high and he took her and rode her until the electrifying feelings in her body, the knots in her stomach, the dryness in her throat culminated in a moment of passion so intense that they both felt as if they were flying. And then they collapsed into each other's arms, and kissed gently.

Marcus took Samoya home in his commander's carriage. It was on the ride home that Samoya decided she would not marry Prince Alif. She would go with this magnificent soldier to Rome. She would sacrifice everything for him. She would become his wife.

'Are you married?' she asked. She thought it was a vital question that needed an immediate answer.

'No,' he laughed. 'Too much war and killing to think about love.'

'Would you like a wife?' she asked.

'Sometime,' he answered. 'But not yet. I don't want to leave a widow and fatherless children at the mercy of other men. I'll marry when I've finished soldiering.'

'When's that?' she asked.

'When I finish this term of duty and get back to Rome. The Persians are defeated and the Goths are quiet. We can have a period of peace. Perhaps I'll marry you. You could come with me to Rome.'

Marcus turned her face to his and kissed her lips. Samoya made no answer. Her heart was beating furiously, her mouth had gone dry and there seemed to be a gap between her stomach and her legs.

Marcus was slightly puzzled by her silence. But she had no intention of telling him she was betrothed to Prince Alif and was leaving soon for Palmyra. Not until she had informed her father that she no longer wanted to marry the Palmyrene prince but a young Roman soldier. Of course her father would be annoyed but he would give in. He always did. And she would take all her wonderful things, her clothes, her jewels in the other direction. To Rome instead of Palmyra. And she would live happily ever after.

'My father will be very angry with me,' Samoya announced. 'You see I shouldn't have been anywhere near the market-place.'

'Then we won't tell him,' said Marcus squeezing her hand.

'And I've been gone a very long time,' she added. 'How will we explain that?'

'He'll know about the riot so I'll tell him I found you unconscious and took you to the garrison and the physicians cared for you until you recovered.'

'Thank you,' Samoya said sweetly, kissing him once again.

The carriage turned into the street where her father's house was situated. And there Samoya received a shock. Camels and their attendants were blocking their way. Slaves were coming and going furiously from the house, loading up the camels then moving them on.

Someone called to her father. Pernel rushed out of the house and over to the carriage. He nodded grimly at Marcus and grabbed his daughter's arm.

'Your brothers are home from the war,' he said, almost dragging her out of the carriage and into the house.

Samoya had no time for fond farewells. She was frog-marched up the steps of the mansion into the great hall without a word. Marcus found a space to turn the carriage and went back the way they had come.

'We are leaving immediately for Palmyra,' said Pernel.

'But, but . . .' said Samoya, unaccustomed to being manhandled so roughly by anyone, especially her father.

'This city is too dangerous. Your brothers will look

after the business here whilst I take you to your wedding.'

'But Father . . .'

'No buts,' said Pernel savagely. 'Change into your travelling clothes. We're going now.'

Wearily Samoya trod the stairs to her bedroom which she found devoid of all her possessions except her black desert clothes. She undressed. Tears began to course down her face. Why hadn't she told Marcus the truth? He would never find her now. She would be hundreds and hundreds of miles away in Palmyra and he would go to Rome. They would never meet again.

With care Samoya put on the plain black bodice, skirt and cloak needed for the desert journey and a plan began to form in her mind. Perhaps she could leave the caravan? Perhaps she could get some of her slaves to come with her. If she offered them their freedom they might. She would have to make sure she took some of her jewels with her. It was no fun being poor. It was a nuisance that they had packed everything without her knowledge. She would have to be clever. Surreptitiously she must find out which camel-load held her jewels. She smiled at the thought of outwitting her father. Her tears stopped. She felt happier. She had made her decision. Once out in the desert she would steal away and go to Rome and find Marcus.

Chapter Four

When Princess Bernice and her lengthy caravan of hundreds of laden down camels rode out of Antioch she was neither pleased nor happy.

Pernel had given permission for his daughter to be married to Prince Alif but he was adamant that he would accompany Samoya to Palmyra, and that he would be staying there for and after the wedding. This did not suit Bernice one little bit. She had her own understanding with the Prince of the Bedouin. Any woman passing through the desert to Palmyra to be a wife at court could be enjoyed by him and, if he so desired, his men as well. But this could not happen if she was accompanied by her father. And especially not in Samoya's case. Pernel, his trade routes, knowledge and associates were too valuable to be upset. Somehow, thought Bernice, she had to separate the father and the daughter. But how?

Bernice was pondering this question when her caravan came to rest at an oasis of sand, stone, boulders and a few scrubby plants. Immediately her slaves began erecting her huge, luxurious tent and other smaller ones. Then, whilst Bernice ate her solitary dinner of roast lamb, unleavened bread and dates washed down with some of Pernel's best wine, her camel drivers set about greasing water skins, twisting ropes, mending saddles and looking after their animals. Only when all of that was done could they eat, play and finally sleep.

Before sundown a group of Bernice's bare-breasted female slaves entered on their knees. Crawling before her they kissed her feet then untied her leather belt with its phallic thongs and laid it beside her bed. They removed her day clothes. They rubbed her well-rounded sensual body with fragrant oils mixed with lemon juice, and after teasing her nipples, they lifted her onto her feather bed.

'Which of us is Your Highness's choice for tonight?' asked Kia, the fattest of the group.

'You are,' replied Bernice, stretching her arms upwards and opening her legs wide.

No sooner had Kia settled her head between her mistress's legs and begun licking her at the top of her thighs when she was interrupted by the noise of jingling bells. Minutes later they heard the unmistakable sound of camel hoofs pounding across the sands. Ordering the slave to stay exactly where she was, Bernice propped herself up on her cushions and waited for her tent flap to open. It didn't take long. Soon Tamoral, the tall, hawk-like and handsome Prince of the Bedouin, accompanied by three semi-naked, oiled and glistening tribesmen, stood in the doorway of Bernice's tent.

Bernice gave Tamoral one of her most cat-like smiles. He looked so commanding, so magnificent in his deep indigo desert robes, his embroidered headcloth fastened with a black woollen head-rope. And so sexy, with daggers stuck in his wide leather belt, his long curving sword hanging low beside his long sturdy legs, a riding crop in his hand, and the outline of his very large and throbbing penis clearly visible.

'Bernice, greetings,' he said in his deep brown voice, his penis instantly gaining further length, as he and it reacted to the sight of the two naked women cavorting on the bed.

'Tamoral!' exclaimed Bernice, squirming slightly as her slave touched her clitoris. 'I had no idea you were anywhere near. I have peppermint tea or coffee.'

'Neither for the moment.' Tamoral had no desire to drink. And he was no lover of the fashionable dark bitter coffee that merchants paid a fortune to obtain and bring back from Arabia. 'We've been shadowing you since Antioch. What were you doing there?'

'Finding a wife for Prince Alif.'

'Whom did you choose?' he asked, sitting down next to her and touching her nipples with the tip of his dagger.

'Samoya, Pernel's daughter,' replied Bernice.

'I heard she's very beautiful,' said Tamoral.

'She is.'

'Did she open her legs for you?'

'She did and I got one of my eunuchs to suck her.' Tamoral was instantly excited. He indicated to one of his slaves to raise his robes and make the Palmyrene princess aware of his glorious manhood. As the slave slowly lifted Tamoral's clothes to reveal his master's light brown cock standing large and thick, throbbing and proud, Bernice let out a deep sigh of longing. She tensed her fleshy buttocks. She knew the feel of that member and in a few seconds she would be feeling it again.

'Get hold of my cock and suck me,' said Tamoral urgently, flicking his riding crop against her hard nipples. He wanted to have her. Wanted to feel her squirming under him. And he wanted to hurt her. Wanted her to feel the pain of his longing. And wanted her to beg for mercy as his crop hit her rounded, bare buttocks. Twisting Bernice's hair between his fingers he aimed her head towards his belly and shoved his cock into her mouth. At the same time Bernice's hands cupped his large sac and juggled his testicles, enjoying

71

the sensation of his moving softness on her hands as her mouth ran up and down his huge erect shaft.

'Who had sex with you in Antioch?' he asked.

'Nobody,' Bernice answered, between licking the sides and head of his thick penis.

'You're lying,' he said threateningly, striking the crop against his hand.

'No, no, I'm not,' Bernice replied, sucking his member harder and faster in anticipation of the stripe to come.

'Men,' Tamoral called to the semi-naked warriors he had left at the entrance. Their cocks had shot to their full size as they watched the Princess being sucked by her slave whilst she sucked their leader's penis. Tamoral handed his crop to one of the slaves.

'Jai, take this,' Tamoral said, 'she tells me she hasn't succumbed to fleshly pleasures in Antioch. I don't believe her. Twelve stripes on her buttocks. Then you can have her.' Tamoral enjoyed humiliating the powerful Princess of Palmyra. He turned to the smallest of the three.

'Tika, pull that slave away.'

Grabbing the buxom Kia by her labia Tika did as he was told.

'Turn Her Highness over. Let's see her ample buttocks.'

These words gave a spur to Bernice's mouth. She worked harder on Tamoral's tool. In high anticipation she quickly changed her position from lying flat on her back to slightly kneeling and offered her big bottom, loose and inviting, to the crop. Jai held his own long and thin and very hard cock with one hand whilst administering to Bernice's raised backside with the other. Bernice winced as the first stripe hit her bare flesh and delicious, sweet pain swept through her body. She rolled and jumped and squealed and writhed as Tamoral gripped her hands, holding her prisoner. The man brought the crop down with considerable vigour leaving twelve deep, bright red weals criss-crossed on her naked flesh.

'Now, take her in her backside,' commanded Tamoral. Jai knelt between Bernice's legs, grabbed her hips, spread her cheeks and pulled her back onto his long thin upright penis. She was open and wet. Her juices had eased down and along to her anus. Jai entered Bernice with a fiery hardness, boring into her, making her reel, roll, quiver and squirm.

Tika slid on his back between Tamoral's legs, his mouth fixing over Bernice's large pendulous breasts whilst his clutching hands stretched Tamoral's buttocks wide apart so that Tika could graze his cock along his master's crevice. And the fat slave, Kia, crawled over and took Tika's pretty shaped tool into his thick-lipped mouth and let his tongue glide up and down, exciting him so that he felt a quickening in his belly and a desire to release himself.

The sun went down and the moon appeared, lighting up the six of them as their bodies rolled and glistened in the moonlight.

Later, alone with Tamoral, Bernice nestled her luscious body into his firm, well-muscled groin and positioned her marked buttocks onto the tip of his cock.

'Can you think of a way to prise Samoya away from her father?' Bernice asked. 'And I mean without arousing his suspicion or incurring his wrath.'

'Can't we bribe anyone?' asked Tamoral. 'Hasn't he got an heir we could use, manipulate and later blackmail?'

'Not to my knowledge,' replied Bernice.

Then she told Tamoral that whilst she was in Antioch she had tried to discover who his heir was, but to no avail. His vast business empire seemed to be a one-man concern. A dictatorship. Bernice also told him that she'd noticed the only other person present during business meetings had been Samoya. Both Bernice and Tamoral dismissed her as a possible heir.

'And is she still a virgin?' Tamoral asked.

'Technically,' Bernice replied. Tamoral's shaft twitched into life at the thought. He could be the first. He placed Bernice's hand on the head of his penis and told her to leave the planning to him. He had no intention of missing the opportunity of an orgy in the desert. He would organise things so that Samoya arrived in Palmyra without her ever watchful father.

'I must say he's not that watchful, I managed to teach her a few things,' said Bernice. 'And she was very quick to learn. Almost too quick. So I brought her favourite slave away with me as a punishment.'

'Where's this slave now?' asked Tamoral.

'In the next tent. Do you want to see her?'

'Yes, have her brought here.'

'I suggest we go to her,' said Bernice. Bernice draped a long, red silk robe over her luscious body and she and Tamoral stepped out of her tent into the sharp coldness of the desert night air. Bernice stopped at a tent considerably smaller than her own but still big enough for at least ten men and women to stand up in and walk around. She lifted the front flap and she and Tamoral walked in. Tamoral let out a gasp.

Irene was kneeling. Her pale, rounded, bare, freshly crop-marked bottom was up high facing them. Her ankles had heavy chains attached to them and her legs were tethered apart to balls of stone. Tamoral moved round to the side of the girl. Her elbows and forearms rested on a carpet thrown down on the sand. Her wrists were bound together. Her head was resting on the sides of her hands. She was blindfolded and her mouth was gagged. Her long blonde hair fell over her shoulders and hung free, not touching her breasts, which were encased in tight leather with only the nipples poking through. This bodice reached to her waist and was then tightened by leather thongs, forcing her flanks to swell out. Tamoral moved back to stare again at her buttocks. There was a large, polished, wooden penis inserted in her anus. It was attached to chains around her waist and upper thighs.

Bernice clapped her hands. From another flap at the back of the tent Bernice's two Nubians appeared accompanied by a couple of large, heavy-breasted women. All of them were naked. All had different sized leather dildoes strapped on to them. One was long and thin, one was short and fat, one was small and thin and the last one large and thick. They stood to attention close by the kneeling girl.

'She was too tight. They are taking it in turns to sodomise her,' said Princess Bernice. 'She had to be opened. In between their own penetrations they insert one of my playthings to keep her stretched. Do you want to watch or indulge yourself?'

'Watch,' he replied.

Bernice ordered the two eunuchs to unlock the chains and remove the wooden penis. The girl let out a sigh. Tamoral didn't know whether it was one of joy, relief or fear. Bernice moved over to one of her heavy-breasted slaves, fondled her nipples and then, pulling her by her short, fat dildo, placed her between Irene's legs.

'You first,' said Bernice.

The big woman positioned herself and then, gripping Irene's hips, lunged into the slave's freshly stretched orifice. The sight of the large olive-skinned woman's pendulous breasts moving up and down as she ploughed the dildo into the blonde girl's anus excited Bernice and she put out a hand to rub Tamoral's cock. But he had moved away to the far side of the tent. 'Change, and change each time I clap my hands,' said Bernice.

Irene knelt in total submission and without a murmur took the constant ramming of her changing and leather endowed partners. Tamoral sat on his haunches and stared at her head. Her hair covering her face was jerking backwards and forwards to the rhythm of the movements. It was the first time he had seen anyone so pale and blonde. And something inside him did not want her violation to continue. He didn't know why. He watched but was receiving no pleasure.

'Stop,' he suddenly shouted, getting to his feet and waving his arms about. 'Go, leave us.'

'What's the matter?' asked Bernice bewildered, as her slaves left the tent wondering what they had done wrong.

'I want her,' he answered.

'Take her. I asked you if you wanted to watch or indulge. So take her now.'

'I want her to keep.'

'What! You can't have her.'

'Why not?'

'Because she's mine.'

'I'll buy her.'

'I've got more money than I need. And, Tamoral, you've got nothing I want,' said Bernice.

'Oh but I have,' replied Tamoral.

'Oh yes, I'd like to know what that could be!' exclaimed Bernice, sarcastically.

'The disruption of Pernel's caravan. Parting father from daughter. And you know very well only I can do it. Only I have enough cunning and enough men. So, I propose we trade the girl for your plan.'

Bernice sat down and considered this. It was not what she had expected. She thought Tamoral would have received great pleasure from watching the blonde slave being sodomised and then doing it himself. But ordering it to stop! That was against his character. He must want her for some devious plan of his own. Bernice calculated quickly. A silly, fat, blonde slave-girl in return for Pernel being sent back to Antioch and Samoya arriving in Palmyra on her own but with her dowry. There was no contest. Whatever Tamoral wanted of Irene he could have. She was worthless.

'Very well. It's a bargain,' she said.

'Good, have her released, cleaned up, rubbed down with oils and put some other clothes on her. I'll take her with me,' he said, then grabbed hold of Bernice's hand and dragged her back to her own tent. 'Time to have you now, bitch,' he said.

Tamoral pulled Bernice backwards onto his chest, manœuvred himself to one side, spread one of Bernice's legs wide across his belly, held her huge breasts with his hands, squeezed her nipples hard, very hard, then let his prick trail upwards so that it entered her luscious, wanton, open and very wet pussy from underneath. He thrust his thick proud penis into her as she writhed and gasped for more, and harder. Then he withdrew and finding her other hole, without warning plundered it ravenously. And he bit her and scraped her belly with his nails. Bernice didn't mind. She loved it. The harder the better. She bucked and writhed. The feel of his shaft stretching her, taking her, filling her up, excited Bernice almost beyond endurance. The tightening in her belly started again. Her legs went rigid, she raised her buttocks and began to shake. Feeling her close to coming, contracting against him, Tamoral pounded and pounded. He needed every inch of her to be subjected to him and then, panting out a great shriek they came together, and Bernice fell asleep.

She woke at dawn to find Prince Tamoral, his men, and Irene had gone. She was well satisfied, though she had a slight niggle about the blonde slave. However, Tamoral had seen to her own needs so there was no cause for jealousy. And she had aroused his curiosity concerning Samoya. Tamoral would make sure the father returned to Antioch and that Tamoral travelled on alone to Palmyra. She looked forward to having Samoya to herself. She thought of the things she would do to her. She found herself becoming wet again.

Then she had another idea. She went to her great box where she kept her papyrus and her seal. She addressed a letter to Pernel. In it she wrote how she was sending her two best, most accomplished slaves as extra escort for Samoya on her journey to Palmyra. Bernice smiled to herself. They would protect her investment. She would give them permission to keep the young woman occupied at night. And during the day they would keep their eyes skinned for marauders and when Tamoral arrived they would be on hand to make sure the Bedouin did what she wanted: remove Pernel from his daughter. And nothing else. The slight niggle in Bernice's head about Tamoral's insistence on taking the young blonde slave had, in a short space of time, grown to full-blown resentment. Tamoral might not do as she had ordered. He might take Samoya and hold her ransom. This way she had witnesses to his behaviour. She called for her two charioteers, Amos and Aaron. She gave them the sealed letter and told them to return to Antioch. To find Pernel. If his caravan had already left they were to join it. They were to stick close to the Lady Samoya. She opened her other box where she kept her playthings. She took out a number of manacles and whips.

'At night you will stay in her tent and you will keep the lady amused,' she said, giving them the various objects. 'You will stay by her at all times and when the Bedouin arrive to escort her on the final part of her journey you will not leave her side.'

'What exactly can we do to her? Whip her?'

'Yes.'

'Can we fuck her?'

'Oh I think so,' said the Princess reaching for their shafts which had jumped up almost to order. She began playing with them. The feel of their skin and their massive hard-ons excited her. 'When you get back to Palmyra you will report straight to me on everything that happens. Is that understood?'

'Yes, Your Highness,' they said.

'And when you arrive you will make sure that she is carrying out my instructions as far as her dress is concerned. Check that her skirts are slashed from waist to toe and that her nipples show through the bodice. If not, that will be a good enough reason to punish her, and if she has done as she's told, I'll let you think of something else.' And lifting her skirts Bernice bent over.

'Yes, Your Highness,' they said, grinning in anticipation at the sight of her bare bottom.

'Amos, fuck me,' she said. 'A quickie, then both of you can go, and enjoy.'

Amos pulled the Princess's luscious rump back on to his huge cock and rammed it straight up into her. He pounded and thrust solidly for a few minutes. Then he came. Amos and Aaron departed. Bernice ordered her tent to be taken down and her caravan to move on to Palmyra.

Irene felt dazed and sore. Uncoupled from her chains she stood trembling and exhausted waiting for the next onslaught on her body. But it didn't happen. Instead she was wrapped in a rough, dark cloth and bundled across the sands to a group of small tents that Tamoral's men had pitched on the far side of the oasis.

The fierce war-like tribesmen gave her a drink she didn't recognise, she thought perhaps it was camel's milk. But it was sweet not salty. Perhaps they had added something to it. Bernice had allowed her only the bitter, gritty desert water. Having drunk it they surprised her by gently tucking her in sheep skins and leaving her to sleep.

She had no idea how long she slept but it was still dark when she shot out of her dreams. She stumbled to her feet. Dazed and sore for a few moments she couldn't think where she was, or even who she was. She was wearing clothes she didn't recognise. And she was clean and fresh smelling. Whilst she slept someone had bathed her with oils and dressed her. But she looked like a man. She had been kitted out with a man's outfit, red and white patterned head-dress, long, white, coarse linen shirt, roped around the middle and complete with dagger and sword and the whole of her had been covered with a russet coloured cloak and hood, a burnouse. Irene was completely mystified.

The previous weeks, crossing the desert with Bernice had been utter misery. She had been treated as a plaything by every member of the caravan. They had done exactly as they liked. They had whipped her, sucked her, chained her. She had endured the wooden penis and the leather dildoes and not one of them, neither man nor woman, had shown any remorse.

She had been made to wear strange leather clothes where her nipples stuck out through holes and her bottom swelled out from the tightened waist. Her belly, sex and buttocks were bare and accessible. Barefoot, she had to wear a collar and chain around her neck and perform like a dancing bear. Although covered from head to toe in the black desert cloak, Bernice had given orders that if anyone so desired they could feel her, suck her or even fuck her *en route*. She had had to resign herself to the cloak suddenly being lifted and hands feeling her sex, a cock being thrust between her legs and possibly inside her. At night she was put in a tent on her own, chained to stone balls, gagged and, starting with Bernice, who enjoyed the ritual of subjecting Irene to various humiliations, was penetrated by a queue of dildo-wearing eunuchs and women. Then later, after they'd finished and she had fallen asleep, she was woken in the night for the use of the camel drivers.

Tamoral cat-napped for a few hours then lay back against his saddle, his arms crossed above his head, thinking. He still had no idea what made him take the slave away from Bernice. Had it been the long, thick blonde hair bobbing backwards and forwards? Or the girl's passive acceptance of her torture? Or had it been the strange sigh that had issued from her when the wooden penis had been withdrawn. Or was it simply the very paleness of her skin, the like of which he had never seen before, that made him make such an odd decision. He hadn't even seen her face; the curvaceous shape of her rump, but not her face. Moreover, he had given himself a major problem. Whatever she looked like, what was he going to do with her? Raiding parties never travelled with women.

So far his men hadn't questioned him. They had carried out his instructions impeccably. There was no sign of rebellion. As yet. He was their undisputed leader. By his wilyness he protected them. They gave him their allegiance. But one false move, one bad decision and he knew his fiercely independent tribe would turn on him. With the swiftness of a desert leopard Tamoral leapt to his feet, marched out of his tent and into Irene's.

Irene had her back to the tent flap when Tamoral entered. Sensing his arrival more than hearing it she had turned quickly to face him, her heart beating fast with fear. She stood in front of him shrouded in the rust coloured burnouse. He marched up to her, threw back the hood and removed the headcloth. Holding a candle up to her face he scrutinised her. Her downcast pale blue eyes were fringed with soft, golden eyelashes. Her creamy white complexion was tinged with a rosy glow on her cheeks. Her nose was short and straight, her mouth was wide, red and full. Her white-blonde hair fell thick and straight, past her large breasts almost to her waist. She was a beauty, he thought. A strange beauty, more akin to a marble statue than a person. And she was his. His slave, he had bought her. He could do what he liked with her. The choice was his if she lived or died. He pulled the dagger from the rope belt encircling his waist.

Irene didn't move. So this was going to be her execution. So be it. Death could not be worse than travelling with Bernice. She would meet it bravely. She lifted her head and stared defiantly straight into Tamoral's hooded, dark brown eyes.

'Do you know how to use this?' he asked, pointing the dagger at her.

'No,' she replied, more gently than she intended. His question had puzzled her. Thrown her off balance.

'I will teach you,' he said. 'And anybody who comes near you again, you will kill them.'

Irene said nothing. She was thinking this was the voice she heard last night ordering her release. It was also the voice that had bartered her for some sort of attack on Samoya's caravan to Palmyra. She owed him no thanks. But if he was offering her the ability to learn how to defend herself then she would take it. But she wouldn't be grateful. Gratitude had no place in Irene's vocabulary of emotions.

'What is your name?' he asked.

'Irene,' she replied.

'It isn't any more. You'll be called . . .' and at that moment he stopped short. He cocked his head as if listening to the softest whisper that had drifted on the wind, over mountains, plains, land and seas to meet him in the desert. 'Dagmar.'

The name came out strange, foreign to him. He said it as if compelled but surprised by the compulsion and the sound. He repeated it this time as if it was his own.

'Dagmar. You will be called Dagmar.'

Irene stared at him, appalled and fascinated. She knew the name. It had been her birth name. The name her mother had called her by when they lived in the north. Before the war. Before they had been taken into slavery. Before the Roman who had first bought them had changed it to Irene. For the first time in a long while she smiled.

'Dagmar. I won't forget,' she assured him.

'Come. Follow me. We're leaving soon.'

'Where are we going?' she asked.

'Wherever I say we go,' he answered.

Outside in the chilly night air some of his men had prepared a fire from camel dung and were busy roasting goat. Others had taken the camels down to the green water edged with rushes to drink. And whilst the camels filled their humps the men filled their goatskins. Tamoral sat her beside him close to the fire.

'You will eat and drink now with us,' he said, hauling the meat from the fire and dividing it into pieces. He speared her portion with a stick, handed it to her telling her not to eat until all his men were present. She reached out a hand to take it. Hurriedly he dashed it to the ground.

'Your left hand is only for washing and pointing to an enemy,' he said. 'Everything else is done with the right hand.'

When all his men were assembled Tamoral told Irene to stand.

'This is Dagmar,' he said. 'A new warrior. She will be taught everything we know. She will be respected and never touched. She is no longer a woman. She is no longer a slave. She is one of us. She will abide by our rules. And I want her welcomed. Dagmar, you will shake hands with every man here. From now on they are your comrades.' And Dagmar, the new Bedu warrior, walked ceremoniously round the fire shaking hands with every man.

'Today we ride. Tomorrow you will learn to be a soldier,' said Tamoral, lifting his food to his mouth.

It was a signal for them all to eat. Dagmar looked on quietly watching every move they made. So the first part of the old crone's prediction was coming true. She munched on the charcoaled meat and wondered what else was going to happen. She had mentioned war. But that had just ended. Peace reigned. The Persians were beaten. The Romans ruled. War could never happen. The ancient must have got that wrong. And Samoya? She wondered about Samoya. Somehow she had to warn her that her caravan was going to be attacked. But how could she? The Bedu were now her brothers. Samoya was in the past.

Before dawn broke, they broke camp. Tamoral gave her a camel newly prepared for her. She had walked into the oasis Irene, the slave. She was riding out as Dagmar, free, the soldier. And she would never be known as Irene again.

Chapter Five

Zenobia believed in fate. Her fate. She also believed in making it easy for fate to find her. She was not one to cower behind doors, windows, walls or veils as if afraid of it. No, Zenobia believed in going out there and meeting fate on the road. Shaking fate's hand, bowing, even kissing it, but most certainly welcoming it with open arms.

Her father paid the Bedouin a large sum to protect them on their journey to Palmyra and they did. Zenobia, covered in her black desert burnouse, spent most of the time up with the leaders of the caravan. She asked many questions but gave them no information. She was thinking, her eyes taking in everything.

She noticed how the countryside changed from the fertile plains with its cultivated fields of grain and orchards of olive and mulberry trees to the mountains where the cedars grew and firs, pines, juniper, and cypress, to the rocky patches where only brushwood and tamarisk flourished. And then the desert where very little vegetation managed to survive. She also noted and filed away in her memory the ridges and the wadis of the desert.

She let her mind dwell on her friends. Especially

Samoya. Zenobia thought it odd that she had agreed to marry Prince Alif. He had a sordid reputation. She wondered what had changed her mind. Samoya had been so intent on becoming a doctor. She would find out more when they met up in Palmyra. They would discuss things. No doubt Samoya would talk about men. Whilst she would think about power. The cycle of their relationship would begin again. And Paul, the Bishop of Antioch. Zenobia really missed him. His sense of humour, His outrageous size and incorrigible sense of humour. She would write and ask Paul to visit her. And then she thought about the Roman commander. But she didn't dwell too long on that thought. She dismissed it quickly. That was far too uncomfortable.

It didn't take long for Zenobia to settle in to life in Palmyra. On their first day in the city her father had bought a large crumbling mansion. Its grounds were not big enough for his liking so he acquired the adjoining land which had been settled on *ad hoc* by nomadic families. They had built up a shanty village of tents and hovels. He had kicked the people out, broken up their tents, knocked down their hovels and had the area landscaped into a beautiful garden for his daughter's benefit.

Zenobia protested at his harshness. Her father retorted that he was a self-made man and if they weren't so idle they too could have made a lot of money. But Zenobia failed to see the sense in that argument, because if the poor people had more that meant the rich would have less. And she didn't want that. But she felt she had a duty not to make the poor, poorer. At her mother's death Zenobia had become a rich woman in her own right. She decided that the families must not be abandoned and set about finding them and providing them with the wherewithal so that they could find somewhere decent to live in another part of that teeming and expensive city. And they never forgot her kindness.

The best architects in Palmyra were employed to redesign and reshape the old mansion. An army of workers; stone-masons, carpenters, plasterers, and artists, those who made mosaics and those who painted murals, were then called in to do the work. It was to be the finest, most modern mansion in the whole of Palmyra. Many people came to stare at it during the construction. They included the old rich who, influenced by Rome and Roman thought and style, pronounced it gaudy and ostentatious. The main work was done quite quickly and she and her father were able to move in. He to conduct his business, whilst Zenobia ordered the finer touches to the building and discussed plants with the gardeners.

Whatever she was doing Zenobia always looked as if she was going to a major social function. She always wore robes of the finest silks coloured with the best dyes and masses of jewellery. Her hair was piled up, Grecian style, and held in place with a headband studded with gems. She wore bangles and necklaces and anklets and ear-rings. Zenobia had a passion for ostentatious jewellery; she possessed an inordinate quantity and wore as much as she could whenever she could. Seeing her, many of the older women tut-tutted their disapproval. But Zenobia didn't care.

Standing on a mound in the garden, wearing a geometric concoction of bright green, orange and purple, with her gems flashing in the sunlight, Zenobia was supervising the planting of an orchard of lemon and orange trees, when she heard a low rumble that quickly developed into a thunderous clatter. She looked up to the surrounding hills. The victorious Palmyrene army was returning from Persia.

Realising they would head for the Great Temple at the top of Palmyra's mile-long central avenue, where they would give thanks, Zenobia gathered up various slaves and ordered them to accompany her. She would go there too and have a prime view of the procession.

By the time she arrived most of the population had had the same idea. The place was packed tight with sightseers. People from every walk of life were everywhere. Hanging out of windows, hanging on to statues. Sitting on top of statues, sitting on the plinths of the statues; as most of these were halfway up the walls of various municipal buildings this was quite a precarious perch. Protected by her circle of hefty slaves Zenobia took up her position close to the steps of the Temple of the Sun. She ordered her tallest slave to put her up on his shoulders. She wanted to get a good view of the victors but most of all she wanted to see their great Prince Odainat. News had already filtered through that the Emperor Gallienus was pleased with his army and especially pleased with him. He had heaped various titles on Odainat as a reward. Zenobia wanted to see if Odainat had the look of an emperor about him. If he would be worth marrying.

Trumpets were blowing. Drums were being struck, cymbals were crashing. The noise increased to a deafening level as the amy approached the temple. Zenobia felt a quickening in her gut as she watched the colours of the banners, the glinting of the long javelins, the cavalry with their distinctive armour covering both man and rider. And the heroes of the whole campaign, the archers, were holding up their special composite bows, letting out war cries, which were echoed by the ululating women in the crowd. Every bit of it excited her, she wanted to be a part of it. She wanted it to happen to her. The glory of a victorious army coming home.

And then she saw him standing high in his ornate war chariot. Tall and handsome with a short, clipped black beard. Every inch an emperor. So very different to his short, fat, bloated brother, King Hairan, who had come out onto the steps of the temple with the High Priest of the Sun and was waiting to greet him.

In that great mass of people, most of whom were dressed in either black or white, Odainat's attention was caught by the small figure radiant in colour and sparkling gems, sitting on the shoulder of a very tall man. He paused as he stepped out of his chariot and before ascending the temple steps. He turned slightly. Their eyes met. He bowed in her direction. A great cheer went up from the crowd. Odainat then continued up the steps to make his obeisance to his King and to the God.

Zenobia watched Odainat stride with his back straight, his Generals in formation behind him and she cheered and waved along with the thousands of others as he entered the temple. Then she ordered the slave to put her down and bade him and the others accompany her home. She had work to do.

'Father, I want the biggest banquet Palmyra's ever seen,' said Zenobia, later. 'I want us to welcome the heroes.'

Her father wasn't paying attention. He was busy trying to organise a new caravan to the East.

'Father!' Zenobia was exasperated. 'It's going to cost a lot of money.'

She knew that would get his attention.

'What is?' he asked sourly.

'The banquet we're going to give for the King and Prince Odainat.'

'Are we?' he asked, bemused by his daughter.

'Yes,' she said determinedly.

'Why?'

'Because it will be good for business,' she replied shrewdly. 'You'll be spending a lot of money to make a lot of money.'

'That's a certainty is it?'

'Definitely. It'll mark the turning point in both our fortunes and our lives,' she said prophetically.

Zenobia's father trusted his daughter's exceptional business acumen and he agreed. Zenobia set about planning the banquet as if it were a military campaign. Nothing that could be foreseen would be left to chance. She would provide everything that returning heroes needed. Food, wine, women, men (for those so inclined), and every item, every person would be hand-picked. She would make certain that it was the most superb banquet anybody had ever been to. Only a woman with great ability could provide such a banquet. Everybody would say so. And Odainat would find her entrancing, exciting and unforgettable. She knew he had mourned for his wife for years. She had discovered that nobody had replaced her in his affections. Zenobia had every intention of supplanting that long-dead woman. Nothing could go wrong. The gods were on her side. They hadn't given her an exceptional brain, able to analyse, think, memorise and act, for nothing. But Zenobia had forgotten that the gods can sometimes play tricks on mortals, and upset even the best laid plans.

From dawn until late at night she worked. Once in bed, over stimulated, she found it difficult to sleep. She lay with her eyes open, dreaming. She imagined the powerful, handsome Odainat touching her. Kissing her, feeling her breasts, touching her between her legs. Slowly with these thoughts she drifted into sleep. But it was at that moment hung between sleep and wakefulness that Odainat became the Roman commander. As ever, she dismissed that image and switched off all thoughts until morning.

Samoya sat dreamily on her camel not noticing anything. Her thoughts were all of Marcus and how she could leave the caravan and follow him to Rome. It would be difficult. Her father seemed exceptionally conscientious. He was polite; let no one else in the caravan realise that he was extremely annoyed with her for going into the market-place against his wishes, disappearing and reappearing with a handsome Roman officer in tow. He made her ride beside him. She had very little opportunity for any conversation with anyone, not even her female slaves. And her father slept in her tent. She was furious. But she smiled and was gentle. After a few days she knew he would relax. Soon his anger would subside. All she had to do was bide her time. Then she would get her female slaves back. And she could begin planning her escape.

Samoya, jerking to the rhythm of the animal carrying her, let her mind wander back to the events of the previous weeks, of her sexual awakening. Samoya stayed deep in her own day-dreams, unaware of anything. No danger signals reached her, she was too involved in her own mind. Samoya constantly thought about the moment when Marcus had carried her to the trestle bed and she had raised her legs and clasped them around his waist and he had entered her. Penetrated. Slid into her wet sex. And she had taken him, all of him. She conjured up the feel of him as his thick full black cock had glided in. The more she thought about it the more she felt her nipples hardening as they had done during the ride with him through the city, and she had allowed her cloak to drop, her breasts pressing against the muscles of his strong arms. And his cock had stiffened further beneath her. She squeezed her inner muscles as she remembered how their united bodies had rolled and swayed. And electrifying sensations had poured through her as he had pounded into her with an exultant passion.

She re-lived her time with Princess Bernice and Irene. She shut out the changing landscape and remembered with a wicked, licentious shudder the Princess's hands caressing her body, and kissing and sucking Irene.

Samoya's wedding caravan passed out of the fields and the woods into the scrublands on the edge of the desert where the sands spread endlessly before them. It was dusk and the leading camel drivers had announced they would camp for the night. In the morning the Bedouin would arrive. They would be their escort on the final half of the journey, which had been remarkably uneventful. Her father began to relax his vigilance. She insisted that some of her female slaves be returned to spend the night with her in her tent. He acquiesced surprisingly quickly. Samoya wondered if he too was tired of the arrangement. She looked at him. He was a good-looking man. No doubt he had his own sex life. It was something she had never given much thought to. Perhaps there was a woman amongst the slaves he wanted.

The long caravan took time to make camp. Samoya, riding up with the leaders had her tent erected first. Slaves brought many thick, beautiful carpets and laid them on the scrubby earth, high poles were secured into the ground then covered with varieties of cloth and skins. Inside wall-hangings were draped to cut out sound and make it cosy. And candles were lit. Masses of very large cushions were spread out as bedding and, weary from her long ride, Samoya lay down and rested. Small low tables covered with tasty morsels for nibbling before dinner were placed before her. Outside, cooks roasted a goat. Pernel sent Phyllis and Hermione to her tent. They were the inseparable friends from Macedonia that Princess Bernice had left behind to help her dressmakers. Olive skinned, fine looking, tall, the strapping girls enjoyed doing everything together. Apart from that Samoya knew very little about them. They hadn't mixed with the other slaves. Samoya was surprised that her father should have sent these two to her. Inwardly wary, she smiled at them, thinking her father had outwitted her. There was something about these two women she did not trust. However, they brought her jewel boxes with them.

And then the squabbling started. At the far end of the line of camels two drivers began arguing. It developed into a full-scale punch up. Pernel, before he had time to supervise the setting up of his own tent, had to take various slaves, travel the couple of miles back down the line and stop the altercation.

Samoya was unaware of this as she sat down to eat roast goat and dates and fresh fruit. When she had finished eating the two women undressed her. It was the first time anyone in the caravan had seen Samoya without her burnouse. The enormous cloak with its hood covered every part of her.

'My Lady you are very beautiful,' they said staring at her erect rosy-pink nipples that were peeping out from the holes in her yellow bodice. 'Do you colour them, your nipples?'

'No,' she said.

'Oh that's a pity,' they said. 'Perhaps we could do that for you?'

'Yes,' said Samoya, excited by the idea. She wanted her body touched again. The slaves putting make-up on her nipples was a good excuse. 'My make-up boxes are there.'

The two women fetched an array of gold boxes and laid them out in front of their mistress. Samoya lay down on a number of cushions. The women knelt on either side of her and slowly began rubbing the colour into the tips of her nipples. The gentle pressure began to make Samoya feel incredibly aroused. When their hands slid away from her nipples and encircled the rest of her breasts she sighed and opened her legs. Her skirt fell apart leaving her nakedness on show.

'Sometimes,' said Phyllis, licking her lips at the sight of Samoya's red-gold triangle, 'it's nice to have a little colour down there too. Would you like me to do that?'

'Yes,' said Samoya, feebly, as her body began to writhe to the insistent rhythm of Hermione's hands on her breasts.

Phyllis turned her body, stretched out a hand and began to stroke Samoya's sex.

'Has My Lady been thinking naughty thoughts?' Phyllis asked.

'Why do you ask?' queried Samoya, breathlessly.

'Because My Lady is very wet,' she said, a finger finding Samoya's clitoris and lightly touching it.

Samoya let out a deep sigh and raised her hips.

'I think My Lady has been imagining somebody stroking her like this,' said Phyllis, and she moved her finger slightly so that it rubbed against the outer rim of Samoya's sex. Samoya squirmed.

'Did the Princess do this to you?' she asked. 'She has a reputation for knowing how to please other women. Did she teach you to open your legs and let her fingers roam over you?' Samoya didn't answer. She was too busy enjoying the sensation of Phyllis rubbing her labia and Hermione caressing her breasts. Instead, Samoya rolled her hips. Her mouth had gone dry. Phyllis's fingers, deliberately not entering her sex, continued to play on the outer rim and it was exciting her more and more. Her pussy was becoming wetter and wetter. She put out a hand and lifted Hermione's dress. She let her hands feel the strong limbs of the slave.

'So My Lady wants to touch us, does she?' said Phyllis. 'Hermione, make it easy for My Lady to feel you.'

Hermione instantly unwrapped her skirt and knelt beside Samoya so that her bare bottom and moist pussy were facing Samoya's mouth. Samoya's hand began to travel up the slave's thighs and then she let her finger touch Hermione's wetness. The softness of the yielding flesh beneath her fingers made her catch her breath. Samoya thrust suddenly and hard into Hermione's willing sex. And Phyllis's fingers continued to rub at Samoya's own entrance, occasionally flicking upwards onto her clitoris.

'Would My Lady like me to suck her?' asked Phyllis. 'Would she like me to put my tongue in her wet pussy?'

'Yes,' gasped Samoya.

'How much would she like me to do that?' asked the

Macedonian slave, beginning to jab her fingers further into Samoya's sex.

'A lot,' said Samoya, rolling her hips whilst thrusting her own fingers further into Hermione.

'Then I will,' said Phyllis. She bent her head over Samoya's mound and gave her clitoris a quick flick with her tongue. Samoya raised her hips wanting more. 'But first you have to tell us what made you so wet in the first place. What were you thinking about? Was it a man?'

'Yes,' said Samoya.

'And did he have a big cock?'

'Yes,' said Samoya.

'And did he shove this big cock into you?'

'Yes,' said Samoya.

Phyllis nibbled on Samoya's clitoris again sending more delicious feelings of wantonness flooding through her.

'How did he do that?' Phyllis asked, removing her tongue, just leaving her fingers playing on Samoya's labia. 'Tell us.'

Samoya wanted to tell them but she was also wary. These were Bernice's slaves and could be spies. She would let them think she'd been fantasising.

'I imagined a man who came along out of nowhere and picked me up,' she said, 'then threw me down on a bed and I opened my legs wide and put them around his waist, crossing my feet over his back.'

'Yes, and then . . .' said Phyllis nibbling again at Samoya's clitoris, whilst she was still playing with Hermione's sex.

'He positioned his penis . . .'

'Like this?' said Phyllis and placed two fingers just inside Samoya's entrance. The feeling of the slave's deft fingers and the memory of Marcus's cock was almost too much for Samoya. For a moment she couldn't speak. Her whole body was tingling. She desperately wanted

95

to feel her sex opened up, ravaged, taken, played with, screwed.

'Yes,' said Samoya. 'And then he plunged it into me.'

As she said that Phyllis rammed her two fingers hard up inside Samoya's sex, and Samoya instantly lifted her hips and jammed her own fingers harder into Hermione.

'So, My Lady wants to be screwed does she?' said Phyllis.

'No, no,' said Samoya, imagining how wonderful it would be to feel Marcus's thick cock pounding into her.

'Her Ladyship wants to *imagine* being screwed.'

'Oh yes,' said Samoya enthusiastically.

'Then perhaps we can oblige.'

'How?' asked Samoya, aroused and desperately wanting to feel a man's cock inside her.

'Well, first we must blindfold you,' said Phyllis. 'Hermione, tie your skirt around our mistress's eyes.'

Hermione did as she was told. Then they removed their own clothing. They stood still for a moment admiring each other's body. They touched eath other's large breasts and smiled.

'Now My Lady, you kneel down and bend over.'

'Why?' asked Samoya.

'Because that is the way we will help you imagine.'

Blindfolded, Samoya knelt down on the thick carpets that had been laid out on the scrubby earth under the tent. Hermione parted her skirts so that her posterior was clearly visible even in the moonlight.

'Such beautiful buttocks,' said Phyllis, stroking it but taking care not to enter any part of Samoya. 'Move your legs further apart.' Samoya edged her legs further apart. And the two girls began to massage and stroke Samoya's bottom, their hands occasionally trailing between her thighs and touching her moist sex. 'Hermione is now going to lie underneath you and spread her legs. You will put your head down and suck her.'

'But that isn't what I wanted,' said Samoya.

'My Lady you are impatient,' admonished Phyllis. 'Just do as I say. In a moment you will feel as if a cock is pounding inside you.'

Hermione slithered down beneath Samoya. She caught hold of Samoya's wrists and held on to them. Phyllis guided Samoya's head so that her face was level with Hermione's sex.

'Suck her,' she ordered.

Samoya's tongue came out and hit Hermione's large protuberance. Samoya's tongue fastened on to it. It was like a tiny penis.

'Is My Lady doing that properly?' Phyllis asked.

'Yes,' replied Hermione, stroking her own breasts and writhing as Samoya's tongue slurped at her wet and oozing orifice.

Samoya felt the warmth of Phyllis's large breasts squash against her back as she leant over her buttocks. Phyllis stretched Samoya's crevice and quite suddenly shoved a finger hard into her anus. Samoya's body jerked with the harshness of the thrust.

'Keep sucking,' said Phyllis softly. And Hermione kept hold of Samoya's wrists as she raised her hips to meet her mistress's exploring tongue.

Phyllis shoved again and again into Samoya's anus. Stretching her. Then she stopped and slowly eased another finger into Samoya's sex. 'So, My Lady would like a man's cock to be entering her wet pussy, would she?'

Samoya, slurping at Hermione, nodded her head.

'Then, My Lady, that is what you shall have.' Phyllis stopped her moving fingers, and whistled. Immediately, the tent flap opened and there stood Amos and Aaron, their naked freshly-oiled bodies glistening and their penises erect. They each held a whip in their hands. Phyllis pointed to Aaron and indicated to him to move stealthily and stand between Samoya's legs.

'My Lady wants to feel a cock.'

Phyllis positioned Aaron's penis. Aaron was careful not to touch any part of the kneeling woman.

'We don't want to disappoint her, do we?' said Phyllis.

'Who are you talking to?' asked Samoya, imprisoned in darkness by her blindfold, and as part of it was covering her ears she was also having difficulty hearing.

'An imaginary man,' said Phyllis. 'And he is going to shove his great big imaginary cock hard up into you.'

Amos stood beside Samoya's feet ready to grab them in case she moved. Phyllis rubbed Aaron's member along Samoya's labia. Samoya squirmed at the feel of it. She tried to turn but Hermione held onto her wrists. Then, in one fast movement, Aaron grabbed hold of Samoya's hips and slid into her anus. Samoya gasped in surprise as his massive cock entered her. She tried to move but she was pinned down by Hermione's hands on her wrists and Amos's hands on her ankles. She shook her head madly in an attempt to loosen the blindfold so that she could see who her violator was. She slumped down to the floor. Aaron's cock stayed inside her as he continued pumping.

'Give her a whipping,' ordered Aaron.

Samoya recognised the voice from somewhere. But where?

'I told you I'd have you, Lady,' he said. Now Samoya remembered. The charioteer. Who was going to be whipped? It couldn't be her. No. She lifted her head away from Hermione's sex. Her head was shoved back again between the slave's legs and pinioned there. Phyllis picked up the whip that Amos had dropped when he had caught hold of Samoya's ankles. Aaron pulled out of Samoya's anus and jumped neatly away as Phyllis landed three harsh stripes in quick succession on Samoya's neatly rounded buttocks. Samoya jumped and writhed with the acute pain. She tried desperately to struggle away from the lash but was unable to. And then the fourth stripe caught her upper thighs. They were even sharper. Then, before she had recovered, two more stripes landed on her buttocks and her legs were parted again. Aaron plunged into her anus once more. Tears of indignation were rolling down Samoya's face. They were caught by the blindfold. And nobody took any notice. Hands began to grab her breasts. She felt a tongue lick the marks on her bottom. Hermione held Samoya's head tight against her pubis.

'I think you know these two,' said Phyllis, ripping the blindfold from Samoya's eyes, pulling her head up by her hair and twisting her round so she could see the two huge Nubians. 'They arrived as you were having dinner. They have orders from Her Highness to look after you.'

As her attention was taken by the sight of them, Hermione snapped on handcuffs around Samoya's wrists. And clanking chains were snapped onto her ankles.

'Now, My fine Lady, we can do whatever we want to you. We have the Princess's permission,' said Amos, coming round to face Samoya. Aaron was still thrusting into her other orifice as Amos coaxed Samoya's head back and slid his rampant member into her open mouth.

The two females began laughing.

'She wanted to be fucked,' they said. 'And she got it. Not quite what you expected is it, My Lady?'

Amos and Aaron continued to invade Samoya's stretched orifices. The two women began to play with each other's body; their hands roaming over each other's breasts and bellies, their mouths kissing. They fell to the floor touching and caressing each other's sex and making lewd noises.

Samoya let out gurgling screams with a great desire to bite on Amos's cock and hurt him as punishment for the indignity she was having to suffer. But almost as if he could read her mind he pulled her head back and removed his cock. Sobbing, Samoya closed her eyes in an effort to shut out the horror of what was being done to her. Why had she ever agreed to marry Prince Alif? She should have stuck to her original intention, gone to Athens and become a doctor.

Without warning, the two females were suddenly silent. Equally without warning Amos fell backwards and the man with the cock in her anus slumped over her body. Samoya was imprisoned beneath his great weight. She could hardly breathe.

For a brief moment nothing moved in the room. It was so quiet she could only hear the sound of her own breath. She opened her eyes at the sound of clinking armour and screamed. But no sound came out. Her mouth was wide open but silent. Phyllis and Hermione lay together in a pool of blood silenced by javelins. Amos, too, was quite dead. Samoya was frightened out of her wits.

Men moved around the room. The candles were dying, the light they gave out was extremely dim. Shadows flitted about. The men grunted. They said something unintelligible. Persians! They were Persians. Her heart was pounding at such a rate she thought they would hear it. With half-closed eyes she followed their progress. Watched them with dread.

They picked up her gold make-up boxes and stuffed them into their pockets. They opened her trunks, took out her jewels and stowed them into a large skin bag. They kicked aside Phyllis and Hermione and laughed. Then she felt the dead weight on her back being removed. Samoya didn't know whether to keep her eyes open or shut, pretend she was dead or let them know she was alive.

They saw her eyes flicker. Three of them in their unfamiliar uniform stared down at her. Aaron was pushed roughly to one side. She saw the glint of a javelin sticking out of his back. She felt a deep sigh of relief. Only to be overcome by another fear. What would these men do to her? And where was everybody else? Why couldn't she hear sounds outside? Was everyone there dead too? Surely a small band of marauders could not have slaughtered her entire caravan?

One of them picked her up and stood her on her feet. They said something to her. She opened her mouth to answer. No sound came out. Terror raced through her body. Absolute terror. She was dumb. Her voice had gone. She had lost the power of speech. There was a noise outside. The men inside panicked. They threw her down onto a carpet and rolled her up in it. She found the warmth of the all-enveloping carpet reassuring. She felt it being dragged along the ground, then her heart swooped upwards as the bundle of her was tossed onto a horse. Samoya lost consciousness as the animal jerked and galloped away.

Chapter Six

*L*ucius Aurelian was strutting up and down his room like a bear with a sore head. He had wanted to push on to Rome but orders had come from the Emperor Gallienus that he must stay in Antioch until further notice. He was furious. Somehow the news had managed to reach the Emperor that the Persians were beaten before he could tell him. Lucius Aurelian was displeased.

He called Marcus. There was no reply. He shouted louder. There was still no reply. This did nothing to improve Aurelian's temper. He unstrapped his belt and sword. Then strapped it back on again. He couldn't be without his weapon. He wasn't called 'old hand on hilt' for nothing. He must remain ever ready. But for what? Not only was Lucius Aurelian displeased, he was incredibly bored.

Three weeks in Antioch doing nothing when he could have been halfway to Rome. Antioch was a pleasant enough city. The people were charming. His hosts had made him, and his second-in-command, more than welcome. But there was something missing.

Perhaps he should avail himself of the city's fleshpots. Go to the theatre. Watch some sport. Visit the dancing girls. Go to a brothel. In theory the latter appealed to him most. It had been a bloody long time since he'd known the delights of sex. It had been even longer since he'd known the delights of good sex.

He stared out at the garden. The smell of jasmine overwhelmed him. It reminded him of the slave his hosts had provided for him. She was called Jasmine. The one thing about the girl he did remember. He rang the bell. To Hades with the world. He would get drunk. The slave arrived. He looked at her as if for the first time. She had been waiting on him hand and foot ever since he'd arrived. But he hadn't really noticed her. She was young and pretty. Dark-haired, brown-eyed. Slim. He could take her if he chose. He stretched out a hand and touched her bare shoulder. Nothing. He felt nothing when he touched that skin. Why not? Why was he so dead inside? He'd always been lusty. The first into a brothel, the last out. The long screw without emotion. Just as he liked it. No entanglements. Simple enjoyment. Pay and leave. And with the slave he wouldn't even have to pay.

'Jasmine,' he said.

'Yes, sir,' she answered, bowing low.

'Red wine, and lots of it,' he said, abruptly.

Jasmine bowed and was gone. When she came back he would make her stay with him. Once he had some wine inside him he'd loosen up. Then his cock would rise and they would screw.

He lay down on his own truckle bed. It went everywhere with him. In peace or in war. It was a constant. He liked the hardness of his own mattress. It was a comfort. He didn't want to get used to the luxury of feather beds. Whatever the day held, and wherever he was, his own bed was the one spot of familiarity in his life. He closed his eyes and waited for Jasmine's return. And in his mind his past and his future curdled, in his body his present was activated. Laughter. He heard

103

laughter. From the river. Girls bathing. Naked bodies. Swimming. Dressing. Brightly coloured clothes. Water swirling. Reeds hiding girls. Women. Soldiers. Another river, darker, muddier. More water. Pure. Cascading. Pools and fountains. And then he saw her. She came out of the pool like a water nymph. Her long hair, so raven dark it was tinged with blue, dripping wet and hanging close to her slim body. He could see her curves through the wetness of her clinging white shift, and her perfectly shaped, well-rounded breasts. The darkness of her nipples pushed hard against the soaking fabric. She held her arms open. He stretched out a hand. Then she was gone. Hidden by a pillar. She reappeared. Magnificent in robes studded with gems sparkling in the bright sunlight. Her curls piled up upon her head and fastened with a diadem. Majestically, she glided towards him. She came up close. He could smell her perfume. Intoxicated by her aroma, his hand rose up and touched her neck. She raised her head. Their eyes met in one startling and intimate glance. He drew her closer to him. Felt her soft, pliable body against his hard muscles. His eyes moved from her eyes to her lips. Slowly he bent his head. His heart was pounding so violently he thought it would burst. His eyes sought hers again, silently asking permission to kiss her mouth.

Imperceptibly she nodded her head. Their lips touched. Gently they made that first contact. Then, as the blood in his body went haywire, he crushed her to him and his lips pressed harder on hers. Her mouth opened to receive his tongue. Their tongues entwined. Searching. Their lips burning, alive. Desire surged through every vein, pore, bone, muscle and sinew he possessed. His entire body trembled. His hands were shaking as they touched her breasts.

She was pressing her body hard against his. He could feel the bone over her pubis. She changed her position. Edged her legs apart allowing his hard, erect penis to press in between her thighs. He could feel her trembling. Then her hands slithered down his body. With cool fingers she touched his burning hardness. He thought he would explode.

She ringed his manhood. With rapture and an almost tranquil ease she began to massage him, stimulating him beyond endurance. The feeling extended upwards into his mind. Gripping his spirit. There was a hazy connection between every particle of him. And yet he didn't want to take her. Not yet. Her tender body swayed this way and that. His turbulent one followed her every movement. Their mouths stayed locked together. His hand lifted her robe. He found the soft and tender place at the top of her thighs. His hands stroked her. He felt her response; the widening of her legs giving him greater access. His fingers began to explore her sex. Suddenly she snaked down the length of him. She took him in her mouth and began to suck. He stood, his feet apart, his muslces tense and trembling, his hands twirling through her hair as her mouth went backwards and forwards.

He bent down and picked her up. Now he was going to take her. Now he had to know her. Had to feel himself inside her. He had to possess her.

He carried her across the marble courtyard through a great wide doorway and laid her down on an enormous bed. Once more their lips touched. Once again he felt her body. Then she opened her legs as he came up between them. She raised her hips. Gently he inserted the tip of his penis and edged himself into her. She sighed. Loving sighs. She moaned. Loving moans. He kissed her again and again. Her lips, her eyes, her cheeks, her ears, her neck. He put his hands over her breasts and caressed them. And then he pierced her.

They were joined. United. There was no hardness, no softness, only a yielding under fitting pressure. Sealed in love. Words whispered. Love. Love you. And in their sweat they rolled, and rolled again and changed over until she was on top of him and stayed there.

Jasmine returned with the pitcher of wine as the Roman commander had requested. Only to find him fast asleep. She put the wine on the table beside him then sat on the floor watching him. She had fallen in love with Lucius Aurelian as soon as he had set foot in her master's household. She had begged to be allowed to sleep outside his door. Wash his clothes. Do everything for him. Jasmine longed to have been born a man, and a Roman. If she had been she would have been a soldier and followed this commander anywhere. She liked his second-in-command too but he was too pretty. Too beautiful for her taste. Jasmine liked rugged men.

Many soldiers had billeted themselves upon her master and had thrown their weight about. Bullied everyone. But not this Roman.

Her master had said his villa was obviously in the wrong position. It was the first house of any real size to be seen before entering Antioch. Tired troops dreamt of it as home. Tired commanders made it so. Her master was thinking of selling, moving to the other side of the city.

Jasmine watched the Roman toss and turn in his sleep. There was something special about him. It wasn't his handsome face, his stocky body. His muscularity. It was his magnetic presence. She wanted to touch him. To calm him down. She lay her face next to his and kissed his cheeks and his lips. When he stretched out an arm she moved closer so that it would land on her head. When his hand caressed her cheek she took hold of it and held it to her breast. When he turned suddenly revealing his manhood, erect and hard, she ringed it with her hand and stroked it. Enjoying the feel of his throbbing skin beneath her cool fingers Jasmine let her hand glide with a gentle firmness from the tip of the head, down to its base and back again. She thought he would wake, but he didn't. He was far away in his dreams and she was enacting hers.

Jasmine took off her clothes, climbed onto the bed

beside him, knelt between his legs, took his member into her mouth and gently sucked it. Then she placed a knee either side of his hips, lowered herself and guided the sleeping man's penis into her wetness.

His arm shot out and knocked the pitcher of wine beside the bed crashing to the floor. The shattering noise woke him.

The slave-girl was sitting on him. They were copulating. Her hair was over her naked breasts. His hands were up holding them. She was levering herself up and down on his shaft. Her head was moving this way and that. She was in ecstasy. He could feel from the tightness in her abdomen she was about to come. He thrust harder. With a great, long sigh she came. Moments later he surged into her. The girl collapsed across his chest. He put an arm around her. To comfort her. But also to comfort himself.

It hadn't been the slave he had been screwing. It had been that wretched witch he'd met outside Antioch. The girl who had laughed at him and demanded a stretcher. She occupied far too much space in his thoughts.

The slave-girl sidled away from him. She covered her naked body. She began to pick up the pieces of the pitcher.

'I'll bring you some more wine, sir,' she said.

'That's not necessary,' he replied.

Jasmine left the room. And he buried his head in his arms. For the moment he was replete. No wine. No need for the brothel. No more women. He had discovered what was missing. It was the girl he had met. The one his soldiers had told him lived in a mansion bigger than they had ever seen in Rome.

'What was her name?' he'd asked.

'Zenobia,' they'd said. 'And rich sir, seriously rich.'

But when he had gone to see her, to pay his respects, the whole place had been locked up, deserted. He'd made enquiries. 'Gone to Palmyra,' he was told.

And she had lived in his dreams ever since.

'Sir, sir.' Marcus's voice shattered his stillness. 'Sir, there's a man outside in a terrible state.'

'Who is it?'

'Says his name is Pernel. He's a merchant, sir.'

'Rich or poor?' asked Aurelian.

'Rich. He was taking his daughter to Palmyra when bandits stole into the camp, killed his daughter's slaves and kidnapped her. He thinks they might have been Persians. There have been rumours about some in that area. He wants us to find them, and his daughter, sir.'

Marcus tried hard not to let his superior realise that he had a very personal interest in the matter. He had recognised Pernel as Samoya's father. He'd had only a fleeting glimpse of the man when he had taken Samoya back to the villa. And at the time Pernel had been furious. He had grabbed his daughter quite roughly and spoken to her harshly. But there was no mistake. Pernel was definitely Samoya's father. It was Samoya who had been kidnapped. Marcus had to find her. He was grateful Pernel had not recognised him. That would have been an added complication. Pernel might become suspicious of his motives. With every right. Marcus had thought about Samoya constantly and had decided she was the woman for him. He wanted to marry her. Take her back to Rome with him. The day after possessing her he had made a detour past her mansion on the way to the garrison. He had wanted to ask her father's permission to court her. But all he met was a couple of surly brothers freshly home from Persia. They had told him their father and sister had gone to Palmyra and had shut the door in his face. Marcus had been devastated. He couldn't mention this now.

'Where did this happen?' Aurelian asked.

'Somewhere on the edge of the desert,' Marcus replied. 'Any chance of a few of our men going to look for her?'

Marcus didn't say that he wanted to look for her. He

108

was too canny for that. People could be untrustworthy: one couldn't afford to take chances. They might, out of sheer bloody-mindedness, decide against the thing you most wanted, just because you wanted it.

Lucius Aurelian considered the proposition carefully. He couldn't leave Antioch without the Emperor's permission. But his troops were getting restless. They needed something to do. A raiding party. Rounding up some of the remaining Persians would not do any harm. It would keep his troops on their toes. He would send runners with them in case he, and his men, were called back to Rome, or, as rumour had it, to fight the Goths.

'Marcus,' he said seriously, 'bring the merchant into me.'

Pernel was brought into the commander's room. The kidnapping of his daughter had aged him considerably. He was well dressed, plenty of silken robes covered his body but his hands fluttered aimlessly as he talked. He was distraught. There were many things about the kidnapping he did not understand. What were two huge and naked black men doing lying dead in his daughter's tent? And they were men, not eunuchs. And the two slaves left by the Princess? Why were they also naked and dead?

Lucius Aurelian stared at the merchant. He seemed genuinely upset at his daughter's disappearance. The merchant bowed.

'I am Pernel, sir, a merchant of this city,' he said.

'I know,' said Aurelian cutting him short. 'My second-in-command has told me. Now you want your daughter found and you want us to do it?'

'Yes, sir.'

'And I agree. One band of marauders gets away with a kidnapping and more will try it. *Pax Romana* reigns here. We will uphold the peace. Marcus will select two hundred of our best men, who no doubt at this moment are drinking and whoring their lives away in the taverns of Antioch.'

Marcus tried to withhold a smile. First hurdle over. He waited with bated breath for the next command.

'I am giving Marcus here the job of leader.'

Marcus let out an audible sigh. Aurelian glanced at him. What, he wondered, was this to do with Marcus? He had never mentioned a girl. In fact, now Aurelian came to think about it, Marcus had not been visiting the flesh-pots. And why not? He was instantly curious. There was obviously some emotional involvement between Marcus and the girl. But when had that occurred? Most of the time Marcus had been holed up with him in the villa. The only time he was loose in Antioch was during the religious riot. It must have happened then. A number of frightened female slaves had been rounded up in the market-place. And now, as he thought about it more carefully, Aurelian realised Marcus had gone missing for a time. Well, when he returned from the sortie Aurelian would ask him about it.

'Pernel, you must go with Marcus. You will show him exactly where you were when the incident took place. Now, if your daughter is dead, then he has my permission to accompany the body back to Antioch. But if she is alive, do you want to continue with your journey to Palmyra?'

'Yes,' said Pernel. 'That is absolutely vital. I only hope she is still alive. You see she is due to marry Prince Alif, a kinsman of the King. It will create a major international incident if the marriage does not go ahead. I have already sent a runner to the King to tell him what has happened.'

Aurelian slyly watched Marcus's face as Pernel made his devastating announcement. He saw the young man swallow hard and bite his lip. Aurelian realised Marcus had received a bitter blow. Other than that he betrayed no interest. Aurelian admired Marcus's self-control.

'Then those are your orders,' Aurelian said. 'If the girl is alive you are to take her and her father to

Palmyra. You and your men will be her escort. You will make certain that she arrives unharmed. At least that she comes to no more than she has already. She is under your care, Marcus. I want your word as a Roman soldier that you will protect her at all times and deliver her safely to Prince Alif.'

'You have my word, sir,' said Marcus enunciating with all the military precision he could muster in an effort not to show his deep disappointment and his emotional anguish.

'Then go,' said Aurelian, 'and may the gods go with you. Especially may the Great Sun God, Elagabalus go with you.'

'May I say one more thing,' said Pernel. 'Whether my daughter is dead or alive, there will be a reward. I shall pay the men in gold.'

'Well then, Marcus, that's an added incentive,' said Aurelian, fully aware that Marcus needed none but endeavouring not to show that he had guessed the young man's plight.

Pernel and Marcus departed. Aurelian stared out at the orchard. He thought again about Zenobia. Yes, he knew exactly how Marcus was feeling. If he heard Zenobia was about to marry his heart would sink too.

Marcus's emotions were in a turmoil as he rode out of Antioch with his men, plus trackers and runners. One hundred were expert marksmen with the bow and arrow, fifty with the javelin and fifty were the finest silent killers with the dagger. Not knowing how long it was going to take or which part of the country they would find the bandits, they also provided themselves with camels for their milk and their dung, live goats to be killed when necessary, goatskins filled with water, plenty of rope, general rock-climbing tackle and a cage on wheels.

For two days he and Pernel rode in virtual silence. They were both extremely worried. Neither wanted to discuss what they might find. Before returning to

111

Antioch for help, Pernel had sent the rest of his caravan on to Palmyra with instructions to camp in the hills outside the city and to await news. If all was well he would join them with Samoya and only a few days would be lost. If she was dead they would turn back without having to pay the taxes it cost to enter the capital.

On the third day Pernel showed them the spot where they had made camp the night Samoya had been kidnapped. Marcus made it his base, too.

'What do you know of this area?' Marcus asked as they ate their dinner of smoked eel and bass which Pernel had provided as an alternative to goat.

'There are wadis and caves to the east,' said Pernel. 'They're not usually used by us or the Bedu, except in an emergency. The water's brackish and the caves have bears and scorpions, also polecats.'

'If they're not normally used then my instinct tells me that's where we start looking. I'll take one hundred men tonight and we'll go on a recce.'

'Do you want me with you?' asked Pernel.

'No,' Marcus said quickly. 'It's only a recce. We'll find out as much as we can tonight.'

Pernel accepted the young man's decision. He liked him, although he did have a distinct feeling that he had seen him somewhere before. And not in the best of circumstances. But as he couldn't put his finger on it, it didn't seem worth his while to occupy his brain with wondering where or how. He was going to find Samoya. That was the all-important thing.

After Marcus and his men had departed, Pernel decided to pray to the Goddess for his daughter's safe return.

The stones were still hot from the daytime sun as Marcus and his band, part bowmen, part javelin throwers, all the dagger men, some of the trackers and a couple of runners, made their way on foot in the moonlight, guided by the stars. There was an eerie silence about the scrub that kept them all alert. And the land wasn't flat. They walked with the utmost care.

Outlined by the moon, caves loomed ahead of them in the darkness. Marcus felt sure that if the bandits were still in the vicinity they would be there. A flat plain with a few shrubs and stones lay in front of the caves. The moon was good for them. It showed them where to go, but it would also be good for the enemy. Their look-outs would be able to see them all too easily. Carefully they crept forward. They came to a wadi, a small pool with a few reeds, a cluster of trees, the remnants of a recently used camp-fire and the fresh clean bones of a gazelle. The terrain had lost its noonday colour, now everything was in shades of grey and black. His men, either naturally dark skinned or bronzed from their various campaigns, had a built-in camouflage. But Marcus was aware of shadows and how much of a giveaway they would be. He ordered the men to cut down branches of the trees and shrubs and carry them with them. They would make their way, slowly, on their bellies, holding the branches in front of them. They would wriggle across the stones like worms, the vegetation hiding their advance.

At the base of the first rock they saw a stallion tethered to a stump. Marcus looked up. He saw the mouth of the cave and moving shadows in the firelight. Marcus knew then they were on the right track for someone. Whether it was Samoya, that he would have to find out. Ushering the men together he whispered his instructions. Twenty-five dagger men were to go with him. The remainder to stay where they were and watch. Any sign of trouble and they were to advance with bows at the ready. Kill first; ask questions afterwards. Marcus decided to approach the cave entrance from the top down. This meant a walk around the base to find a suitable place to climb up. Stealthily and with judicious use of the rope and tackle he and four others made their way to the top. Marcus tucked some bits of branch into his belt. He then instructed them to hold on to the rope whilst he slithered down and looked into the cave.

Marcus didn't know what to expect, although the worst thoughts were in his head. Almost at the mouth of the cave he stopped to tuck the branch into the neck of his uniform so that his face was covered but he could still see through the leaves. He balanced his feet on the rock face and with extreme caution edged his head down. The fire was dying. He could see the men.

Six of them. And wearing the familiar uniform of his enemy, the Persians. But no woman. For as long as he could he stayed upside down, trying desperately to see into the darkness beyond the men. He couldn't. He twirled around to get some breath and let the blood run back to his feet. It was in the moment of turning that he saw a flash of red-blonde hair and rags. Quickly he spun himself head-down again. It was her. He knew it was her. His heart leapt. He almost let out a whoop of joy. That red-gold hair was difficult to hide and the embers of firelight lit it up. He recognised her arms, her neck, her shapely body even though it was dirty, covered in a filthy shift and the breast-plate of a Persian's uniform. He gave a gulp of relief.

He saw her move. He strained his eyes. She appeared to be offering the men a drink from a goatskin bag. In turn they took it from her, drank, smiled, then handed it back. When she had finished one of them patted the ground furthest from the cave opening and safest from wild animals and made way for her to lie squashed in beside him. Another covered her with a rug. All of them lay down to sleep.

They were not molesting her. They seemed almost patient, as if dealing with a wounded bird. Marcus was confused. Whatever he had been expecting it wasn't what he was witnessing. He swung himself upright, thinking. For a woman who had been kidnapped she gave out no sign of fear. Marcus was used to the smell

114

of fear. It rippled through the troops prior to a battle before the drumming and the war cries started. And no smell of fear was drifting into his nostrils. There was more to this than was immediately apparent. Marcus signalled on the rope to be hauled up. They returned to the base of the rock.

Marcus held council. He told his men what he had seen. And that had the Persians been misusing Samoya everything would be simple. They could charge in not worrying about killing. But they seemed to be treating Samoya with kindness. Marcus felt honour-bound to take the Persians prisoner. This would involve a different tactic and the utmost caution. The Persians were trained killers, soldiers as they were. But his men would have the element of surprise on their side. And speed. And speed was of the essence. In the sandy soil Marcus drew a plan of the cave, the fire and the sleeping arrangements. Twenty of them would abseil down the rock face. Forty would stay on top of the rock holding the ropes. The rest would stay at the bottom with their arrows ready in case any Persians managed to escape. Out of the twenty Marcus told the first six to abseil into the cave and allotted a Persian to each man. They would take up their position, a dagger to each Persian's throat. The others would stay, javelins ready, at the mouth of the cave. He would abseil in and take Samoya. When he and Samoya had departed, the men at the entrance must move in and bind the Persians, taking them prisoner.

Marcus sent a runner to tell Pernel his daughter was alive and well and that they proposed to ambush the Persian bandits that night, and that he should prepare the cage. He would be returning with prisoners. But Marcus remained deeply troubled. Why would a rich young woman not be showing any fear whilst living with a bunch of Persian ruffians? He would discover the reason. He pushed the thought to the back of his mind. He had a mission to fulfil and he would do it to

115

the best of his ability. Failure never crossed Marcus's mind. He was in no doubt that he would rescue Samoya.

For the entire day Samoya had felt odd. She had woken at dawn with a strange tension in her belly. The fire had long since gone out. The cave was cold. She had huddled back under the skins and put her nose to the carpet which was full of familiar smells. It was the one the Persians had used to wrap her in when they had taken her from her tent. And it had remained hers to sleep on. Without turning her body she had scanned the faces of the sleeping men surrounding her. Life had taken an odd turn the night they crept into her tent and stopped her rape. For that she was grateful but now she needed to escape.

They had left her alone. Had shown no inclination to touch her, or to violate her. Indeed, it was quite the opposite. It was as if she was their good luck symbol. They had tucked her own jewels under her carpet and were kind to her. Prehaps they thought she was Persian, captured by the Palmyrenes and taken into slavery. And born dumb. They had rescued one of their own. She had very little on her to identify her as the daughter of the owner of the rich caravan. Her hands and feet had been shackled. They had broken those on the second day of her captivity. The Persians had shared their food with her and left her to sleep for two days. On the morning of the third day they went hunting. There was a strange and for her humorous exchange, when their leader gave her a javelin, endeavoured to explain to her that if any wild animals came near she was to spear them, and mimed how she was to use the weapon. Samoya nodded. She saw no point in letting them know she was an expert. There was, she thought, a certain advantage in being dumb. A few hours later, from the mouth of the cave she saw them running across the stones. Some of them carrying goatskins with water spilling out, others throwing spears, trying to catch an antelope. She saw she had the advantage. She threw her javelin and killed the animal. They brought it home. Smiling. She was one of them. From then on they took her hunting with them. She had listened to the men talking and being quick at languages was soon able to understand them. She had managed to talk to them by a series of simple signs and wondered if her power of speech would ever return.

They watched her. Not as a prisoner but because they worried about her welfare. In the beginning this was a surprise and a novelty. After a while, when the initial shock of capture and the thrill of survival had worn off and boredom had set in, Samoya found it stifling. Every day was the same. She wondered if the rest of her life would be spent in a cave with bandits. She longed for civilisation. For talk and people and ideas. Even for the men to change camp. They showed no inclination to move on. They hunted and fetched water. They ate, drank, told stories round the fire and slept to start again the next day. There was a rhythm to their life. But it was not one she wanted to continue forever. She began to think how she could escape. In this desire there was also a sadness. The men had cared for her. Her escape would mean betrayal. But she could not stay where she was. How she was. She had to leave.

And that morning as the sun rose higher lighting up their primitive hide-out, Samoya, with the strange tightening in her stomach, had let out a long sigh. She was homesick for comfort. She had glanced at the various rumpled skins on the cave floor and those covering the men. She was thirsty but knew there would be nothing to drink until they went down to the wadi. The water obtained from the wadi was brackish and initially had made her sick. She stared at her dirty arms and hands, her torn nails. She was dishevelled and filthy but there was very little she could do about it. By the time they had climbed the rock face with the water, there was very little left to drink let alone wash in.

The feeling had remained with her all day. They had hunted and cooked out in the open near the wadi. But she had been strangely unhungry. Her gut was twisted, excited by something unknown. They had returned with part of the gazelle for her to eat before sleeping. She was perplexed. The day was almost over and had progressed the same as any other, yet the tightness in her stomach had not lessened. Round the fire in the cave the men told their stories. Ancient tales of Persian history and valour, of Xerxes and Darius and Alexander and of Shapur, their current Emperor, and his treatment of their enemy, the captured Roman Emperor Valerian. And the feeling in the pit of her stomach persisted. When they lay down to sleep, she couldn't. She stared out into the moonlight.

Her mind whirled on different and more and more outlandish modes of escape. Perhaps she could take some of her precious stones with her each day they went hunting. And leave them somewhere hidden. That, she thought, was a positive start. She must not be without money, in the desert or anywhere else. Samoya slid her hand under her carpet and grabbed the bag of jewels. She was about to remove some stones when Marcus came hurtling through the entrance of the cave.

She recognised his singular beauty and the darkness of his skin immediately. Rescue. She clutched her jewel bag tightly. Marcus was swiftly followed by six others. Samoya stayed absolutely still holding her breath so that the men beside her would not wake. The precision with which Marcus had planned the attack paid off. Complete with jewels, Samoya was snatched up into the air and whisked out, and down the rock face. Marcus put her up on the tethered stallion and they began their trek back to Pernel. The sleeping men were captured with a speed they could not comprehend. Disarmed, they were roped together then lowered onto the rough ground below. Surrounded, they were marched to Pernel, the rest of the Romans and the awaiting cage.

From the moment Marcus held Samoya in his arms again he felt the tingling. With joy and relief he kissed her neck. Her thin body pressed hard against his, which despite the danger they were in gave him an immediate erection. He longed for her. Wanted to touch her breasts, kiss her, take her. He wanted to tell her he loved her. Then he remembered his promise to Aurelian. And he was silent.

Samoya leant against him. Unbelieving. Marcus. The man she had dreamt of had rescued her. She felt his lips on her neck. She clutched him tighter, trembling, remembering their last ride together. Her whole body was alive with his touch. She was shaking with love and anticipation. She didn't know where he was taking her. But she hoped they'd be alone. Samoya knew what he was going to do. He would ride away and find somewhere quiet. He would kiss her lips, and feel her breasts. He would lay her on the ground and come up between her legs. He would hold his penis at the entrance of her sex and then he would thrust into her. Samoya was growing wet at the thought. She desperately wanted to say something to him. She opened her mouth again and again but no sound, nothing came out.

Marcus held her tightly. She bent her head and kissed his arm. Instead of reacting by kissing her neck he moved away from her. Disbelief flooded through her. Why was he doing that? Samoya thought it was because she was dirty. Smelled of the caves. She kissed him again.

'No,' he said, harshly.

It cost him every ounce of self-control he had to say that simple word. He wanted desperately to find somewhere where he could gently take her in his arms, tell her he loved her then touch her, kiss her, enter her.

Deep resentment raged through Samoya's body. How

dare he! She sat up straight and pulled away from him. They rode on over the stones, past the wadi and back to base camp, in a disagreeable silence.

They were the first to arrive. Pernel was quite horrified when he saw the filthy state his daughter was in. He kissed her and made a fuss of her, babbling constantly, overjoyed to see her.

'We'll go to Edessa, I've friends there, you can bathe and change and . . . and . . .' he kept kissing her with relief. 'Samoya, was it terrible? I got help as soon as I could . . . darling daughter . . .'

But Samoya did not, could not reply. She opened her mouth and croaked. Pernel stared at her in horror. He opened her mouth and looked inside. Somebody might have cut out her tongue. But no. In anguish he shook her. She cried but silently. He let her drop like a rag doll. Then he fell in a crumpled heap on the floor. His beautiful daughter was dumb.

'Did she say anything to you?' Pernel asked Marcus.

'Nothing,' he replied.

'She's not speaking,' he said, near to tears. 'My darling daughter is not speaking. What shall we do?'

Pernel stared at Samoya who was standing close by him opening and closing her mouth but with no sound coming out. He had his beloved daughter back in one piece but would Prince Alif want to marry a woman who was dumb? Pernel shook his head sadly. He took Samoya into his tent, sat her down and covered her with a burnouse. They would go to Edessa. Perhaps if she was cleaned up, whatever had happened to her to make her dumb would be released.

Marcus was also perplexed. What had made her dumb? Like Pernel he reasoned that the Prince might not want a wife who couldn't speak. This was his chance. He must take this opportunity to tell Pernel he was in love with Samoya. That he wanted to marry her whether she was dumb or not. Yes. That's exactly what he would do. But he was stopped in his tracks as the prisoners arrived.

'Into the cage with them,' he ordered.

The Persians were truculent. Seeing the cage they began to twist and turn in their chains.

'Whip them,' said Marcus, uncharacteristically savage. He was disgruntled. He hadn't wanted them to arrive just then. He had wanted to walk calmly into Pernel's tent and ask for Samoya's hand in marriage. Now he had to think about Persians. 'Show the prisoners what Romans do to Persians who disobey orders.'

Samoya heard the noise. She came running out of the tent as the men were being lashed. Horrified and shocked by the sight of her rescuers' bare backs being subjected to the whip she ran towards the Romans.

'No,' she screamed, suddenly finding her voice and with tears pouring down her face. 'No, no, no.'

Marcus and Pernel turned and stared at her. Samoya rushed into her father's arms and began hammering on his chest.

'They saved me,' she cried. 'They saved me. Please don't do that to them.'

'Daughter, your voice. Your voice has returned,' said Pernel, weeping for joy.

'Yes,' she said, croakily. 'But please stop them whipping those Persians.'

Marcus ordered his men to stop the punishment. He watched Samoya and her father return to their tent. He was utterly downcast. Now he would have to escort her to Palmyra. She would have to marry the Palmyrene prince.

Samoya came out of the tent. They stared at one another with unspoken longing.

'My father says we're to go first to Edessa,' she said. 'And then to Palmyra.'

'I know. And you're to marry Prince Alif,' he said, flatly.

'Yes,' she said, smiling a false smile but Marcus didn't realise that.

'And do you want to do that?'

'Of course,' she replied, defiantly. She was still furious with him for pulling away from her. She was not going to tell him all she wanted was him. That she had dreamed of running away and finding him. Of going to Rome. Of becoming his wife.

'In that case My Lady,' said Marcus, bowing, 'it is my duty to escort you to your wedding.' He turned sharply on his heels and marched away from her. Samoya watched him with tears in her eyes.

'Marcus,' she called. But he didn't hear her. He closed her off from his mind. He had work to do. The Persians must be taken to Antioch. He and a small group would escort her and her father to Edessa and then Palmyra.

Samoya pulled her burnouse closer around her as if that would protect her from her own feelings. She was alive. Soon she would be back in civilisation. She would be Prince Alif's wife. A strange tremor rippled through her loins. Princess Bernice had said that Prince Alif enjoyed certain sexual practices. Well, she would find out what they were and she'd learn to enjoy them, too.

Samoya stalked off into the tent. Her father was waiting for her with many questions.

'Father,' she said putting her arms around his neck. 'Please don't ask me. I don't remember a thing except that I'm going to Palmyra and will be married to Prince Alif. And I'm really looking forward to that.'

Pernel was too relieved to hear her voice to realise she was lying.

Marcus decided that as soon as they arrived in Palmyra he would make for the brothels. He had been faithful and chaste long enough. He was going to have his sexual fill. And there was no way he would ever see Samoya again.

Chapter Seven

'Your husband's gone hunting,' said Princess Bernice, and tugged at the gossamer-thin, pale blue silk cape Samoya was wearing. The cape landed on the floor. Bernice, as voluptuous as ever, was sitting on her great carved chair on a dais in her apartments. She put out a hand and nipped Samoya's freshly oiled and erect nipple where it peered through the delicate hole in her dark-blue silk bodice.

'My husband! But that's not possible. I haven't got a husband!' exclaimed an astonished Samoya.

After her unpleasant journey to Palmyra – via Edessa, Marcus had ignored her in the surliest and sulkiest way – Princess Bernice had welcomed her to the palace and taken her to her apartment. There, for two weeks she had been kept isolated, and not allowed any visitors. She'd had no news of the outside world. A couple of silent female slaves had stayed with her night and day. They woke her in the morning, bathed her, shaved and oiled her sex, dressed her and fed her until it was time for her to go to bed. Today was the first time she had seen anybody else.

Bernice's two huge Nubian eunuchs had suddenly arrived. They announced they had come to collect her, to show her into Princess Bernice's presence.

And now Princess Bernice was informing her about her husband when she did not have one.

'Oh yes you have. When he heard you'd been kidnapped, Prince Alif arranged a proxy marriage. He said you'd either re-appear to enjoy the fruits of marriage or you'd be dead and he'd have to find a new wife. Very little disturbs Prince Alif's plans. And he had planned to go hunting after your wedding.'

Samoya was thunderstruck. She could not believe her ears. From the dais where she was standing in front of Bernice, who was now fondling her breasts, she stared around her at the great brown marble room. It was long, high and stately. There were no murals but every now again magnificent carpets hung down breaking the coldness. At the far end, opposite the dais, was a balcony. This was hung with heavy, red damask silk curtains. The room was empty except for her, the Princess, and the two impassive faced Nubians who stood fanning their mistress with great palm leaves.

'The rest of you is dressed as I commanded isn't it, my dear?' asked Princess Bernice. She parted Samoya's diaphanous skirt to reveal her belly and her bare, shaved sex. Princess Bernice stretched out a finger and traced the line of Samoya's pubis.

'What a dear little pussy,' she said, and suddenly stuck her finger in and shoved it up and down. Samoya was taken aback by the swiftness of Bernice's invasion but it didn't stop her becoming instantly moist.

Licking her lips Bernice trailed a finger gently on Samoya's clitoris. Samoya began to sway to the rhythm of Bernice's finger. She had been starved of contact for over a fortnight. Bernice smiled licentiously then took the corner hem of each piece of Samoya's blue and purple slit, silk skirt and tucked it into Samoya's waistband. Bernice slid her hands along Samoya's thighs, eased her whole body round, tucked the corner hems of the back of her skirt into the back waistband revealing

Samoya's neat, bare buttocks and sensuously stroked them.

'And now we will prepare you for your wedding night.'

'When's that?' asked a totally bemused Samoya. Nothing was as she expected it to be.

'When your husband returns. We do not know when that will be. You must stay in a permanent state of readiness for his arrival. First you must drink.' Bernice handed Samoya an extra large goblet full of water.

'No thank you,' said Samoya.

'It's an order, not a request,' said Bernice. 'You will drink every last drop and then some more.'

Bernice watched as she drank, then refilled her glass.

'I can't,' said Samoya.

'You must and you will,' said Bernice, a hint of malice in her voice.

When Samoya had downed the last drop Bernice clapped her hands and a group of female slaves arrived. They came though a small side door on their knees and bowed, lowering their heads to the floor. Samoya noticed they were identically dressed. All of them had leather collars around their necks, from which strips of leather fell from a steel ring and criss-crossed over their bodies but leaving their breasts bare, enhancing them. They wore leather bracelets and leather anklets and very short leather skirts. As they knelt down their skirts raised up and their buttocks were displayed. When they stood up Samoya noticed that the skirts did not cover their pubis. And each one of them was shaved.

'These are your slaves.' Bernice clapped her hands and they crawled over to the base of the dais where they stood with their legs apart.

'They are to do your bidding. They are for your pleasure,' said Bernice standing up. 'They must be ready for sex at all times.'

Princess Bernice came down from her dais and walked along the row of slaves. She was inspecting them. She rubbed their breasts, their nipples and parted their legs and felt each slave to make sure she was wet.

When she had finished Bernice clapped her hands again and a row of tall, handsome, well-muscled naked men entered and bowed. They, too, wore leather collars and leather wristlets and anklets.

'They have been chosen to give you pleasure. You will notice the size of their penises.'

The men walked into the room, their cocks huge and stiff, and stood in front of the females. Samoya felt an instant rush of desire.

'Come, we will inspect them.' Bernice stepped down from her dais. Her two Nubians then unwrapped Bernice's robes, took them off layer by layer, leaving her huge breasts hanging loose and her hips and full buttocks naked. But leaving her special belt with its two leather dildoes around her waist. 'Do whatever I do,' she said, taking Samoya's hand.

Bernice walked down the line of male slaves and gave each man's penis a rub. Samoya followed Bernice's example and felt the thrill of power as her cool hands touched their thick, large, erect, pulsating members. The men, standing to attention, their eyes staring straight ahead of them, their muscular bodies glistening with oils, their hands hanging limply by their sides, had no option but to submit to whatever the two women did to them. In each case Samoya ringed the head of the cock, took her hands down along its length, pressing subtly against its ridges, then brought her hand back up again curving over its cap. She felt herself opening, getting wetter as the cock in her hand extended and throbbed still further. She squeezed their balls, squashing them gently between her fingers. They had to submit to her. Samoya enjoyed the freedom of being able to do whatever she wanted with another person's body.

'Now we will have a display.'

Bernice clapped her hands. Each man turned to the

woman behind him and picked her up. She then wrapped her legs around his waist. They turned again to face Bernice and Samoya. Each woman was so positioned that her wet and open sex was hovering over her partner's erect penis. Bernice clapped her hands. As if it was a well-rehearsed dance, each man thrust his cock up inside the sex of the girl he was holding.

The precision and the speed of their action took Samoya completely by surprise. She found herself getting wetter and wetter as she watched. Bernice came up behind her and put her two hands over Samoya's breasts and began caressing them.

'Isn't that a beautiful sight,' she said, as they watched the couples heave and sigh. 'And they are all yours. You can have them do whatever you want. You can watch them copulating. You can have sex with them yourself.'

Bernice felt Samoya's body tense and let out a gasp of anticipation.

'Yes,' Bernice grinned, pulling down the soft transparent silk that covered Samoya's breasts and began squeezing her nipples, 'if that's what you would like you can have one of those big thick cocks rammed up inside you. Or, would you like to be sucked?'

She snaked her hands down over Samoya's belly and began to feel Samoya's bare, open and willing sex. As she did that Bernice began to move one of the leather dildoes along the crevice between Samoya's buttocks.

'Shall we make them stop and have them bend down and suck you?'

Bernice's insistent fingers playing first on her nipples making them erect, then on her clitoris, with the leather cock sliding and gliding between her legs made Samoya desperate for more.

'Yes,' said Samoya, rolling her bottom against Bernice's naked belly.

'In that case, as you are now a princess of the Royal household you must command them to stop copulating and command them to suck you. After I clap my hands you must issue your orders.'

Bernice guided Samoya up on to the dais and behind her throne. She leant Samoya's shoulders against the wall that was padded and hung with a great tapestry.

'You must stand with your legs well apart and your hips jutting forward.'

Samoya stood quite still whilst Bernice made certain she was in the correct position. Samoya looked out at the sea of coupling beneath her. Bernice clapped her hands.

'Stop,' Samoya ordered in a loud ringing tone.

Every one of the couples stopped in mid-thrust. The men lifted the women down. Samoya noticed with delight that their members were still very thick and erect. She wanted not only to be sucked, she wanted to feel at least one of those inside her.

'I command you to come forward one by one, kneel before me. And suck me.' Samoya hesitated. Which should she choose first, the men or the woman? 'Come forward as couples. The man will honour me first, then the woman.'

Obediently the slaves did as they were told. When the first slave's tongue slithered into her vulva she shivered with delight. When it began to nibble on her clitoris a further wave of desire swept through her body. Samoya closed her eyes. She gave herself completely to the sensuality of the constantly changing, exploring tongues and the different hands spreading her thighs further apart so that the tongue could go deeper. Hands gripping her flesh, digging nails into her skin. And sometimes a finger would stray. It would begin to massage her anus. She could feel herself opening further, wanting to surrender to the lewd pleasure. She wanted a cock. The more the tongues explored her sex the more her hips began to sway and roll. And the more she wanted a firm shaft inside her. She held her own breasts, enticing her own nipples to a firm erectness. And she thought of Marcus. Not when she had last seen him, angry and surly. She wanted the Marcus who had laid her down onto his bed, crawled up between her open legs and satisfied her longing. She wanted to feel a body on hers. She wanted to smell the sweat of a man. She wanted to feel the hardness of a man.

Suddenly, there was a great noise. The sound of trumpets and the drumming of drums. Samoya's eyes flew open. The huge, high doors at the far end of the room were parted to reveal a procession of men in flowing robes and turbans, some holding hawks on gauntleted hands, others holding trumpets. The procession marched into the room and the men took up their position around the walls.

Samoya was at a loss. She had no idea what she was supposed to do. Bernice was sitting on her throne. Samoya could see from the back of her that she was still naked. All the slaves were now prostrate on the ground, except for the man between her own legs. He was still kneeling, his tongue firmly lodged inside her wet sex. The trumpets were blown again and a great cry went up.

'Prince Alif, Prince Alif.'

Mesmerised, Samoya kept her eyes firmly on the doorway but to her complete surprise no one came through it. Instead the red curtains over the balcony were suddenly pulled apart. Samoya had the first view of her husband. He was wearing a magnificent golden robe and a high turban heavily encrusted with jewels. That was all she could see. Samoya felt a wave of relief. She had not known what to expect. Nobody had described her husband to her.

'So far excellent. Now prepare her for me,' commanded Prince Alif from the balcony. The red curtains were closed and he disappeared.

Within seconds of Prince Alif's announcement the slaves who had lain prostrate on the ground jumped up and grabbed Samoya. In one fast movement they removed her clothing, pinioned her arms behind her and lifted her up. When she was held high others came over and snapped thin but sturdy chains on her feet and on her wrists. She was carried over to a slim, cushioned trestle table that a number of slaves had immediately placed in front of the throne. Samoya noticed that it was fashioned exactly to her body shape. Bernice watched in silence as Samoya's back was put onto the upper part of the trestle. Leather straps attached to its base were fastened around her neck, under her arms and across the top half of her breasts and around her waist. Her open legs were fastened in the same way, leather straps surrounding her thighs, her calves, her ankles. Two cushions were placed under the buttocks raising her open wet sex for all to see. The straps around the top of her thighs were tightened making her pubis bulge further forward. The chains holding her hands were joined together under the table.

Holding a swansdown powder-puff Bernice came down from her throne, stood between Samoya's legs and began to run it over Samoya's sex and her clitoris. The gentleness of each tendril of the swansdown excited Samoya. She wanted to move and heave but the leather straps totally restrained her. The more Bernice flicked the more of Samoya's clitoris was coaxed into view and the more open and wet she became. And she felt her bladder filling up. She cursed Bernice for making her drink so much water. There was a heaviness in her lower parts that made the enticing sensations of the swansdown on her ever-enlarging clitoris turn into exquisite pain. Samoya forgot about the people in the room watching her. She could only think sexual thoughts. She wondered what would happen to her next. Would she be penetrated? She desperately wanted to be. Would Prince Alif do it to her?

Then the trumpets sounded again. Samoya heard once more the cries of 'Prince Alif, Prince Alif'. Princess

Bernice moved away from Samoya's legs. Someone tipped the trestle so that Samoya could see the approach of Prince Alif. She let out an involuntary gasp. He was the ugliest man she had ever set eyes on.

He was no more than five feet high and he was strutting towards her, a leering smile on his thick lips. His hooded, sleepy eyes drooled sex. His turban with its glittering great diamond in the centre was still on his head and his golden cape was draped nonchalantly about his shoulders. What Samoya now saw, which she hadn't seen when he was on the balcony, was his naked muscularity. And as he swaggered across the marble floor and up onto the dais his cape floated out behind him and his thick tool swayed proudly from side to side. Prince Alif had the biggest cock Samoya had ever seen. It was not erect, but hung huge and menacing almost to his knees.

Samoya tensed her buttocks in fear. How could she take such a massive instrument? It was impossible. Was this why she was strapped down? She turned her head. The slaves were now standing in a semi-circle around her on the dais. Prince Alif's noble friends had moved up closer. They stood, clothed in great capes in formal rows in front of her below the dais. They were waiting to see her being taken. She was their sport. They were eagerly waiting to see if she could accommodate Prince Alif's substantial member. Samoya decided to take the line of least resistance. She relaxed. Prince Alif removed his turban and handed it to Princess Bernice who was standing to one side, a smile hovering about her lips, as if to say 'let's see how she copes with this'. Prince Alif walked between Samoya's legs. He began to stroke her thighs, her sex. He lifted his great penis and held it, still flaccid, at her moist outer opening. He trailed the tip up and down, up and down her moist labia. Despite herself Samoya found the contact excited her. She edged her thighs outwards. Prince Alif took hold of the lips of her vulva and pulled them open. He put the bulbous tip of his penis against her engorged clitoris and rubbed so that of her own accord she opened still wider. She could feel the whole of herself expanding, her muscles, suffused with desire, were swollen and wanting to take his enormous penis. Then Prince Alif took one step backwards and aimed it at her abdomen.

Samoya felt a great jet of wet warmth flood onto her. It flowed down onto her clitoris, over her thighs and down along between the crevice of her buttocks. He was emptying the contents of his bladder over her. She was being covered in Prince Alif's golden shower. It was an endless stream and it made her want to empty her own bladder, her water to join his. Then she remembered where she was. People were watching her. Seeing her debased. Samoya found that stimulating. There was something so wholeheartedly erotic in her being strapped down and used, that instead of making her curl up with embarrassment she uncurled, unfurled and opened herself to total abandonment. She was no longer Samoya. She was a princess. She was an exhibitionist. She was a whore. She was a goddess. She enjoyed sex. She wanted it in all its forms. She craved for it. She craved for Prince Alif's massive penis. Prince Alif bent forward over her. With one hand he grabbed one of her breasts and tweaked her nipple. His other hand landed on her belly just above her pubis and pressed. It was agony on her full bladder.

'If you let any water out I'll have you whipped,' he snarled, lasciviously.

He leant back, positioned his huge cock against her opening and thrust. Samoya could feel his hugeness entering her. Spreading her wider. And she took him. What little leverage her bindings gave her she used to heave her body towards his. To force him further upwards, to take every inch of him. And then he began to drive into her with a frenzy. Intoxicated by her restraints and his fervour, her head was lolling this way and that. And she was gasping. Her bladder became fuller and fuller with the pressure of his body. Then he stopped, pulled out and deliberately pressed again on her belly and she couldn't hold it. It was sweet agony but she had to let it go. Desire and pain were too great. Slowly the stream issued out of her.

Prince Alif laughed. His eyes glinted with voyeuristic delight. His thick lips were drawn back over his teeth and he let out a croak of achievement and pleasure.

'Take her to my chamber,' he announced.

The slaves came forward and unstrapped Samoya from the trestle. Keeping her hands chained behind her back they presented her upright and naked to the entire assembly. With her red-gold hair tumbling over her petite breasts, accentuating her tiny waist, her soft rounded stomach, her shaven sex, she looked quite beautiful. Everybody bowed. Prince Alif came up to her. Put his penis just below her knees, close to her calves and rubbed. Samoya was surprised to find this, too, was an erogenous zone; she responded instantly by jutting her hips forward. Prince Alif bent his head, spread her sex with his thick stubbly hands, put his tongue to her sex and slurped noisily. He licked Samoya's clitoris. Her thick, throbbing little morsel of sensitive flesh grew thicker and more wanton with his expert attentions. He licked it again and again.

Princess Bernice came up behind her, pressed her great orbs into Samoya's back, and let her sex rest neatly on Samoya's chained hands. Samoya moved her fingers so that she parted the lips of Bernice's juicy wet sex and began to play with her, feel her and enter her. Bernice pressed closer so that Samoya's fingers could go deeper. Bernice brought her own hands round to the front, clasped Samoya's breasts and played with them. Samoya could feel her desire, her eroticism increasing as she realised she was the centre of attention. Prince Alif was sucking her and Princess Bernice playing with her breasts whilst she massaged Bernice's sex. Samoya looked out across at the slaves and Prince Alif's entourage who formed her audience. Every man in the room was staring at them whilst frantically rubbing their own cocks. When Samoya's fingers were firmly entrenched inside Bernice's sex, feeling every furrow and furl of the other woman's inner body, jerking to the rhythm of Alif's tongue working madly on her, Bernice leant forward and in a hoarse whisper that everybody could hear said, 'This whore is playing with my sex.'

Prince Alif immediately removed his lips from Samoya and stood back.

'Did you ask her to?' he asked.

'No,' said Bernice.

'Then she will have to be doubly punished,' he said. Prince Alif raised his hand.

'Clothe her and follow me,' he said.

The slaves picked up Samoya's pale blue cape and draped it over her shoulders. Then Prince Alif stepped down from the dais followed by Princess Bernice who was naked except for her belt with the leather truncheons attached. After her came Samoya and Bernice's two Nubians closely followed by Prince Alif's young nobles and the various slaves. They walked through the great doors, down a long, wide corridor, through another great room, down some steps and through another long corridor and then they entered Prince Alif's chamber. The room was as dark as night and lit by torches on the walls. It took time for Samoya's eyes to adjust to the darkness. In the centre of the room was a great bed covered in white bearskins. There seemed to be an arrangement of what looked like sticks on the walls. She screwed up her eyes in an effort to see what they were but as she did so the two Nubians quickly guided her to a place near the bed. Her cape was taken away. A leather collar was placed around her neck. A chain was fastened to the ring on the front of the collar. Her hands were unlocked but then drawn upwards, bound together again and the chains keyed to a bolt fitted into a rafter above her head. New chains were fitted to the rings on her anklets. These chains were then drawn taut, forcing her legs and feet apart, and attached to different pillars. The chains from her wrists allowed her leeway. Samoya twisted and noticed that everybody was standing in what seemed to her to be pre-arranged positions. And they were watching her. She couldn't see Prince Alif or Princess Bernice.

Suddenly she felt a sharp retort across her bare buttocks. She jumped and let out a great howl. Then another biting stroke of the lash came down. Frantically, she twisted again and howled louder. Tears were streaming down her face. But there was no mercy. The lash came again and again, marking her rump or her thighs, wherever it landed.

Realising her efforts to retain any sense of dignity were futile, she couldn't take the agony, the burning, any more and slumped. Water was thrown over her face and body. Prince Alif stood in front of her holding a long tawse that was split at the end into six long strips, his huge phallus erect, excited by the sight of her pale body turning to the whip. He clasped her sex.

'Your punishment for not holding your water was twelve lashes. Your punishment for touching Princess Bernice without permission is six lashes.'

'No,' cried Samoya.

'We don't give mercy here. You will learn to obey and thank us for your punishment. But now I want to watch you being fucked. You will bend your pretty, bright red little bottom over and present it nicely to my friends.'

Prince Alif trailed the whip along the inner lips of her sex, then tickled the soft tender flesh around her anus with the wet leather strips.

'I am giving them permision to take you where they want. Back or front, it's up to them.'

Samoya twisted on her chains. Hands held her hips, other hands parted her buttocks and she was thrust

135

forward as a very stiff cock penetrated her other orifice. Prince Alif stood rigid in front of her, his head level with her belly. He was the barrier against which she could be screwed. He held her breasts, at the same time hitting the side of one of her legs with his member every time she jerked.

Samoya turned her head. Each one of Prince Alif's entourage was being attended to by a female slave whilst they waited their turn to penetrate her. She looked over to the great bed. Princess Bernice was lying with her legs held high in the air by two slaves, another slave was on his belly pounding into Bernice's sex. From where she was swinging on the chains Samoya could see Bernice's hands moving wildly up and down the cocks of a couple of slaves beside her. And she could make out the outline of a woman's full breasts bouncing up as she squatted over Princess Bernice's face.

'Change,' ordered Prince Alif and the man penetrating Samoya's anus moved and another man took his place. He lunged for her open sex as a blindfold was tied around her eyes. From then on Samoya knew only sensation. The feel of a series of cocks entering her from the back and from the front and the feel of her naked flanks being whipped. Occasionally a hot tongue found the furls of her inner lips and then she was spread futher and a thin, icy cut would break onto her most tender flesh. She howled and moaned but to no effect. The whipping continued. She swung, she twisted and turned on her chains and finally, she was taken down, wrapped in cool silk and carried to the bed. There Princess Bernice put lotions on her weals and welts and gently caressed her breasts whilst the rest of the assembly watched. But this gave little relief because the surface of the bearskin tickled her scars, irritated and annoyed her, and caused the burning to continue.

Samoya looked about her through tear-stained eyes. She was aware that every man in the room had known her whiplashed body; had felt her inner self, her muscles closed over his penis. She lay quite still smarting from her thrashing but still excited and wet, as if the beating she had received had heightened her sexuality. Prince Alif climbed onto the bed with her. He pressed his thick-lipped mouth to hers.

'You performed well, my dear, better than expected. I congratulate you, Bernice. She is an excellent choice.'

Prince Alif began to lick her breasts and her neck, his short stubby body clambered over her, his thick fingers invaded her sex and her anus. Though not tied down, Samoya was too weak and exhausted to make a single movement of protest.

'And now my dear wife, I want you to perform some more,' he said.

Samoya thought that was impossible. What else could she do that hadn't already been done?

He began to lick her stretched and open sex, his great tool flopping along her legs. There was something exciting about the feel of it not quite erect and touching her inner thighs and other hitherto unknown erogenous zones.

'You are going to suck Princess Bernice. I want to see that pert little tongue of yours working inside her. She likes that, don't you Bernice?'

Princess Bernice, who was playing with herself as she watched her kinsman's lips and tongue enter Samoya, nodded her head. Bernice rolled her voluptuous body onto the bed and sat on her haunches hovering over Samoya's mouth.

'Put your tongue out and lick her,' commanded Prince Alif, changing his own position so that his cock was now level with Samoya's sex. Bernice's open, wet, pink shaven pussy was slowly lowered onto Samoya's waiting tongue, who pressed it in and then rolled it upwards to catch Bernice's over-large, engorged and protruding clitoris between her teeth. Samoya nibbled and Bernice made circular motions with her hips.

Excited, Bernice greedily grabbed Samoya's breasts holding firmly to her nipples and squeezing every time Samoya's teeth captured Bernice's baby penis. Samoya's hands were stretched out and suddenly she felt a thick, warm, pulsating, erect cock placed in each one. She began to rub them along their shaft, moving her hips, forgetting about the pain of the stripes marking her body.

And then Prince Alif pounced. He thrust himself into her with full force and she jerked wildly, her tongue hitting the very depths of Bernice's wanton sex as his massive penis filled up every tiny space in her pussy. Samoya could feel Bernice's muscles contracting and dilating, contracting and dilating. She was moaning, her hair flowing every which way as her head rolled and her mouth opened.

'Give me a cock, someone. I want a cock in my mouth,' Bernice yelled as she went up and down on Samoya's mouth and watched Prince Alif's drive into the girl who was sucking her. One of the young nobles with a short thick member obliged. He held Bernice's head as her mouth travelled up and down his length, whilst her sex moved rapidly along Samoya's tongue and her hands massaged Samoya's breasts.

Then Samoya felt her own body contracting. A great force tightened in her belly and began to move downwards. She was going to come. Alif, who was also on the point of coming, realised this, pulled out his prick, and sprayed all over her belly. He denied her her climax. But he knew what he was doing. He left her still open and wanting more. Prince Alif hadn't finished with her yet.

Samoya felt the jet of his creamy liquid landing on her belly as Princess Bernice jerked into her climax and the two men whose cocks she held spurted into the air. Bernice rolled away from Samoya's mouth and into the arms of some waiting females who began to rub her body with fresh oils. Prince Alif pulled Samoya to a standing position and threw her into the arms of some waiting slaves. They held her tightly whilst massaging her breasts, her belly, her buttocks and her sex with masses of sweet smelling oils so that her body was slippery to touch. Prince Alif pointed to the man who had first invaded Samoya's anus. He was a tall, light-skinned, handsome man with black hair and blue eyes. He was bone idle except when it came to anything to do with sex, then his prick was upright, the one part of him that worked.

'Lie there, Jojo,' he said, indicating the place vacated by Samoya. The man lay down. Prince Alif stretched Jojo's legs apart and came up between them. He rubbed his gigantic cock against Jojo's flaccid one. It jerked into life. Prince Alif then took the other man's penis in his mouth and began expertly to suck it. With every movement of the Prince's mouth and tongue Jojo's cock became stiffer and stiffer. He ordered one of his other soldiers to put his member into Jojo's mouth.

'He likes to be fellated,' said Prince Alif to Jojo. He looked over to where Samoya was being caressed by the slaves.

'Now bring her over here,' he ordered. Samoya was brought to stand beside Prince Alif.

'See this nice stiff cock on this handsome young man,' he said leering at her and once more rubbing his phallus between her calves. 'I want you to sit on it. Place yourself on him with your back to his face and sit on his delicious member. Only my dear, make sure it's your arsehole that takes it.'

Samoya was helped up onto the bed by the slaves who now poured lashings of oil over Jojo. Samoya put her feet either side of Jojo's hips and her anus neatly over the tip of his shaft. Prince Alif knelt between Jojo's legs. He took hold of Samoya's shoulders and pressed her down so that she was instantly impaled by Jojo's cock. He began thrusting hard into her.

'Now my dear, as Jojo is firmly ensconced in the place

he likes best I want you to lie back, your back resting on his chest and open your legs wide. I want to see that cock of his sliding in and out of your most private place.

Samoya lay back, gliding on the masses of oil which had been massaged and poured over both of them. While Jojo was pounding in and out of her, Prince Alif took a feather from one of the waiting slaves and began to tickle her clitoris with it. Samoya cried out. She wiggled her hips. Jojo thrust deeper. Alif played the feather more and more on her sex, inviting her clitoris to appear, large and excited. Then he began to spread her sex. He ringed the base of Jojo's cock allowing a couple of fingers to stray along to Samoya's anus.

Every slave in the room was wondering which one of them would be picked next. 'You, come here,' he shouted to a slave. The man he had picked was short with a fat stubby penis. It stood up proudly and was throbbing with excitement. He strutted to the bed.

'Screw her,' ordered Prince Alif.

Holding his own erect penis the slave came up between the two pairs of open and stretched legs and played himself on Samoya's juices making it thicker, stiffer. Prince Alif held open Samoya's sex-lips and helped the slave insert his tool. The slave gasped at his master's touch and the delicious excitement of being able to feel Jojo's cock as it worked in Samoya's other orifice. Samoya thought she would never be able to take two penises. But she was wrong. The slave inserted and rode her. Jojo continued to ride her. Then Prince Alif ordered another slave forward and instructed him to put his erect cock into Samoya's mouth. Every orifice she possessed was being plundered for the Prince's benefit. Prince Alif was enjoying himself. He stood to one side and began to stroke himself as he watched his wife take the three tools of pleasure.

Princess Bernice decided to join in the exhibition and knelt in front of Prince Alif taking his huge testicles into her mouth as he continued to play with his own shaft.

Then Princess Bernice stuck out her bottom, proffering it to the nearest person who chose to take it. One of Prince Alif's entourage immediately stood behind her and pushed his member hard into her. Bernice happily jerked backwards and forwards as Prince Alif stuck his bulbous shaft into her wide open mouth. She had difficulty taking it. She eased herself backwards and in so doing took more of the first member in her backside.

A couple of female slaves slid under Bernice's arched body and began to play with her huge breasts whilst she continued to be sodomised whilst sucking on Prince Alif's huge cock.

All the time this was going on Prince Alif was becoming more and more excited as he watched Samoya being penetrated back and front and the cock moving up and down in her mouth.

Bernice was right, he thought, the woman was a natural whore and perfect for his purposes. He would enjoy being married to her. There was no doubt she loved sex. He would keep her. He would make certain she was available to him or his friends for sex night or day. He must remember to give Bernice some extra slaves as a present for her excellent choice.

Prince Alif noticed Samoya's body straining upwards, going rigid. She was close to orgasm. This time he would let her. She could climax. He would take her again. There was another ceremony that must be performed. But he'd keep that for another time. He'd show her off tonight. He'd see to it that she wore the most beautiful clothes which would enchance her red-gold hair, and her pert upright breasts, which he had been careful not to mark with the whip. And those clothes, however voluminous, would be slit, allowing him immediate access to her sex whenever the desire moved him. He would spread the folds of her robes apart and spread her legs, feel her, touch her with his penis, screw her if he wished. She was his wife. And she was an exhibitionist. She would be stimulated by it. Enjoy it. And every man in the palace would want to have her. And he wouldn't allow it. Not then. Later perhaps, when he had marked her as his. For now only his special guard could enjoy her. Yes, tonight she would come with him to the King's palace. He would make her sit beside him, do whatever he wanted when he wanted in front of everybody. Prince Alif's shaft quivered inside Bernice's mouth at the thought. Oh, he'd enjoy that. He'd enjoy the look of shock on the King's brother's face. Odainat was such a prig. He needed a good seeing to. If he was anybody else Prince Alif would have given it to him a long time ago. Sadly, the beauty of his body was lost to the debauchery of King Hairan's court. He would not participate. With these thoughts Prince Alif's juices began to form quickly and almost before he realised, his climax was upon him. And as he withdrew he squirted his liquid into Bernice's mouth, over her lips and down her neck.

Samoya knew she was about to come. The whole of her body was trembling, the oils allowed her to glide on the men's hard bodies, one underneath and one on top. She had never known anything so wonderful, so exciting, so erotic.

She didn't want it to stop. She certainly wanted it to happen again, and again. As she rose higher and higher, Jojo's hands held her breasts, and pinched her nipples hard. The tightening in her belly travelled fast through her body and in a massive explosion and trembling violently she came, and so did the two men. Prince Alif took hold of Samoya's hands and undid the chains around her wrists. He ordered a couple of slaves to take off the collar and the anklets. He put her cape over her shoulders. Then he stood her beside him on the bed.

'My wife will be joining me at the banquet tonight,' he announced.

Everyone in the room bowed. Samoya felt as if she

had passed some sort of test. Prince Alif then handed Samoya to Bernice.

'You will dress her. She will look magnificent,' he said. He left the chamber taking his entourage with him.

Chapter Eight

'*I*'ve been waiting for a week to see the King and I must see him today,' said Prince Tamoral, indignantly.

'What's so important?' drawled Princess Bernice as she lounged on a marble bench covered in exquisite cushions in one of the arbours in Zenobia's garden. Bernice had deliberately chosen the spot; it afforded her both shade and privacy.

'I cannot guarantee anybody's safety across the desert unless I have an increase in monies for my men,' answered the Bedouin prince.

'Now's hardly the moment to ask,' said Princess Bernice. 'And if you've been here for a week why didn't you let me know?'

'My dear Princess I didn't want to be side-tracked by your beauty and my lust,' he said smoothly.

'Oh! Well why hasn't the King given you an audience before this?'

'I don't know, except I was told he was exceptionally busy,' said Prince Tamoral, knowing full well from his various spies inside and outside of the palace, that the King had a fresh intake of boy-slaves and breaking them in was occupying all his time. 'But I must leave tonight.

My men will be getting restless. I want you to ask him to see me at the banquet. It is urgent.'

'Where are your men?' asked Samoya inquisitively.

'I left them over there,' said Tamoral, pointing to the hills overlooking Palmyra.

'Really, they're normally with you!' purred the Princess, her mind turning briskly, wondering why he would have done that.

'We can't afford to pay the taxes for all of us to enter the city,' said Prince Tamoral. 'If we had the increase, we might. Please, I beg you get me an audience tonight. I won't take up much of his time. Just a quick question. Then his answer. But if it's not the right one your trade will suffer.'

'Blackmail, Tamoral!' said Bernice.

'No, a matter of fact.'

Zenobia was surprised to overhear the conversation. She didn't think anybody had arrived as yet. But then the grounds were enormous. The two of them must have arranged an assignation before the banquet. Zenobia, who was lying out of sight, decided to stay exactly where she was; the rest of their conversation could prove very interesting.

Princess Bernice gave a deep throaty chuckle and put a hand on Tamoral's knee.

'My dear Prince,' she said, moving her hand along his thigh and touching him between his legs. 'My very dear Prince, what's in it for me?'

'The safety of the caravans,' he replied, feigning innocence of her meaning.

'I'd be more interested in sex,' said Bernice, blatantly. 'We could leave quickly now before the processions and the nonsense begins. We could go to my apartments. You see I didn't know you were in Palmyra. You naughty, naughty man, you didn't let me know. I've missed that lovely big thick cock of yours. I could do with it now, erect, and inside me. It would set me up for the evening – which promises to be deathly boring.

Anything where Odainat is present is boring. And tonight he is guest of honour. This rich, upstart, Zenobia bitch has decided to give a banquet in honour of our glorious commander and his victorious troops. Now isn't that just too boring for words! A banquet. If she'd decided on a sex orgy it might be a different matter!'

'But dear Princess, for you a straightforward banquet will be different matter,' replied Prince Tamoral.

'Oh Prince, you are sharp today. Did you sleep on a bed of swords last night?' Bernice took hold of one of Tamoral's hands and put it over her breasts as she continued to rub his thighs and the top of his legs. 'You know I should be very angry with you.'

'Why?' asked Prince Tamoral.

'Because you took that blonde slave from me on the promise that you would part Pernel from his daughter.'

'She was kidnapped.'

'I know,' said Bernice, 'but not by you. When I heard about it I rejoiced. Ah, I thought Tamoral has done the trick. Very clever. Then she arrived in Palmyra not only with her father but with a contingent of Romans as well! But Tamoral you didn't keep your part of the bargain. So I would be interested in having that blonde slave returned to me.'

'You can't,' said Tamoral, defiantly.

'And why not?' asked Bernice, annoyed, unused to being denied anything she wanted.

'Because she's dead,' replied Tamoral. He knew Bernice was angry but there was no way he intended handing over Dagmar to the Princess's not so tender mercies.

'Oh really!' exclaimed Bernice, instinctively knowing Tamoral was lying. 'How did she die?'

'In a raid. Some Persians carried her off.'

'My but those Persian bandits are getting very clever!' she said sarcastically.

'Exactly why we need more money,' said Tamoral ingenuously.

'More money makes you more vigilant?' she asked.

'It helps, but it also enables me to recruit more men,' he said simply.

'Yes, I can see that. But it is unusual for you to come unaccompanied to Palmyra. I thought perhaps you were keeping that blonde girl out of sight. So I wasn't reminded of our bargain. And that's why you didn't tell me you were here.'

Tamoral had forgotten how astute the Princess was. He decided to head off that line of thought. It was far too accurate for his liking. He thought the best course of action was to be seen responding to her caressing hand. He opened his legs fractionally wider so that she could put her hands beneath his robes and grab his balls.

'Tell me Bernice, what happened when Samoya arrived in Palmyra?'

'We kept her in her woman's quarters for weeks. Then told her that she'd been married by proxy and sent her father back to Antioch, without her dowry, naturally. A very rich little girl, that one. Very rich indeed. And highly sexed. Prince Alif was well pleased with my choice.'

'What did she do when she saw him?'

'Nothing much she could do, she was strapped down with her legs wide open, he showered her with a stream of his royal water then took his pleasure.'

'She took him?' said Prince Tamoral, surprised.

'Oh yes, she took him and his entire entourage as well. She loved it. She was sexually indulged in every way. And her pleasure was heightened even more after the switch. She twisted and turned with her lovely little backside going backwards and forwards.' Bernice could feel Tamoral's penis rising under her caresses, stimulated by her description. 'I was being pleasured in numerous ways myself at the time but did have a moment or two to watch what was happening to her. Saw those men kneeling down, sliding their tongues into her, fondling her breasts, bending her over and taking her in every orifice. Alif made her lie down on the bed on top of Jojo. He took her up the arse whilst another slave went straight into her honeypot. Then I sat on her face and she pleasured me with her tongue. Good tongue she has, a very good tongue, found all the right places. Alif was very impressed. He's bringing her tonight. It wouldn't surprise me if he performs a decadent display with her at the banquet in front of everybody. That'll liven up the proceedings. He's very proud of that enormous tool of his. And he's found a woman who can take it. I bet he'll show it off.'

Bernice than parted her beautiful clothes and put one of her hands between her own legs and began stroking her sex.

'I'm very wet. You could have me now. You're wonderfully stiff, let me suck you and then I'll sit on you.'

'Here?'

'Yes, why not?' said Bernice.

'No,' he said. 'There isn't time.'

'There's always time for sex,' Bernice replied.

'No. I need to speak to the King. You organise that, then I'll come to your chamber after the banquet.'

Tamoral kissed Bernice's neck. She smiled at him.

'Very well,' she said, inwardly seething. How dare he refuse her. She would get him his audience with King Hairan but she would speak to Hairan first. She would make sure he didn't get his increases. No, better than that. He would get an increase but it would be so derisory that although he'd have to take it, it would be an insult. From her vantage point Zenobia watched Tamoral walk away and saw Bernice set her jaw as she looked after his departing figure. Zenobia smiled to herself. She knew the look on the face of a thwarted woman when she saw it. She'd better get inside fast and talk to her father. Zenobia had no doubt that Prince Tamoral would not get what he wanted. She and her father had better make their own private arrangements with the Bedouin so that at least their caravans were safe.

Zenobia walked quickly and determinedly through the gardens and into the fabulous villa. She was surprised to hear that Samoya was in Palmyra. She had not heard of her arrival. But then if she'd been locked away in the palace and not given a proper wedding she would not have heard. So, she was Prince Alif's wife. His sex object. Poor girl. She wondered how that had come about. Samoya had seemed so determined to become a doctor. Sex must have had something to do with it. Zenobia was pleased with herself that she had managed to thoroughly curb all of her own sexual instincts. Every time that Roman commander had entered her mind she had transposed his face with that of Odainat's and had concentrated on the idea of marrying the great Palmyrene warrior prince. And tonight her dream would be fulfilled. No one else anywhere in the world was capable of entertaining on such a lavish scale. She was certain of that. She had mentioned this to her father. He had said that it was probably true. The only exception would be the amazing Egyptian Firmus.

Within the last couple of days Firmus had been to see her father. Had put a business proposition to him. Become a partner in a papyrus factory in Egypt. Firmus needed an outlet in Palmyra, with a Palmyrene resident at the helm. That way their taxes would be reduced. Her father had hesitated, said it wasn't his line of operations. Zenobia had looked at the great fat man and had trusted him immediately. She saw an opportunity, decided to go in with him and, without consulting her father, put her own money into the venture. She would have an income from Egypt. She could go there, visit the pyramids. See the land of her ancestor, Cleopatra. Zenobia was convinced she had Cleopatra's blood running in her veins. She felt they had much in common. But Cleopatra had killed herself. Zenobia had no intention of killing herself. Not for love, not for a country, not for anything. She would live and enjoy, marry Prince Odainat, make him king and she would be a great queen.

She thought again about Samoya and shuddered. Married to Prince Alif! The nastiest, most scheming man she had ever met. Fractionally worse than the debauched King himself. Well, she would be charming to him tonight. She would be charming to everyone tonight. It was her banquet. Nothing must go wrong. If Alif wanted to use it as an excuse for another sex orgy, so be it. Hopefully she would have achieved the object of the exercise by then and have left.

On her way to her father's office, Zenobia made a detour through the great banqueting hall. She gazed at everything purposefully. It was the best, the finest, the biggest in the world. It was fabulous. And there was nothing tasteful about it. It was extreme, excessive, stupendous. She loved every inch of its glitter and gaudiness. She loved it even more when she thought how the Romanised matrons would criticise her for her appalling lack of taste. The whole place, the villa and the banqueting hall was inordinately ostentatious and it shrieked money. And money was what she had and she was going to flaunt it. Soon she would have power as well. The hall was beautifully proportioned with the finest marble pillars supporting the heavily carved ceiling. For every inch of the building she had employed the very best craftsmen. She had paid them well and they had rewarded her with matchless work. The most beautiful silks were draped along the walls, there was an abundance of carpets littered with extravagantly designed and brightly coloured cushions. The largest, thickest garlands of the most exquisite flowers bedecked the columns and the tables. On the tables rested the finest embroidered cloth, the most beautiful goblets, and priceless gold plates and gold candlesticks, and when the food arrived that would be the most wonderful anybody had ever eaten. She heard the murmur of voices. Zenobia looked at the far end of the hall. On a newly erected stage, not far from the great doors and almost opposite the raised podium where the Royal table was set, Greek actors were practising their lines. She smiled, recognising the script. Her second most favourite Greek comedy. *The Birds* by Aristophanes. She had thought about putting on his *Lysistrata* but decided as that was about women withdrawing their sexual favours from men until they stopped the war it wasn't quite appropriate for a welcome home for victorious soldiers.

'My Lady,' said one of the actors as she passed by. 'Are you sure everyone will understand Greek? We do have an Aramaic translation available.'

'We Palmyrenes are not barbarians,' she replied, haughtily. 'We speak Greek, Latin and Aramaic here. At least those with any culture do. Of course everybody will understand it. And if they don't, they should.'

Dismissing him with a wave of her hand, and satisfied that everything was going according to plan with a military precision that would have left a general proud, Zenobia went to find her father and tell him about the conversation she had overheard with Tamoral and Bernice. He told her to watch out for the meeting between Tamoral and the King. Afterwards she must find an excuse to speak to Tamoral herself. She queried why *she* should do that and not him. Her father told her that no one would suspect a flighty young woman decked out in jewels and finery to have a business head on her shoulders. She must discover the terms offered by Hairan and if necessary make her own arrangements with the Bedouin. Her father told her he trusted her implicitly to make the best possible deal with them.

Zenobia went to bathe and rest and dress. Tonight she would be all smiles and gentleness to everyone. She would give the greatest performance of her life. Her father watched the determined figure of his departing daughter and thought she was better than a boy. Better at organising, better at gathering information, better at acitng on it than any man he had ever known. He also realised she was wanting to ensnare Prince Odainat. He was pleased. It would be a good match. He would give it his full approval.

Marcus had indulged himself in every tavern and brothel in Palmyra. He had drunk to excess. He was in a sorry state but now, suddenly, he had to pull himself together. He had wanted to get back to Antioch, and go on to Rome. But with every despatch came another order telling him to stay where he was. And now there was his latest command. Wearily Marcus held his head in his hands. He despised himself for entering and then enjoying every variety of sex the flesh-pots had to offer but he couldn't resist it. Whether it was as a voyeur or as a participant Marcus threw himself wholeheartedly into the job of giving himself pleasure. He felt he needed it. Anything to try and get rid of the taste and feel of Samoya. He had fallen in love with her and that love hurt.

Marcus failed to understand why she was so cold to him after he had rescued her. He would have taken her back to Rome with him. Why hadn't he done so? Then he remembered he had made a promise to his commander, Aurelian, not to touch the girl but to deliver her safely to Palmyra. And he had done it.

He lay in his lodgings with his head aching from the previous night's over-indulgence. What hurt him most was that she seemed so pleased to be going to Palmyra to marry a prince. Of course, he reasoned he was only a lowly Roman soldier, but he wouldn't always be in that position. He was rising through the ranks. He would become a commander.

And the longer he stayed in this desert city the more he heard about the ruling family and their outrageous decadence. He forgot that he had been participating in his own debauchery as he wondered what Samoya had been up to. He had heard Prince Alif was an incredibly unpleasant man with the biggest cock in the land. And that he had sex orgies. Surely his beautiful Samoya was not having to submit to that. And if she was, was she enjoying it? It was bad enough imagining it happening to her but the thought that she might like it racked Marcus's emotions.

Marcus thought of Samoya's slim body and its delicious curves. The sweet taste of her mouth and the smell of her hair. The softness of her clothing wrapped around his legs as they had travelled on horseback on that first exciting ride. He remembered the feel of her buttocks against his prick. How she had moved so that she was gliding on him. And the moment when he had taken her in his arms, embraced her, held her tight. How the two of them had fallen on the bed in a frenzy of desire. How she had opened her legs for him and he had entered her with a passion he had never known before or since.

Marcus picked up a nearby pitcher and drank from it. He didn't know whether he liked Palmyra. It certainly wasn't a wonderful place if you didn't have any money. The fun was mainly for the rich, the very rich. He had his salary but he was glad old Pernel had paid him in gold. That had helped to get him better lodgings than he otherwise might have had. It was cooler than most. His room faced due north and onto a shady courtyard where a fountain played and date palms grew.

He was hot. Noon was always hot in Palmyra. No respite from the endless power of the sun. He poured water over his head and lay down on the cold marble floor, endeavouring to cool his over-heated body as well as his over-heated emotions. He had to sober up before the evening. He'd had specific instructions to attend the banquet in honour of the returning and victorious warriors of Palmyra and Rome.

Marcus thought how extraordinary the lines of

Roman communications were. He had been lying half-awake on his bed, his head pounding, his mouth tasting like a drain, his eyes as red rimmed as if he'd been in a sandstorm, when his landlady had knocked on the door.

'There's a big fat man at the door says he got to see you,' she had said.

Marcus had followed the nimble old woman downstairs and was met at the entrance to the building by a large, jolly man who had introduced himself as Paul of Samosata, the Bishop of Antioch. That had completely flummoxed Marcus until the Christian explained that he had a message from his commander. The bishop went on to tell him how he had been invited to a banquet that a great friend of his, the Lady Zenobia, was giving in Palmyra. A messenger had bought the invitation to him in Antioch the very morning that Lucius Aurelian, had visited him on official Empire business. When he heard the messenger's news the commander had asked if the bishop would deliver a letter to Marcus in Palmyra. And then the bishop had handed Marcus a letter complete with Aurelian's seal. It had ordered him to attend the Lady Zenobia's banquet that night on behalf of the Empire.

Marcus poured more water over his head. When he thought he had the whole day to himself he now had to prepare himself for an evening of total boredom with senators and dignitaries representing Rome. And all he could think about was Samoya. Would she be there? Would she see him? Would she notice him or ignore him? Marcus thought he'd better go to the baths. Lie there and thoroughly cleanse himself. And he made a mental promise. He must not drink tonight. Whatever happened, he must remember that he most definitely must not get drunk.

Zenobia was waiting for the arrival of her royal guests. She looked up and down the room. Everything was set according to protocol and precedence. The high table was vacant, waiting for the King and his family. The lower tables in serried rows were for favoured representitives of the city: Senators, Generals, important men of the various religions. The High Priest of the Sun God was there and the High Priestess from the temple of the Goddess Allat. Respected and rich merchants with their wives dressed befitting their wealth and their status. Though in Palmyra if you had wealth you also had status.

Zenobia, knowing that everyone would expect her to try and outdo everyone else in finery and jewels had in fact done completely the opposite. She was wearing a robe of the simplest, purest, most virginal white. It was finely pleated, fell in folds to the floor and modestly covered her breasts. Her hair was softly curled around her ears with only a few gold pins holding it in place. She wore a necklace of pure gold around her neck and two slim gold bracelets on her arm. She wore no rings. No matter that her surroundings were one of unbridled luxury she presented a personal image of chastity and frugality.

Zenobia sat at the middle of her table between her friend Paul, the Bishop of Antioch and a philosopher acquaintance of his, Cassius Longinus, who had recently arrived in Palmyra and was looking for work. Cassius was as thin and lean as Paul was large and ebullient. They were talking about the latest philosophic fad in Rome. Neo-Platonism. Next to Cassius sat Timogenes. Zenobia loved him. He made her laugh. He was the strangest mixture. Effeminate, covered in feathers and baubles, yet desperately wanting to join Odainat's army. Every time he came to visit her he had designed himself another weird and wonderful uniform. But when she talked to him about history Timogenes could fully explain and recount every battle there had ever been in the known world. He kept rooms full of tiny carved soldiers where he enacted the ancient battles for his own pleasure. Because of his homosexuality Prince Odainat would never allow him in his army. Zenobia thought that was wrong. He would make a fine soldier.

Zenobia glanced further down her table to Prince Tamoral. He sat resplendent in his bedouin robes. She had placed him where she could see him at all times without any difficulty. The moment he moved to speak to the King she would see. And she would be able to watch his unguarded expression when he returned to his seat. From that she would know if and how to approach him. Zenobia was listening to the conversation between Paul and Cassius and had just decided to ask Cassius to become her personal tutor when the trumpets sounded. The Palmyrene Royal Family had arrived. Everyone stood up and bowed as they made their way through the doors and down the length of the room to take their places at the high table.

Zenobia found it difficult to hold back her feeling of total revulsion as she saw the gross, bloated and debauched King stumble along at the head of the procession. He was wearing a purple robe which did nothing to disguise his enormous belly hanging over his short legs. And his crown kept slipping from his bald head. That gave Zenobia an enormous feeling of satisfaction. Behind the King strolled his handsome, weak, and slimy looking son, Prince Maaen. He walked straight and was wearing army uniform. Then came a bevy of fat, though pretty, young boy-slaves who crawled behind the father and son. They were clothed in transparent fabric showing off their chubby young bottoms. After him came Princess Bernice. She was wearing a cape of deep red, covering a robe of see-through yellow silk, her great breasts were wobbling and her dark brown nipples were clearly visible. As she walked the robe parted allowing the assembly a glance of her legs, her thighs and occasionally a flash of her pubis. She was followed by two huge bare-chested Nubian eunuchs waving palms above her head and a host of crawling, well-rounded, female slaves, naked but for their short leather tunics. As they crawled everyone was able to see their bare buttocks and their moist half-open vulvas.

After this group had seated themselves at the high table, their slaves on the floor under it, Prince Alif arrived. Zenobia felt a fresh wave of revulsion wash over her as she watched him strut through the great doors, a glittering turban on his head and a floor length, heavily embroidered cape completely covering his short muscular body. Behind him walked twenty handsome young men, his personal friends, the young nobles, wearing costumes designed to show off their large, semi-erect penises. Prince Alif took his place and his young men stood against the wall behind him.

Then Samoya walked in and Zenobia let out an involuntary gasp. What had they done to her? Her face was heavily made-up, her eyes darkened with masses of kohl, her mouth strongly rouged. She wore a high feathered head-dress but no jewellery. But what amazed Zenobia most was her diaphanous robe of light blue, deep red and fiery orange criss-crossed with strips of leather. The strips formed a halter from her neck around her bare breasts. Her nipples had been coloured a dark shade of brown, her breasts were glistening with freshly applied oils. From the base of her cleavage the pleats fell in folds. The centre pleat was edged with leather. As she walked, her waist and belly, her shaved mound, her naked thighs were visible to everyone in the room. Under her robe she wore a thin chain belt. Attached to its ends were two penis-shaped truncheons which flopped from side to side as she made her way towards the high table. Zenobia was horrified and astounded. And vowed to release her friend from her appalling state.

When Samoya arrived at the table Prince Alif took one of her breasts in his hands, pinched her nipples and announced to all the assembled guests, 'My wife,

Samoya.' And sat her on his knee. Everyone in the room, though outraged by the entire procession and Prince Alif's performance in particular, duly bowed.

Then the trumpets were blown again. Zenobia breathed a sigh of relief. Prince Odainat had arrived. But he was not going to be outdone by the eccentricities of his family. He rode into the banqueting hall on his charger. With his upright soldierly bearing, his mane of long curling black hair, his tightly cropped beard and his great golden cape embroidered with the insignia of Prince and General of Palmyra flowing out over his shoulders and along the horse's back, he was instantly recognisable and a great cheer went up from everyone. The horse moved elegantly and at a slow pace down the centre of the hall. Odainat pulled it up beside Zenobia, his hostess. He dismounted and bowed to her. Their eyes met and he flashed her the message. I want you. And Zenobia knew in that moment she had won. Every scheme, every moment of planning was worth it. He wanted her. And she would have him.

A groom removed his horse. Odainat marched to the high table where he sat beside his brother the King. Then his Generals and other high ranking officers of the Palmyrene army and a few Romans marched into the room. They sat at the table closest to the stage which Zenobia had allotted to them. These men were followed by a group of gaudily dressed slave-girls and they sat, as arranged, between each soldier. Then came the dancing girls, the acrobats and the jugglers. And the eating and drinking began in earnest.

Marcus was amongst the soldiers. He looked around the great hall and up at the high table. He could not see Samoya. He let out a sigh of relief and drank water with his first course. He didn't know why she wasn't there but he was glad. He couldn't bear to see her belonging to another man. The slave-girl beside him was most attentive but he was morose. After a while she urged him to take a little wine in his water. As he was perfectly sober and everyone around him was getting tipsy he decided he would. He'd better relax. It wasn't long before the slave-girl was pouring his wine without the water.

Odainat sat amidst his relatives pretending that he didn't know that the boys under the table were playing with the King's genitals. Or that Princess Bernice had her group of females stroking her thighs and licking at her sex. Once he glanced in Prince Alif's direction only to see that beneath his cape he was completely naked and he was holding his new wife's hands over his huge penis, making her play with it. Prince Maaen sat close to his father. He seemed aloof, disdainful, as though he didn't want to be there but would stay if only to get drunk. Odainat sat quite disgusted. He looked down at the rows of tables in front of him and saw Zenobia, sweet and virginal and charming. What a difference, he thought. I will marry that woman.

They were at the thirteenth course. The dancing girls were dancing again, the wine was flowing liberally, acrobats were hurling themselves over one another when Prince Tamoral looked up and saw the King. His head was lolling backwards. He was panting. Obviously his young boys were performing to perfection. Tamoral judged the time to be right for him to ask for his increase. And with so many people moving around he wouldn't be missed from his place. Whilst chatting conversationally to Paul and Cassius, Zenobia watched Tamoral walk up to the high table, bow and whisper to the King. The King's head nodded and nodded. Tamoral's face was expressionless as he talked. Then she saw the King shake his head. And she noticed Bernice's cat-like smile of triumph. Tamoral, keeping his face as rigid as a mask, bowed, backed away from the King and wove his way through the acrobats and jugglers towards the great doors. He wasn't going to return to his seat. Quickly Zenobia jumped up and stopped the Bedouin prince in his tracks.

159

'Prince,' she said, gently tugging at his arm. 'Are you unwell?'

'No, My Lady,' he said quietly, trying to disguise his fury.

'Then I would be honoured if you would sit by me. My companions are most interesting. I'm sure they'd amuse you. And besides I need to discuss some business with you.'

Tamoral hesitated. He wanted to leave. But perhaps it was better if he contained his anger. There was no point in giving the King or Bernice an unnecessary advantage. Tamoral was sure Bernice was behind the King's refusal to give him more money. Well the day would come when he would repay her. Now it was wiser to bide his time. He smiled at Zenobia and followed her back to the table. He was intrigued. What sort of business could this slip of a woman need to discuss with him?

Odainat had only half heard the exchange between Tamoral and the King but he felt the Bedouin's anger. He watched him depart and then saw Zenobia approach him. How very diplomatic of her, he thought. He then looked along the table at his own dissolute relatives. In one way or another they were all eating and sexing. Odainat felt a wave of disgust envelop him. What they did in the privacy of their own apartments was up to them but their public manners were a disgrace. Of course they were all drunk and getting more so. The King seemed oblivious to the anger of the Bedouin. His only interest was his great bloated body being stroked and crawled over by his mass of fat boy-slaves. Maaen had slouched forward onto the table. He was in a drunken stupor. Odainat watched some of the female slaves put their hands over Bernice's shoulders, and caress her breasts. Bernice was stuffing food into her mouth and rolling her body from side to side. No doubt some of her other slaves were beneath the table sucking her pussy. But perhaps from the sudden jerks she was making, somebody was playing with her sex with one of her leather dildoes.

Odainat knew Bernice was partial to the perverse pleasures of such accessories. He knew she kept them around her waist so that whenever the desire overcame her she could put them to good use. He remembered once he was walking behind her and her entourage along a corridor in the palace. Suddenly she had stopped, leant her back against the wall and spread her legs. She had grabbed a slave by her hair, made her kneel down and lick her pussy. On her command her two Nubian eunuchs, ever in attendance, had untied her belt. She had placed one of the leather cocks at the entrance to her vulva. Then had told the girl to insert it and rub vigorously until she came. Odainat had been both ashamed and aroused. He had gone to his chamber and rubbed himself until he had climaxed. But he had done it in private. What she and the King were doing now was monstrous behaviour in public.

But, Odainat had to remind himself, whatever he did, however he behaved, the King's word was law. With that thought as his starting point Odainat began to think the unthinkable. Perhaps if the King's word was law and the law couldn't be changed, the King might have to be.

He turned his head away from them only to be faced with the girl Samoya. She was very pretty he thought, but with the clothes she had on and her incredible feathered head-dress she looked more like a foreign concubine than a wife. He watched slyly as Alif told her to spread her legs wide and then a slave's head came between her thighs.

Odainat swallowed hard. He did not want to be affected by their sexuality, but he was. He found his own cock moving. He bent his head and continued eating. Zenobia had provided an incredible banquet. He thought he had never tasted such delicious food and in such variety. The hummous and tabbouleh were excellent but the dried fish that she'd had brought in from the Mediterranean was superb. As was the mullet, eels and bass from Syria's lakes and rivers. The duck had come in an orange sauce. The snipe with a variety of spices that had titillated his palate, preparing his taste buds for the succulent charcoaled goat and lamb. Of all the desserts she had offered, honeyed pastries with dates and nuts, fruit in rose juice, his favourite had been mulberries in wine served with yogurt.

Odainat downed the remainder of the wine in his goblet. He looked out over the entire assembly. They were merry and drunk. Some of them were leering at their partners. Some of them were leering at people who were not their partners. He noticed a couple of the soldiers had passed out. Including the Roman. A pretty young slave was endeavouring to shake him awake. But none of their behaviour was as gross as his own family's. Nevertheless, he was aroused. For the first time in years he was thinking sexual thoughts. He would like to touch the untouchable. He would like to make love to enchanting Zenobia. He would join her for the rest of the banquet. Odainat pushed back his chair and made his way down steps and along the tables, noticing that everyone of any importance in Palmyra was there. Even the High Priest, sober and looking extremely disapproving. Odainat walked more slowly, calculating as he went. Instead of asking her to marry him now why not do it now?

She looked up at him as he approached. Their eyes met. She smiled. She stood up to greet him and bowed. He took her hand. He felt people's conversation stop. Now what should he do? Having singled her out, properly he should take her up to the Royal table. That was the last thing he wanted to do. Although he was sure she knew what was going on but had chosen to ignore it. Nevertheless, it would be too embarrassing to take her there. Zenobia came to his rescue.

'Prince Odainat,' said Zenobia with lowered eyes, 'I

think it is time for our special performance. We have the famous Greek Theatre Actors with us tonight and they are going to perform Aristophanes's, *The Birds*. Would you come with me to the stage to make the announcement?'

How clever she was, thought Odainat. She had saved him. His reputation. He who knew exactly what to do on a battlefield had hesitated. But now she made it look almost as if his arrival at her table was pre-arranged. He smiled down at her, put her hand over his and they walked slowly to the stage.

'Your Majesty, Your Highnesses, Senators, Generals, Officers, High Priest, High Priestess, ladies and gentlemen,' Zenobia began in a clear ringing voice that immediately grabbed everybody's attention. 'This evening's banquet is to do honour to Palmyra and to the sons and daughters of Palmyra. Especially Prince Odainat and those who fought with him against our mortal enemy the Persians.'

Odainat standing beside her was struck by her voice, her carriage, and her beauty. He stopped listening to her words, he made mental plans. Before the night was over he would make her his wife. But these thoughts were cut short when he sensed a subtle change in atmosphere in the room. He looked up at the Royal table. Prince Alif was leaning over talking to the King. They were looking at him and Zenobia. Something wasn't quite right. Odainat turned his attention back to Zenobia's words.

'And so in conclusion I offer for everybody's entertainment, Aristophanes's *The Birds*.'

'Oh no you won't,' shouted the King.

The guests who were about to applaud sat, their hands half way to clapping, frozen and silent.

'My kinsman here,' said the King, slurring drunkenly, and leaning his belly against the table in an effort to stand upright. 'My kinsman, Prince Alif, has a much better idea. And being King I recommend it to you all. And I would remind everybody that Prince Odainat, worthy champion though he is, is only a prince. I am the King. And I have a son who will be King after me. And my word is law. Prince Alif speak.'

Odainat and Zenobia stayed warily and stiffly on the stage as they watched the arrogant prince rise and be helped up on to the table. Zenobia thought she had never felt so humiliated, so angry or so revolted as she saw him throw off his cloak, reveal his fleshy nakedness and take his great penis in his hand.

'This is my weapon,' he said and shook his cock from side to side. 'And this is my wife.' Samoya was lifted up to stand beside him. Alif parted her dress and put a stubby hand over her pubis. 'And we are going to perform for His Majesty, and you – a royal display of fornication. Slaves, carry my wife to the stage.'

Whilst Samoya was carried aloft down the centre aisle past the rows of tables, Odainat and Zenobia left the stage.

As Odainat helped her down the steps he looked at her impassive face. He knew she was shaking with fury. He stood close to her and whispered.

'Marry me.'

'Yes,' she said.

They didn't look at one another. They carried on walking. They were aware that there was an instinctive and deep understanding between them. They were making a momentous decision but quite deliberately on their part nobody in the room guessed a thing from their manner.

'Tonight,' he said.

'Tonight!' she exclaimed softly.

'Yes, then we can begin to change all this.'

'When do you suggest we announce it?' she asked. 'Before or after Prince Alif's performance.'

'I suggest we don't, just ask the High Priest to come with us. He can perform the ceremony. We can announce it after it's done. And that way we miss the Royal production.'

164

'Let's take Prince Tamoral with us as a witness,' said Zenobia. She had not yet had time to put her proposition to him. Which was just as well. As a Princess of the Royal house she would be able to offer him different terms: good ones but to be reviewed in six months time. Things might have changed by then.

'That's an excellent idea. It's always best to have the Bedouin on your side,' he said.

Whilst all eyes were on Samoya being taken to the stage Odainat, Zenobia, the High Priest, and Prince Tamoral slipped out of the banquet. It was after they had departed that the slave's ministrations to Marcus suddenly bore fruit. Blearily he came round from his drunken sleep. And the first thing he saw was Samoya standing alone on the stage. Marcus blinked his eyes a couple of times. He could not believe what he was seeing. He watched as slaves made their way up to the stage with a wooden frame and set it up. Then they made Samoya stand against it and attached her wrists and her open legs and wide apart ankles to it.

'What's going on?' he asked, his vision coming and going.

'We're going to watch a display of lewdness,' said the slave-girl.

'Oh right,' said Marcus, and clambered to his feet.

'Hey what're you doing?' asked the slave-girl, desperately trying to push him back on his chair.

'I must have her,' said Marcus pointing to Samoya.

'But you can't,' said the slave.

'Oh but I can. I've done it before, and I'll do it again.'

The slave-girl heard his words with horror. He was obviously so drunk he didn't know what he was saying.

'No, no,' she said. 'Look, you can have me later.'

'I don't want to have you later. I want to have her now.'

'You can't,' the slave wailed.

'We've known each other intimately before and will do again,' said Marcus.

165

'Don't be ridiculous,' said the slave.

'That's the Lady Samoya, Prince Alif's wife. See, there he is beside her.'

Marcus looked up to see the naked prince with an enormous erection standing beside Samoya. He pushed the girl to one side. She grabbed him.

'Help me,' said the slave-girl to the others at the table. 'Help me to hold him down.' A couple of the men helped pinion Marcus to his seat whilst watching Alif part Samoya's robe, insert his manhood between the calves of her legs, his buttocks moving backwards and forwards, and put his thick long tongue at her private entrance and begin to suck.

'Some advantages to being small,' muttered one soldier to another. 'I couldn't do that.'

'Yeah, yeah, Alif,' shouted the King. 'Very clever but we want to see a more lascivious display.' Alif ordered his slaves up onto the stage and they tipped the wooden frame backwards. Prince Alif stood on a stool, his erection positioned to lunge when the King clapped and shouted. 'Take her, take her.'

To a great roar of approval Prince Alif slid his huge member into Samoya's wet opening. In their excitement, the men holding Marcus relaxed their grip. Marcus broke away from them and rushed up to the stage screaming at the top of his voice, 'How could you do this to me, Samoya, you bitch?'

He knocked Prince Alif down and pandemonium was let loose.

Chapter Nine

*B*y the camp-fire light Dagmar looked both dangerous and enchanting. Her long, thick blonde hair was held in two bunches, soft tendrils had escaped their binding and framed her beautiful face. She was talking to Tamoral's tribesmen, arranging a hunting expedition for the following day. When Tamoral and the stranger rode into camp Dagmar quickly covered her hair with her headcloth, pulled the burnouse closely around her body and made a quick exit into her own tent.

Tamoral introduced Marcus to his men. Marcus sensed danger. He knew that he was under an obligation to the Bedouin prince who had saved him from the King's troops in Palmyra. He was shown a tent to use for the night and immediately retired; he had no intention of putting one foot out of place. Also, he was physically exhausted from days of riding (Tamoral had expected to find his men camped in the hills but he had been gone so long that Dagmar, sensing trouble, had ordered them into the desert) and he was mentally in torment. He wondered what had happened to Samoya and what would happen to him when he was eventually handed over to Aurelian.

At dawn next morning, after a turbulent night's sleep,

he was lying on the river bank hidden by the reeds. He was gazing peacefully at the apricot and salmon-pink sky and dabbling his feet in the water when he heard a movement. Thinking it was a duck or a heron he propped himself up on his elbows and caught a flash of naked buttocks, which quickly disappeared in a neat dive beneath the glassy surface. A few moments later he saw a beautiful woman swimming towards him. He held his breath and watched as she stood up and he was able to see her tiny waist, the womanly curve of her well-rounded belly, the swell of her large hips and the length of her shapely limbs. She picked up a length of cloth and began vigorously to dry her hair.

Suddenly the unknown woman gave a scream and disappeared. Marcus jumped up, leapt into the water, found her and hauled her back to the river bank. Soaked, they lay side by side. She looked at him surprised.

'Crocodiles?' he said, staring into her eyes, fascinated at finding them blue. She held his gaze and laughed.

'There are no crocodiles here, it's not the Nile. I slipped.'

Then he kissed her. He had not meant to do it. But her naked body in his arms, the touch of her breasts, the texture of her wet skin, had overwhelmed him. A force greater than all his good intentions ran riot within him. He did it without thinking. And to his delight she responded. Her lips opened beneath his pressure. He held her body tighter to his. He stroked her back. He could feel his excitement rising. She moved a wet hand beneath his tunic and held his balls. She rolled them gently. He held his breath, revelling in the exquisite tremors sharpening his appetite for her body. Then she let her fingers trail along his shaft, until they reached its head. She left a thumb under the rim and allowed her fingers to play individually up and down the shaft, up to the top then down again to the base. Under her expert handling his cock stiffened and stiffened. His whole body shook with desire.

He wanted to splay her legs, go up inside her, take her. He wanted to feel every ridge of her inner-self meeting the ridges and veins of him. His hands encircled her large soft, malleable breasts. He ran the inside of his fore and middle fingers in a tiny squeezing scissor movement against her nipples. Her mouth opened wider to take more of his tongue and she moved her legs apart. His hand moved along her belly to the blonde down of her pubis. He parted her labia. She sighed the moment he touched her. She raised her hips, silently inviting him to enter. The touch of each other produced a lightness, a tenderness that was full of electric tension. Anything they did, anywhere they touched, ignited the fires within them. With the tiniest of movements he pressed inwards beyond her corolla, and her legs were apart and stiff waiting for the next vital touch whilst her hands still played along his shaft.

And then he was on top of her. Entering her, taking her, touching the tip of her womb. Their open mouths were fastened together, their tongues entwined, her hands, held by his, were outstretched, her heels were digging into the ground, her hips raised off it, taking him as his stiff cock raided her moist, willing, wanting sex.

They returned to the Bedouin camp separately. They made certain to keep away from each other and tried, except for the simplest of platitudes, not to talk to each other. They were both aware of Tamoral's watchful and jealous eyes.

Tamoral lay on his rugs in his tent. He was playing with himself; he had woken from a dream where he had been having sex with Dagmar. Tamoral felt a combination of disappointment and frustration and that made him extremely irritable. It was his own fault they were bound for Antioch. When they got there he would be rid of the irritant. He had promised Odainat he would deliver the Roman to the garrison in Antioch. He would keep his promise. Aurelian expected him. And Tamoral had to remember, however much their fortunes wavered, the Romans were masters of the world. It did not do to anger them, too much. It was a far better policy to have them indebted to the Bedu. But whilst he was doing that he was missing out on good money guarding Zenobia's father's caravans.

Tamoral held his cock with a strong hard grip as his hand worked its way up and down, up and down, his mind imagining Dagmar under him, her legs open wide then winding them across his back as he fucked her, hard. He gripped his balls with his other hand. He had told her not to allow a man near her unless she wanted him. And she had made it very clear she didn't want him. He had given her every opportunity. He had gone to her tent and she had faced him, dagger at the ready, snarling like an animal. He had stood close to her. She had moved away. He had touched her hands. She had recoiled. He had pretended he had wanted something else. And had left full of resentment. He had taught her how to use a dagger, and a sword. He had taught her how to kill. Now he had to be careful in case she turned it on him.

Jealousy was tearing him apart. He would have to get rid of her before he did something he might regret. He thought of all the women he had screwed. He thought of Princess Bernice and her licentiousness, but it wasn't until he imagined caressing Dagmar's full breasts, and entering her swollen opening that he climaxed.

As he dressed, the solution came to him. He would send Dagmar with some of his men to Palmyra. Having released her from slavery he knew she was honour-bound to him. And completely trustworthy. He would order her to stay in Palmyra as his spy. Not that he would put it like that. He would tell her that he thought the situation in Palmyra was volatile. That he had already heard rumours that the High Priest was complaining about the amount of Christians and other sects in the city. This could lead to religious riots as it had in Antioch. And that King Hairan had put up the taxes again but the people were not getting the benefit. They were working harder for less money. There was talk of the once wealthy senators and merchant rebelling as they saw their high standard of living slipping.

He wouldn't tell her what he really thought. That if he had got the correct measure of Odainat, and more importantly his wife, sooner or later there would be major changes at the palace. He could not see that couple bowing for longer than was absolutely necessary to that bloated debauched fool King Hairan. Tamoral would tell Dagmar he needed her to be his eyes and ears and let him know if there was trouble. Also, a few months away from her and perhaps his passion would die down. Or, she would come back and fall in love with him, the Bedu chieftain.

Tamoral stepped outside his tent. The men and Dagmar were preparing the camels for the hunt. The Roman came up to Dagmar. She turned and said something quickly to him. Marcus walked away. But in that instant Tamoral thought he sensed lust, thought he had captured a glance between them that said 'I want you'. Tamoral decided he couldn't live with that daily torture. He called to Dagmar and told her she wouldn't be going hunting. He was sending her on a mission to Palmyra.

Two days after Dagmar's departure Tamoral and his men met Lucius Aurelian and part of his legions at a crossroads. Tamoral handed Marcus over to him. Aurelian was not best pleased with Marcus for acting like a fool at the banquet but he paid Tamoral well. If he hadn't saved Marcus he might be dead. Aurelian was fond of the young officer and thought he had probably been punished enough for his folly. Life with the Bedu could not have been much fun.

Then to Tamoral's profound dismay Lucius Aurelian

headed in the direction of Palmyra. He had a special message for Prince Odainat from Gallienus, the Emperor in Rome.

Samoya twisted on her chains and wondered how much longer her torture would continue. The days and nights had become one. She was kept in a chamber with no windows and occasionally taken out to another chamber with a hole in the ceiling. Then she could see the sky and knew it was day but which day, which month, which season it was she had no idea.

The room was not uncomfortable. There was a bed and plenty of silken cushions on the marble floor and between the hooks and whips and crops on the walls great patterned carpets hung down. Samoya moved her manacled hands and opened her legs. The chains jangled.

A naked female slave came in and began to massage her body with sweet smelling oils. Samoya closed her eyes and gave herself up to the luxury of the gently moving hands on her face, her neck, her shoulders. Then those hands moved down, caressing her breasts, fondling her nipples, pulling slightly at the nipple rings she was wearing. She bent over Samoya, her breasts rubbing against Samoya's, resting against the skin of her thighs, her legs. Their soft touch, their hard nipples exciting Samoya.

She could feel her wantonness begin. She could feel herself opening, becoming wet. How long would it take before the slave's fingers would move down over her belly and, taking fresh oil in her hands, grease her thoroughly? Then turning her over and massaging her buttocks, starting with large circular movements getting smaller and smaller as she moved her hands closer and closer to her crevice, playing with the soft erotic skin of her anus. Samoya held her breath. She was anticipating every movement. It was a familiar ritual. One she enjoyed. Then the slave-girl would invade her. A finger would be pushed in and rubbed up and down, up and down. And her body would go up and down, up and down. Wanting it. Wanting more. She would be turned over again. Lying on her back, the slave would pass by the rings and chains attached to her open labia, which pulled her sex down and clinked and clanked every time she moved. Letting everyone know she was not simply Prince Alif's wife, she was his sex-slave. To do with as he wanted. When he wanted. And with whom he wanted. The slave's hands continued their work and Samoya lazed in the luxury of contentment and fulfilment.

Then the door was opened. A large, black, sexually powerful naked male came in. His only apparel was wide leather handcuffs studded with silver, and similar anklets. Samoya had not seen this slave before. Her eyes went immediately to his cock. It was long and thick and very stiff. He took a whip from the wall. As he retrieved it, Samoya thought how she never got used to it. A part of her longed for it, a part of her hated it but the initial feeling of fear never left her.

The female slave jerked her finger hard up inside Samoya's sex causing her to moan and writhe with pleasure. The woman adroitly moved her hand and invaded her anus.

The male slave took Samoya from the cushions where she was lying. Samoya could feel his penis against her hips. It excited her. She wanted to touch it. She wanted to bend and suck it. She licked her lips. The man took her manacled hands and jerked them upwards, attached them to a hook on the wall. This gave her enough leverage to bend over but no more. Her legs were spread apart and held down with spikes driven through a link on her anklets through to an iron ring set in the floor.

'Bend over,' commanded the man.

With her arms half up and hanging, her legs firmly apart, the chain fixed to her labia clearly visible, she offered him her neat small bottom. Holding his prick he stood between her legs. He let her feel its erect warmth as he rubbed the soft skin of her thighs, in between her knees and her sex. Then without warning he penetrated. He took her second hole and she, although well oiled, let out a scream. He didn't care. He pushed in further. The harder he pushed the more she screamed; he gaining pleasure from the sound she was making. Without coming he stopped.

'Stay as you are,' he ordered. He brought the whip down on her bare buttocks. Once, twice, three times. Then he let out the chains. He wanted her more open. Samoya yelled. She let out a piercing sound and begged him to stop. The more she begged the faster and faster he lashed her. Then he took her anus again. Her sex he was leaving for the prince.

The door opened and Princess Bernice came in. She was naked except for her ever-present dildoes around her waist. She looked at the big black slaves sodomising Samoya and removed a fine, thin riding crop from the selection on the wall. She stood behind the black man and without warning brought it down with considerable, and vicious, force on his bare thrusting buttocks. She did it again and again, leaving deep weals across his haunches and making him pound into Samoya faster and faster. And the harder and faster he went, the more Bernice enjoyed herself. Then she came up between them and ringed his cock with her hand.

'What do you say?' she asked.

He pulled out of Samoya and lay flat on the ground in front of Bernice.

'Thank you, madam, thank you,' he said and licked her feet.

'Now unhook Samoya,' said Bernice, 'I want her on the cushions, on her belly with her bottom uppermost.'

Samoya was unhooked, and the spikes were withdrawn from the floor. Her buttocks were sore. The two slaves carried Samoya to a pile of cushions, and fastened the chains from her bound hands to another hook close by. They arranged her with her legs open whilst Bernice untied her playthings and inserted one of them in Samoya's wet sex.

Bernice played with her for a while. Making her more open, more wet, as the leather dildo glided backwards and forwards past the chain that kept her labia open. Bernice slid the leather cock inside Samoya, and shook her buttocks, making sure they were soft, relaxed and quivering. Then she walked away and picked up a crop and applied it to Samoya's flanks. Samoya shrieked. She knew nothing would stop Bernice's fierce hand and if she moved she might receive it on her belly, her thighs or across her breasts. Bernice, excited, threw the crop to one side.

'Now you may fuck me,' she said to the black man.

'Thank you madam,' he said, and penetrated her violently.

Bernice slowly slid to the floor taking the female slave who had oiled Samoya with her so she could bite and suck on her nipples whilst the man continued to pound into her. He continued until she was satisfied and then Bernice rolled over and commanded him to penetrate the slave. None of them touched Samoya. They had their instructions. Prince Alif would come when he saw fit. He had instructed them that although anybody could take her anus only he could enter her sex. One by one Alif's coterie of young nobles entered the chamber. They came in wearing robes displaying their sex and bringing with them the slaves they wanted to use. And Samoya lay chained naked on the cushions as all shapes and sizes of male members were thrust into the opened orifices of the slave women, and sometimes of the slave men. She watched them being led to the pillory and chained there; she watched them writhe and struggle, their limbs turning this way and that, then relax and

175

moan sweetly as their particular lover took them, easing and thrusting into sex, anus, or mouth.

Samoya did receive some vicarious pleasure when she saw a group of Alif's young nobles grab the slave who had whipped her, drag him to the whipping-post, and apply the rod to his buttocks and his thighs. When they had finished they parted his crevice and shamelessly used his backside for their pleasure.

Samoya lay untouched anxiously waiting for her husband. She knew he would charge in, his great cock lolling between his legs, stand over her, take it in his hands, rub it until it had gained its full enormous length and then plough it into her. She waited in vain and in their depraved abandonment nobody noticed his absence. Samoya assumed he was out hunting.

Some time later when everyone had gone, her personal slaves came in. They bathed her, poured some healing liquid on her burning flanks, dabbed at the weals on her thighs, brushed her hair, coated her body in fresh oils, left food and wine and water beside her bed, changed the candles in the candlestick-holders, unlocked her chains, leaving only her handcuffs and anklets on, and departed. She was alone and hurting and still surprised that Prince Alif had not arrived. He normally made sure he turned up as she was being chastised. Samoya was too exhausted to eat. She clanked across the room and blew out the candles, settled a long silk robe over her bruised body, bundled up the chains falling from her labia so that they didn't pull in the night and settled down to sleep.

Sleep wouldn't come. She thought about her life, her ambitions and how they'd all been thwarted. She thought about Marcus. And how drunk he'd been at the banquet. Also how furious the King had become when Marcus had lurched up onto the stage and thumped Prince Alif. She thought Marcus had killed him. But he hadn't. Which was fortunate. Roman or no Roman, Marcus would have been instantly executed for killing a member of the Royal Family. She had watched helplessly as Marcus had been dragged away by the King's soldiers. And everybody seemed to be clambering over everybody else. People were running backwards and forwards as if they didn't know where they were going, just as long as they didn't stay in the banqueting hall. She had been left alone and isolated in her humiliation and misery, strapped on a plank on the stage, powerless to do anything with nobody wanting to help her. And then Prince Odainat had arrived with Zenobia. That had stopped the furore.

He had climbed onto the stage, drawn his sword and told everyone not to move. Then he had announced that he had married Zenobia. He had pulled Zenobia up onto the stage with him and had been followed by the High Priest and the Prince of the Bedouin. Then she remembered nothing more. Try as she could, Samoya did not know who took her down from the stage or how she was returned to her quarters in the palace.

In the darkness of her room Samoya's spirit gradually sank down into sleep. But in her twilight state, not quite in the depths of slumber, she heard the door open. No, she thought. No. I cannot take any more. Please. Please. But there was no point in saying a word. She knew the more she begged the more she would be chastised. She kept quiet but opened her eyes, trying not to let her fear show. Terrified, Samoya held her breath. Someone in a soldier's uniform, holding a candle in one hand, a bloody dagger in the other, was creeping across the room. Then in the pitch-black darkness Samoya let out a strangled gasp. She recognised who it was.

'Zenobia!' she cried.

'Samoya!' exclaimed Zenobia shining the light on her face.

'What are you doing here?' asked Samoya in astonishment.

'I've come to rescue you,' Zenobia replied.

177

'But . . . but . . .' said Samoya.

'No buts, quickly, come with me.' Samoya slid off the bed and clanked.

'What's that?' asked Zenobia.

'My chains,' Samoya replied.

'Are you chained to the wall?

'No.'

'Then try and hold them so they don't clank. We'll get them off you soon. Run. We must get away from here fast.'

'Zenobia, what's happened?'

'The King and Prince Alif are dead,' said Zenobia. 'Don't ask any more questions, just follow me.'

Both of them terrified, but for very different reasons, they ran through the deserted corridors of the palace and out into the gardens. Samoya was in pain and wanted to ask where the guards were. Why everything was so silent. But she kept running. Zenobia was agitated. She ran as if being pursued by devils or ghosts or both. Zenobia helped her over the palace walls and then they ran along the dark, quiet streets to Zenobia's villa where she lived with her husband. Zenobia had told Prince Odainat she hated the palace and would not go there.

There were guards on the new high gates of Zenobia's villa. They saluted the two women and let them pass. Zenobia took Samoya to a guest-room where the first thing she did was to wash the dagger and replace it in the belt around her waist. The she turned to Samoya who was sitting quietly on a bed.

'Now, where are those chains of yours?'

'On my labia,' said Samoya.

'How do you get them off?' she asked.

'You don't, replied Samoya, opening her legs.

When Zenobia saw the marks left by the crop and the whip on Samoya's thighs and buttocks and the chain hanging from the lips of her vulva, one half of her wanted to cry, the other half to shrink away from her friend. But she steeled herself. She bent down and looked at how the chains had been fixed. Then she called for a slave to bring a file and when she did, Zenobia ordered her not to leave until the chain was broken and Samoya was free. Then she said she would give Samoya some of her clothing and told her she was to dress herself properly. She would also give her some gold coins.

'Without money you're as unfree as a slave,' she said. 'Go home to Antioch. Put all this horror behind you and go. And don't come back until I tell you you can.'

'Please tell me what has happened. You tell me that King and Prince Alif are dead . . .'

'Yes,' said Zenobia. 'And my husband is now the King.'

Samoya's hands flew up to her face.

'Oh!' she exclaimed. 'That means, you are the Queen.'

'Exactly,' said Zenobia. 'And I am giving you a Royal command. Nobody except the King can countermand me. You are not to return to Palmyra unless I say you can and nobody must ever know I was in the palace tonight. Is that understood?'

'But the King . . . Hairan, how did he die?'

'In his sleep,' said Zenobia enigmatically.

'And Prince Alif?'

'I don't know, but I do know he's dead. I've seen the body. You are a free woman. And a widow. Find a nice man to marry. Or perhaps return to your original idea and become a doctor. The world is open to you again.' Zenobia stopped and stared at the slave busy working away on the chain link with the file. 'As soon as that slave has finished I will give you some of my own to accompany you on your journey.'

'Oh Zenobia . . .' Samoya began. Zenobia rounded on her.

'Never address me like that again,' said Zenobia severely. 'From now on it's Your Majesty.' Then noticing her friend's crestfallen face added, 'But what did you want?'

'I wanted to know about Marcus, the Roman. What happened to him?'

'He should be in Rome by now. He left here in disgrace. On Odainat's orders the Prince of the Bedouin took him to the garrison at Antioch.'

Samoya felt relief and sadness.

Zenobia looked up at the sky. Smears of bright orange were streaking across the darkness.

'Dawn is breaking,' she said. 'I have a lot of work to do.'

'What about sleep?' asked Samoya.

'I'll sleep when today is done,' she said. 'I have to see my husband, the King, and my friend Firmus is arriving from Egypt.'

With fast, decisive steps Zenobia made for the door. Then she came back and kissed Samoya.

'I will always look after my friends,' she said, 'but I won't hesitate to kill an enemy. Samoya . . .' Zenobia took her friend's face in her hands and kissed each eyelid tenderly. 'I want you to know. I'm pregnant.'

And then she was gone.

Samoya, exhausted and in pain, left the slave sawing away at the links, and lay down to sleep. When she awoke the chains had been removed and over a stool lay a beautiful gown of the softest orange silk edged with creamy satin and slippers of midnight blue embroidered with gold and some gold hair-clips and some bangles. Beside this were two leather pouches filled with gold coins.

Samoya stretched lazily in her bed. She was happy. She was going home. She would see her father. See her brothers. What else would she do? Go to Athens? Go to Rome. No, she wouldn't go to Rome. The affair with Marcus was over. She felt a pang as she said that. Well, perhaps it wasn't but she had to accept it was. Her reverie was interrupted by strange and unfamiliar sounds. A sort of trumpeting. She slipped out of bed and looked over the balcony. Nothing there except lots of trees and bushes. She ran through into the great bathroom and looked over that balcony. There in the courtyard below stood a number of elephants. Samoya had heard about them, read about them, had seen drawings of them but had never seen the odd looking creatures before. She watched their keepers hose them down and clean them. The biggest one had an elaborate chair set on the centre of his back. The others were being loaded with carpets and boxes. They obviously belonged to someone who was exceedingly rich because they were decked out in beautiful silk cloth thickly embroidered with gold.

'Princess . . .'

The voice behind her startled Samoya. It had been so long since a kindly voice had addressed her and called her Princess. She felt tears shoot into her eyes.

'Yes?' she said, turning in her bed to see an old woman entering the room.

'I'm Habibah,' she said. 'The Queen has sent your slaves for your journey.'

A number of men and women entered the room and bowed to Samoya.

'Are you refreshed from your sleep?' asked Habibah.

'Yes,' replied Samoya.

'Then the Queen thinks it wisest if you leave immediately. She has provided camels for your journey. They will be waiting for you outside the Temple of the Goddess Allat. I will show you out of here. The Queen said please will you hurry.'

'Do I have time to bathe?' Samoya asked.

'Yes, Your Highness,' said Habibah.

Samoya walked through the bedroom into the adjoining bathroom where she lay and soaked her body in the sweet smelling waters of the marble pool. Habibah helped her to dress, horrified by the marks on her body. Some of the other slaves arranged her hair. Then she was ready for her trip to Antioch. She smiled at Habibah and impulsively kissed her.

'Oh, I'm so happy,' she said.

They were walking in procession through the main hall of the great villa when a side door opened and Odainat appeared with a group of senators. Instantly Samoya and her group fell to the floor and stayed there.

'Call the High Priest,' he was saying. 'I, and my wife, will be annointed immediately.'

'And when will you take up residence in the palace, Your Majesty?' asked a stern looking senator.

'We won't,' replied His Majesty. 'It doesn't have very pleasant memories for me. My wife intends to extend this villa. We will stay here.'

'A wise choice, Your Majesty,' said another senator, bowing obsequiously.

'Yes,' said the King. 'Well, I give you permission to leave.'

The senators bowed and departed. The King was about to return to his chamber when he noticed Habibah.,

'Habibah! What are you doing here?' he asked. 'Why aren't you with your mistress?'

'She didn't need me sire, she's talking business with her friend Firmus.'

'Oh yes . . . Well you may stand and go on your way.'

Samoya stood up first. King Odainat stared at her, struck by her quiet beauty. Where had he seen her before? Then he remembered. She was Alif's wife. Poor girl, he thought. That villain Alif had treated her abominably. He wondered what she was doing in the villa but was glad to see her. Glad that she had not been a part of the general carnage at the palace that night. Quite suddenly he had an idea. He politely asked Samoya to enter his chamber.

There Samoya came face to face with soldiers at attention and Princess Bernice who was in chains and

182

Prince Maaen, King Hairan's son, who wasn't, but he was glowering.

'Princess Samoya,' said King Odainat. 'By marriage you are a member of this family. I know you have been badly treated. However, as I am now King . . .' Samoya watched a grim expression flit across Prince Maaen's face as Odainat said that. She knew what he was thinking. With his father dead, he should be King.

Odainat continued. '. . . I would like to make amends. I would like to put you under my personal protection and marry you to my nephew, Prince Maaen.'

The shock of his words almost made Samoya faint. Instead she bowed her head. Oh what horror. She couldn't believe Odainat would do such a thing. She looked up at Prince Maaen. She wondered if his blank face covered the same degree of loathing as hers. All she could think of was, why? And if only . . . If only she hadn't slept so long. If only she hadn't watched the elephants in the courtyard. If only, if only. Was it a whim or had this marriage been planned by him and Zenobia? Samoya looked down at the beautiful dress she was wearing. And the jewels and the bangles. Surely her friend was not so perfidious. Zenobia had wanted her to leave. She was sure of that. So why should Odainat demand she marry Prince Maaen?

'You have said nothing,' said Odainat. 'Perhaps you are surprised?'

'Yes, sire,' said Samoya.

'Prince Maaen is naturally unhappy at the unexpected death of his father. I propose to send him to Damascus to recover. There he will order and check new weapons for our army. The finest in the empire are made there, did you know that?'

'No sire,' she said.

'He is a soldier, and a good one . . .' Odainat smiled at his nephew, who bowed to his King, trying not to show his hatred. 'I am a soldier. My life has been transformed since my marriage. I want my nephew to know the benefits of a successful marriage. I want you, Samoya, to forget the past. I want you to remain as part of my family and marry Prince Maaen.'

There was nothing she could do. Nothing she could say. The King had made up his mind.

'Thank you, Your Majesty,' she said and bowed.

The senators reappeared with the High Priest.

'High Priest,' said King Odainat, welcoming him with open arms. 'My poor, sad brother is dead. I am now the King. I want you to organise our coronation at your great temple.'

The High Priest bowed. He stole a glance at Prince Maaen and saw the anger on his face. The High Priest knew that the young man was no match for the older soldier. Prince Maaen would never hold the city and its dominions together. The High Priest acquiesced but asked the King as his first act of kingship if he would drive out the new religious sects proliferating in the city. The King pretended not to hear the question but went blithely on saying he wanted the High Priest to perform another ceremony immediately. 'After the sadness of my brother's death we need something to lighten us all. I want my nephew, Prince Maaen, to marry Princess Samoya, the widow of our late kinsman Prince Alif. We want you to marry them now.'

The High Priest looked at the young woman. She seemed in a daze. Then he looked at Princess Bernice in chains. He wondered what was going to happen to her. The King noticed the High Priest's glance.

'Princess Bernice is leaving us,' said King Odainat, deciding not to denigrate his sister by informing the High Priest that he had banished her for her licentious ways. 'She has agreed to join the temple of the Goddess in Antioch.'

The King snapped his fingers at the guards surrounding Bernice.

'Remove her now,' he commanded. Bernice was taken away, knowing she was fortunate to be alive.

The King and Queen led the wedding procession. And before she knew it Samoya was sadly back with a new husband in the bedroom she had left so happily a few hours before. The King smiled indulgently. Zenobia smiled but looked strained. Samoya caught her eye but Zenobia didn't give a thing away. It was too late now. She had tried to get her out of the palace before Odainat saw her. 'Let's find Maaen a wife,' he'd said, when they were changing to receive the senators. Shivers had gone down Zenobia's spine as Odainat had ticked off the various young girls of the nobility and, for one reason or another had turned them down. Zenobia thought of beautiful Samoya. She was already in the family. Her dowry had already been paid. She was now a widow. If Odainat saw her, he would think her perfect. As soon as she could, Zenobia had called for Habibah. 'Get her out of the palace as soon as you can,' she'd said. But the gods had decreed otherwise. And Samoya was married again. Zenobia might be Queen but she was powerless against Odainat's word. She was upset, but nobody would see. She could smile better than anybody.

After the King and Zenobia had gone, Prince Maaen and Samoya stood in silence and alone. She was terrified. He was waiting for their new Majesties' footsteps to cease sounding on the marble. When there was no more sound Maaen leapt at her, grabbed the pouches of gold she was holding, put them in his own baggage and ripped her dress from top to bottom.

'Right, perform,' he said. 'Get on your knees.' Maaen pushed her to the floor. 'Pleasure me.'

Samoya lifted his tunic with shaking hands. His cock was lying limp, without desire. She put it in her mouth and began to work her tongue along its tiny shaft, begging it, willing it to grow. Nothing happened. He pushed her away. Then he undid his belt.

'You can do better than that,' he said. 'I know, I've seen you. Show me your buttocks. Go on, bend over.'

Samoya bent over and lifted up the remnants of her robe. Maaen trailed his finger along the whip and crop marks.

'Who am I?' he asked.

'My husband, Prince Maaen,' she answered, meekly.

'Wrong,' he said slapping her behind. 'Wrong. I am your master. Your Master. And what do you say to your master?' He gave her bare buttocks another slap.

'Thank you, master.'

'Exactly,' he said, tilting her head so that her mouth was jerked open. He lifted his tunic. Now his cock was stiff. He put it in her mouth.

'Suck me, Samoya,' he commanded, tearing the rest of her robe. He pumped in and out of her for about half a minute then pushed her backwards and turned her over.

'I want to take you from behind,' he said. 'What do you say?'

'Yes master.'

'Now, head down, shoulders on the floor, bottom raised.'

Samoya knelt in the pose he ordered.

'Spread your legs,' he said. Samoya inched them apart. He stood between her thighs and lubricated his cock with sweet-smelling oil, then thrust into her moist opening until he came. Afterwards, Samoya stayed exactly how she was, head down, shoulders on the floor and bottom raised and waited patiently for him to tell her to move.

'Get up,' he said eventually.

Samoya got up. She stood in front of him, naked and forlorn. He rang for a slave. 'You'll stay here and eat. I want you fatter. Something I can get hold of. Something

I can rub my cock against. Something I can whip.'

'Yes master. How long will I have to stay here?' she asked.

'Until I return from Damascus. And when I get back I want to find you big, large, fat. I want to find you kneeling with your legs spread open, waiting for me. I also want your second orifice stretched to accommodate me. I am going to order rings to be inserted. There's a good brothel-keeper I know. I'll get him to come in every day. He'll stretch it. Every day a bigger ring. He's used to it. He's done it for all my boys.'

A slave entered. Samoya desperately tried to hide her nakedness by grabbing hold of the bedlinen and holding it in front of her. Maaen laughed and snatched it away, deliberately humiliating her, and threw it at the slave.

'Take it away. Wash it,' he said. 'A whore's been screwing on it.'

Then he ordered cakes and pastries and cream, lots and lots of cream. He told the slave that Samoya must not eat anything else. Morning, noon and night, pastries, and cream. Pastries and cream.

Maaen waited until the order was brought then he picked up her money pouches and handed his baggage to the slave and the two of them departed. Samoya heard him turn the key in the door.

Once more she was in a locked room. She couldn't bear it. Something inside her snapped. She took the tray of pastries and threw them out over the balcony onto the trees and bushes below. The birds could have them. She wasn't going to eat them. Not now. Not ever. She was leaving. But she had to dress. She couldn't go naked. She looked around the room. Nothing except mountains of cushions, and the torn remnants of her robe. Well, that would have to do. She picked up the bits and tied a length around her breasts and another between her legs up to the waist, then she wound another strip around her waist and tucked the other edges into it. At least she was decent.

She looked over the balcony. It was a long way down. But there were ledges. And she was agile. She stopped as she looked. Where would she go? What would she do? She was defying the King. She would be an outlaw. Dispirited, she retreated back into the room and sat on the bed. The bed where she'd woken so happily that morning. Where she'd stretched and found Zenobia's robe and the pouch of gold. Gold! She'd put some coins beneath the bed for the slaves to find later. A small thank you. Quickly Samoya searched under it. There they were – the three gold coins. And she had the haircombs and the bangles. She wasn't rich but she was no longer penniless.

Samoya heard the sound of the elephants again. She ran through to the bathroom and looked out. More things were being loaded up. A mass of carpets were rolled waiting to be lifted. She remembered how the Persians had taken her from her tent. That would be the ideal way to make her escape, inside one of those carpets. But she couldn't climb down from where she was. It was a straight drop on to marble. No ledges, no vegetation to hide her. She would have to climb over from the bedroom and carefully make her way round to the elephants.

Dagmar and the tribesmen had arrived at the palace only to find everything was locked up and silent. The sentries on the gate had redirected them to Zenobia's villa.

'What's going on?' she'd asked.

'You'll find out when you get there,' she'd been told.

And that's when Dagmar had discovered King Hairan and his kinsmen Prince Alif were dead and Odainat was now King with Zenobia as his Queen. And she was in a meeting, too busy to see them for some time. After they'd been given peppermint tea, Dagmar was told by a prancing and very effeminate young man, who said his name was Timogenes, that they could avail themselves of the gardens whilst they waited.

'Spend some time there, smell the flowers, look at the birds, gaze at the fountains,' he had said.

Dagmar was delighted but she guessed immediately that it was not her fellow tribesmen's idea of fun. She had told them they could go into the centre of the city but to return sober in a couple of hours.

Dagmar had then asked the young man if she could wash and change before seeing the Queen. He had directed her to the back of the villa where there were special quarters for transient guests. Declining help, she had carefully washed and changed into Bedouin ceremonial dress, which included her ceremonial dagger and her sword, both heavily bejewelled but very sharp, for an audience with the Queen.

Dagmar had been pleased that Tamoral had insisted she take it all with her. You might need it, he'd said. How right he was. She tucked her travelling robes and burnouse into her goatskin bag, slung it on her shoulders and went for a wander along the twisting and turning paths of the villa's garden.

She had found a nice sweet smelling, shady arbour, close to a small fountain and was sitting quietly watching the butterflies and the bees when she was hit by flying pastries and splattered with great gobs of cream. She had looked up but couldn't see anybody. Ever resourceful, and realising she was hungry, Dagmar proceeded to eat some of the pastries, lick up some of the cream then tried to clean the mess off her robes in the small fountain.

She was back watching the butterflies when she saw a foot and then a bare leg come down through the branches of the tree above her. She gripped her sword, waited and watched. More and more of a thin, lithe body came into view. An escaping slave, she thought. Well, she wasn't going to do anything to stop it. Then the half-naked person lost their footing and landed in a scratched heap in the bushes beside her. Dagmar drew her sword and stood over the huddled person, who she now saw was a young woman.

'What are you doing?' she said, prodding her with the tip of her weapon.

Samoya could not believe her ears. That was Irene's voice. Irene. Bernice had told her she was dead. Irene, and alive. No, it couldn't be. She twisted slightly to see if her assumption was true. And she saw a man.

'Oh!' she cried, and burst into tears.

'Hades!' exclaimed Dagmar, recognising Samoya immediately. Rushing up to her, crushing her in her arms. 'Samoya! I thought you were an escaping slave.'

'You're more right than you know,' replied Samoya, kissing her, happy to be with someone who she knew really loved her. 'They told me you were dead.'

'What's happened to you? Why are you dressed like that? And look at your body. It's got whip and crop marks all over it.'

'I know. And that's why I'm escaping,' Samoya said choking with tears.

'But your husband is dead,' said Dagmar, holding Samoya close, rocking her like a child.

'My first husband is dead. My second husband is very much alive. You see I was married this morning to Prince Maaen. And he's nearly as bad as the first one. Wants to whip me and bugger me and . . . well something snapped when he locked me in and told me to fatten up.' Samoya was now almost hysterical. 'He said I could only eat pastries and cream. I threw them out of the window.'

'So, I've you to thank,' said Dagmar.

'I can't stay here, I really can't,' said Samoya. 'But it's the King's wish. I'm defying the King, so I can't go home.'

You couldn't go there anyway. I heard your father is

dead and your brothers are arguing about their inheritance,' said Dagmar.

'Dead! My father dead!' Samoya burst into tears.

Dagmar cradled her in her arms. She felt at a loss, didn't know what to do but knew she had to get her away as quickly as possible.

'Ssh, Samoya, ssh. Cry later. We've got to think of something and you can't go anywhere looking like that!' said Dagmar.

'I know, Irene, I know,' said Samoya. Hearing her old name suddenly brought terror into Dagmar's heart.

'Samoya, listen, I'm not Irene any more. I'm Dagmar and I'm a Bedu. I'm a warrior. A man.'

'You're a man!' exclaimed Samoya, remembering very well the touch of her sex.

'Well, everybody thinks I'm a man. I'm taller than most men and my voice is quite deep. Don't give me away, Samoya. Never give me away.'

'I won't, I won't,' said Samoya fervently.

'And, most important of all – I'm free.'

'Free?'

'Yes.' And Dagmar told her how the Prince of the Bedouin had bought her from Bernice and had given her her freedom. 'Now I'm representing the Bedu. See, these are my ceremonial robes I'm wearing . . .'

'You wore those crossing the desert! They're terribly heavy,' said Samoya.

'No, I've got my . . .' And then she stopped. 'Samoya, that's the answer. You can wear my ordinary clothes. I can get some more.' She delved into her bag and dragged out her white fine wool desert robe. 'Here, put it on quickly.'

Hidden in the arbour, under cover of the foliage, Dagmar helped Samoya untie the knots of the remnants of her torn dress. When Samoya was naked, Dagmar looked at her noticing all the marks of the whip, the belt and the crop criss-crossing her beautiful body and with affection gently took Samoya in her arms, held her tight and kissed her tenderly.

Gently their lips met and Dagmar's hands began to rove over Samoya's body, fondling her breasts and her nipples. The loving care of each caress made Samoya moist between her legs. Slowly Dagmar's fingers meandered down past her belly to her pubis. Samoya edged her legs apart. Dagmar began to play with Samoya's soft dewy sex-lips. Sliding and gliding, opening her. She began to feel the emergence of that tiny excitable morsel of flesh at the top of her warm, damp hidden gateway. The soft pressure made Samoya let out a gasp of joy. And she began to swell, open like a flower under the warmth of the spring sun. Dagmar licked her nipples, then lay Samoya down on the bench in the arbour and kneeling, buried her head between her legs. Sweet joy. Samoya felt Dagmar's tongue roam, flick and enter, then withdraw and suck. Samoya raised her hips, writhing, undulating with each movement. Dagmar gripped her thighs, spread them further apart so that her tongue could go deeper.

With an unexpected urgency Samoya's hands began to grab at Dagmar's robes. She wanted to feel Dagmar's breasts, touch her sex, put her tongue between Dagmar's thighs, lick her. Dagmar changed her position and pulled Samoya down onto the marble floor. She gathered up her robes and offered her sex to Samoya's willing, open mouth. The two women lay there hidden amongst the trees, sucking, playing with one another, exciting each other, caressing one another, feeling the joy of gentle passion and soft love until quietly their bellies tightened and the juices inside them ached to burst forth. And they came.

When Samoya was dressed to Dagmar's satisfaction and they were discussing the pros and cons of Samoya leaving with the Bedouin, the elephants trumpeted again.

'I wondered if I could be wrapped up in a carpet and go with the elephant people,' said Samoya.

'That's not such a bad idea,' said Dagmar. 'Let's see if we can do it. Do you know whose party it is or where he's going?'

'No, it might be Zenobia's Egyptian friend Firmus, but anything's got to be better than staying here.'

'That's for sure,' said Dagmar and the two of them walked through the garden to where packages and bundles, goatskins and parcels, bales of silk and rolls of expensive carpets were being loaded onto trailers drawn by the huge, magnificent elephants.

Chapter Ten

Princess Bernice was gazing nonchalantly out from a window of the temple in Antioch when she saw the rising dust of an army coming across the plain. Straining her ears she was able to hear the familiar sounds of Palmyrene battle-cries. King Odainat's army was returning victorious from the war with the Goths. And she was delighted.

Bernice smiled to herself thinking how her life had changed since she had watched its departure. Then she had been a voluptuous captive leaving Palmyra who had endeavoured to charm her gross and ugly captors into releasing her. She remembered how she had grabbed their cocks and sucked them, had played with them, had let them take her one by one and all together. And still they had obeyed the King's orders and delivered her to the temple. Now she was a slimmed down priestess who for three years had been incarcerated, a virtual prisoner, with only women for company in the place dedicated to the Goddess and to good works. And where sex had been totally denied her. She had missed it. Initially she had tried to seduce some of the acolytes but her transgression had been reported to the High Priestess and her punishment had been to be locked away for a month on bread and water. No whippings. Somehow the High Priestess knew she would have enjoyed that. She received just a little plain food pushed through the bars of her bare cell, a pitcher of water every three days and no contact with anybody. Then, and since, she had resorted to playing with herself; that had kept her sexually alive.

Now, with the King's return she would be released. The High Priestess had already written to him suggesting that she had been punished enough for her licentious ways and was a completely reformed individual. Bernice thought that amusing; because she was denied access to sex, didn't mean she had stopped wanting it. What she had stopped was showing she wanted it. She had refrained from seducing anybody. Zenobia had received the letter addressed to Odainat and had written back to the High Priestess saying as soon as the King was back on his throne Bernice would be welcome in Palmyra.

Looking at the army drawing closer Bernice remembered how, in chains, and from the hills outside Palmyra where she and her captors were camped for the night, she had watched the legions march north. The army, headed by the Roman commander Aurelian, and King Odainat, followed by Prince Maaen and some of his young nobles had aroused her curiosity. When Odainat had sent her away there had been no hint of war. She had had to wait until she reached Antioch for her curiosity to be satisfied.

The High Priestess had told her how the Roman commander Aurelian had arrived unexpectedly in Palmyra, made Odainat a Duke of Rome, offered him more lands and territory in return for his and his army's help in defeating the Romans' constant enemy the barbarian Goths. And he had gone taking Prince Maaen with him. The High Priestess failed to mention any wife and so Princess Bernice kept her own counsel as far as Samoya was concerned. From time to time travellers had come to the temple and Bernice had asked if anything was known about Samoya. She had heard conflicting stories. First that she had been locked up in the old palace. Second that she had run away. Finally that she'd been killed by wild animals in the desert. But nobody knew for sure and after a while, when she enquired people had given her a blank stare and asked 'Who?' And Bernice had given up enquiring.

Bernice thought that it must have been a shock for Zenobia – Odainat called to war so soon after their reign began. But soon she had borne him a son. That would have kept her busy, and Palmyra too. According to all sources Zenobia had been running the city exceedingly well.

'Bernice.' The old High Priestess Verenia had come into her room. 'You will prepare yourself to meet the King.' Then, after imperiously giving her orders the old woman departed as quickly and as silently as she had arrived.

Bernice bathed and put on her finest linen gown and then with considerable eagerness went to the temple steps with the rest of the priestesses and the acolytes to greet the King. Everybody was excited but Bernice was more excited than the rest. Her temple days were finally over. She could return to Palmyra.

She arrived just before the procession. The banging of the drums and the sounding of the trumpets continued but there wasn't the usual shouting and screaming. There was no cacophony of human sound. Bernice thought that very odd. Then she saw the standard bearer and some foot-soldiers. After him she saw a crown glinting on top of a magnificently dressed figure on a horse. But it wasn't Odainat. It was Prince Maaen. Prince Maaen was King. A deep fear descended on Princess Bernice. What had happened to Odainat? And where was his cortège? Palmyrene heroes are brought home for burial and laid to rest in great tombs.

Something's happened, she thought. Something terrible's happened to my brother Odainat.

Maaen brought his horse to a halt at the temple steps and everyone bowed low. A soldier helped him dismount and, ignoring the entire assembly, he marched up to Bernice.

'Greetings Aunt,' he said, kissing her hand. 'I am the King and I have a mission for you.'

'Where's Odainat?' Bernice asked, almost in a whisper.

'Odainat! He's dead. I killed him. I stabbed him in the back at the victory banquet,' said Maaen, in an offhand way, confirming Bernice's worst fears and opening up new ones: the possibility that Prince Maaen might be mad. But Bernice kept her face devoid of all emotion. 'Now, I want you to go to Alexandria in Egypt and see a man called Firmus. Odainat's widow, Zenobia, is his partner in a very lucrative papyrus business. I want you to tell him that I am now the King, and I propose to be his new partner and all profits in Palmyra will be paid directly to me. I will provide you with an escort, camels and horses and all the money you need.'

Dismissively Maaen threw her a pouch of gold, ordered four of his soldiers to stay with her until she had delivered his message, and whispered to them to kill Bernice afterwards. Then he announced that as soon as the army had eaten and rested he was going on to Palmyra to kill Zenobia and her son and sit on his rightful throne.

When Maaen said that, Bernice gave an anxious glance towards the High Priestess. But the High Priestess was not completely sure of Bernice or her motives so pretended not to see and looked the other way. Noticing this, Bernice then decided she had other things to think about. She had no time to grieve for Odainat or worry for Zenobia. She surveyed the four men Maaen had picked out to accompany her on her journey to Egypt. They were big, brawny and masculine. After three years' enforced celibacy she was going to have real fun with them. Princess Bernice salivated and grew damp between her legs. She thought of the taste of a penis. The feel of it in her mouth, the touch of it along her thighs, entering her sex. Thrusting. By the time she rode out of Palmyra, Princess Bernice had very stiff nipples and an extremely wet sex.

Whilst Prince Maaen entered the main municipal buildings for a celebratory feast, Princess Verenia left the temple and went to see Bishop Paul. He was not her favourite person. She did not approve of his religion, his father-orientated sect, nor his licentious ways. Verenia knew his palace was no more and no less than a harem where he indulged all his sexual whims. But he did collect Zenobia's taxes and he was utterly loyal to her.

Bishop Paul was most surprised to see the High Priestess. He was horrified when she informed him that Prince Maaen had killed Odainat, had proclaimed himself King and was intending to kill Zenobia and her son.

'You must go to Palmyra and warn her,' said Verenia, desperate in case anything should happen to her old pupil. 'She trusts you and you won't have any trouble getting into the palace to see her immediately.'

What Verenia did not know was that Paul had already planned to go to Palmyra. He was in deep trouble with his church. A number of his parishioners had raised a petition to have him thrown out of his palace. And the fathers in Alexandria had convened a synod which had expelled him from the bishopric for his heretical views. But none of this mattered as long as he was under Zenobia's protection. And he was. The two of them were locked in a deep friendship. They would always totally support one another. But forces were gathering against him. The Alexandrian Christians were discussing the possibility of going to arbitration to a pagan emperor in Rome. They were convinced that way they would get him removed. But the Emperor had more on his mind than the internal squabbles of a minor religious sect. Nevertheless, Paul felt he had to go to Palmyra to make sure that the Queen stayed with him despite any ruling from any future emperor in Rome.

When Verenia gave him the news Bishop Paul did not hesitate and before the High Priestess had returned to her temple he was galloping out of the city on the road to Palmyra ahead of the army.

Samoya awoke in a glow of contentment and luxury. She stretched gracefully and smiled at the dawn sun streaming in through her windows, lighting up the fantastic wall-hangings, and making the pure gold threads gleam. She pushed back the silk sheets and scrutinised her body. In the three years she had been in Firmus's harem in Alexandria she had filled out, her breasts were full and rounded, her belly curvaceous, her hips and buttocks ample, although her waist had stayed diminutive. But then she had worked at that by keeping a tight belt around it.

Samoya slipped out of her bed and made her way into the adjoining marble and mosaic pool, which was as big as her enormous bedroom. Soon the rest of the household would rise but Samoya liked the first hours of the day to herself. Naked and happy she floated in the water thinking how lucky she was. She thanked the gods she had had the good sense to escape from Palmyra. She never wanted to see that city again. Although she had to admit, seeing Alexandria for the first time was a shock.

Having lived her life under Palmyrene rule she had not experienced the dirt, horror and degradation of a conquered nation. The beggars, the filth, the starvation, the difficulty of life in Egypt under the Romans was something she found very hard to accept. Once she asked Firmus why the Egyptians didn't rise up against the Romans. He said they would if there was a leader of sufficient magnetism to galvanise them into action. But there wasn't much likelihood of that happening.

To stop herself thinking of the poverty that lay beyond the boundaries of the villa Samoya turned over and swam a couple of lengths of the pool. And she thought of Dagmar and how she had helped her escape. There were times when Samoya longed to see her again. She often wondered what had happened to her. Had she stayed in the palace or gone back to the Bedouin?

Memories of that fateful journey came flooding back to her. How she had been wrapped up in a carpet, the smell of the elephant nearly suffocating her, when Firmus had chosen that particular one to be unfurled for his tent at nightfall. And she had rolled out at his feet. Thinking about it now, Samoya realised he must have taken pity on her, but then she had been too scared to think anything at all.

'And who are you?' he had asked, smiling indulgently at her, and picking her up in one of his huge hands.

Aware that she was very slim and feeling even tinier as he seated her on his vast lap, Samoya had glanced up at him. He was very tall and large to the point of enormous but he exuded sex. His face, though benign in expression was very sexual. He had high cheekbones, a slightly hooked nose, shaggy eyebrows and heavy, hooded lids over sleepy, dark brown eyes, which totally belied his piercingly sharp business brain. His mouth, surrounded by a well-trimmed beard was wide and sensuous. When he smiled Samoya noticed that he had good, gleaming white teeth. He also possessed the attribute of a tremendous presence, a sense of power. The power of great wealth.

When he had asked her who she was, Samoya had wondered whether to tell a lie or the truth. She had looked up into his eyes and decided to tell the truth.

'I am Princess Samoya. I was married early this

morning to Prince Maaen and I'm running away from him,' she had said.

'And I don't blame you,' said Firmus, surprisingly. 'A strange person, quite probably deranged, definitely not somebody I'd ever want to do business with. Who ordered your marriage?'

'King Odainat,' she said.

'Oh dear,' he replied. 'Then my child you are disobeying the King. And if you disobey the King and run away you are an outlaw.'

'I know,' she replied, simply.

'And that doesn't bother you?'

'Not as much as staying married to Prince Maaen,' she said.

Firmus had roared with laughter. Then he had removed her Bedouin clothing and seen the stripes and marks covering her buttocks, her belly and her thighs.

'You poor, poor child,' said Firmus. He clapped his hands and two of his personal slaves appeared.

'Bring me the gold and silver cloth I bought this morning,' he said.

The two men bowed and left his tent. Moments later they came back with a bale of fabric. Firmus shook it out and draped it around Samoya.

'Cut it there,' he said to them, indicating with his fat hands. The two men cut it. 'Now, you're looking beautiful. Bring me some food. You are hungry?'

'Yes,' she said.

Firmus bade Samoya sit on some cushions and they waited in silence whilst a feast of Palmyra's finest delicacies was brought in and laid before them.

'You will sleep with me tonight,' he said when they had finished eating.

Samoya bowed her head in acquiescence. He had saved her, fed her and now he was probably going to fuck her. Well he could do whatever he wanted. She was too tired, too exhausted to protest. But she felt a deep sinking feeling. Her instinct had told her this man was different and now she was discovering her instinct was wrong. Well, she'd sleep properly and tomorrow she'd run away. Firmus had lifted her up and carried her over to the vast bed which had been prepared for him.

'Sleep,' he'd said, settling his great bulk beside her, then cradled her in his huge arms. 'Sleep well. You will come with me to Alexandria. I will protect you. You will not have to go back to Palmyra.'

He had not touched her. Joyously she realised he was not going to. She had curled into a tight ball, her back resting against his and comforted by the contact had fallen into a deep, carefree sleep. The first she had had for a very long time.

After that there was a pattern to their travelling. Each day she rode with him on his elephant. Each night she ate with him in his tent and slept with him in his bed and each evening he had cradled her and kissed her neck but never once had he molested her or attempted to caress her body.

Then, one night he had tucked her up in his bed and not come in beside her. Instead he had left the tent. And she had been unable to sleep. She had lain in the darkness listening to the call of the wild animals and wanting him. She missed his body, his smell, his gentleness. When he had returned in the early hours of the morning she had held her arms out to him.

'I missed you,' she said.

And he had smiled and climbed in next to her and she had kissed his mouth, his neck, his chest. His body was smooth and hairless and responded to her touch. Then she had slithered down his great bulk and found his erect and throbbing penis and had taken it between her hands and lovingly stroked it. She had made a perfect 'O' with her lips and fastened them round his cock, teasing him, playing with it. She had cupped his balls in her hands and moved them gently but firmly from side to side, all the time taking his shaft further and further, deeper and deeper into her mouth. She had moved one hand up so that it caressed the ridges of his penis whilst her mouth went up and down. And when he'd begun to moan she'd felt elated. She had desperately wanted to give him pleasure.

She had moved her legs so that she was crouching over his cock, her feet flat beside him. He took her haunches in his hands, steadying her, enabling her to glide on the tip of his phallus. He could feel the wetness of her, feel her opening, feel her soft, creamy warmth slowly easing down on the tip of his pulsating penis. Gradually, she had lowered her wet and open self onto his hard and fully erect member. She had gasped as it went slowly up, filling every space, making the two of them one. When he was firmly locked inside her (he had aided her movements by rocking her up and down until he was so deeply embedded and she felt secure), he removed his hands from her buttocks and she leant over him and he caressed her rose-bud breasts. Then she lay flat over his belly, her hands reaching up to his shoulders, gripping them as he heaved and shuddered into her. Her tiny body slithered this way and that on his vast smooth frame and all the time his cock stayed pounding inside her, providing her with infinite pleasure.

His hands stroked the length of her spine and held her bottom tightly. She put her legs together over his so that she could feel his testicles against the top of her thighs. That excited her. Firmus began to move his hands in small circles over her buttocks towards her anus, then slowly held it apart and his fingers began to trace along its opening. Exciting her more. The combination of gentleness and affection, together with the longing and the caressing made her wetter and wetter. She had become more and more open and erotic thoughts flooded into her brain. She began to squirm.

Firmus, feeling her responses and noticing the look of lustful wantonness upon her face, suddenly held her by the waist, lifted her off his cock and placed her pussy over his mouth. His long thick tongue began to explore every furl and crevice of her sex. He pushed his way deep inside her vagina and slurped and sucked. Then his teeth started nibbling at her clitoris and the fingers of one hand came round playing with her bottom and her pussy. With the other he stroked her nipples and her breasts.

Samoya could hardly hold her ecstasy. She was writhing this way and that. Every orifice she possessed was willingly imprisoned by him, sensations were renting her body, taking her higher and higher. Samoya didn't know whether she was coming or going as his tongue and his fingers roamed into and over her. Then he lifted her up once more and put her back on his thick and throbbing member. She rode him, leaning first to one side then to the other, her inner muscles gripping him, her torso upright, her breasts pushed forward. His hands played with her nipples and she put her hands behind her back to hold his sac, her little fingers spread out, tracing along the soft erogenous zone of his inside thighs.

Then he pulled her down, crushing her tiny body to his with one hand, the other snaking down between them, touching her clitoris, rubbing that hard little morsel of flesh so that her wanting was almost unbearable, and when he thundered into her she met him with similar, convulsive jerks. They came together in a massive, writhing climax. She collapsed over him, gently kissing his soft sensuous mouth before drifting away into the land of dreams.

The remainder of their journey to Alexandria was passed in exploration of each other's body. It was also one of daytime titillation and night-time satisfaction.

When they approached his gigantic villa Firmus had told her that he was planning to put her in charge of his harem.

'You will have trouble with Soodebeh,' he said. 'She

was my favourite and she will be jealous. But I will back you no matter what she says, or does.'

With Firmus's words Samoya realised her halcyon days of being alone with him were over. Now she would have to work.

'Firmus,' she said, hesitatingly, 'we have spent so long by ourselves I hadn't thought but . . . do you want to share . . . me . . . and yourself? I mean is there anything I can do that you will really enjoy? Anything that you particularly like?'

'I enjoy most things,' he said. 'So you can surprise me. I give you *carte blanche*. Do whatever you want.'

Splashing around in the great pool Samoya thought of the 'performances' she had arranged for Firmus. Of the dancing girls with their split trousers who could pick up gold coins with their pussy. And how they would lift their legs to his shoulders to that he could slowly bend and suck their sex, first one and then the next. And how, robed in voluminous cloth, he would walk down a procession of girls, with their breasts held up and on display, their legs apart, but covered with fine multi-coloured cambric that had a hidden slit which he could push aside and gently feel each girl's sex. When he found the one that was wet and to his liking he would part his own clothing, lift the girl onto his erect cock and penetrate her.

Samoya discovered that Firmus enjoyed watching women playing with one another. She organised elaborate plays where this was incorporated. She designed fantastic costumes for the women to wear and let them roll about the stage sucking and feeling each other's bodies. But whatever happened during the day and in the evening, most nights she was in his bed. And she was happy. Except . . .

Samoya tried to figure out what it was that was lacking. She had love and affection. She was the mistress of a fabulous house. She had more gorgeous clothes than she could ever wear. She had Firmus and she had sex. Occasionally, if she was particularly aroused she would take one of the women and play with her but . . . Everything was too beautiful, too secure. It was pleasure and more pleasure but none of it was intellectual. There were no books to read. Nobody with whom she could have a good conversation. She was imprisoned in a cultural desert. Even Soodebeh had not been that much of a challenge. She had very soon buckled under when she realised that Samoya was in control and Firmus agreed with everything Samoya said or did. She had no *frisson* of danger. No extraneous excitement. Samoya hesitated to even form the word boredom but that was what she was really feeling. Acute boredom. She was a beautiful bird in the most beautiful cage. But did she want out? And could she get out if she wanted to go? Samoya was thinking about this when Firmus arrived at the pool.

'Samoya, my darling,' he said, throwing off his robe, stepping into the pool and swimming up beside her where she was lazily and dreamily floating. 'I have some news for you.'

'So early!' she exclaimed.

'A special messenger. He's come from somebody called Verenia, High Priestess of the Goddess in Antioch.'

'Oh!' said Samoya, suddenly all colour leaving her face. The world she thought she had left behind was crashing in on her security and from a most unexpected source.

'Samoya, what's the matter?' asked Firmus, anxiously. 'I haven't given you the news yet.'

'Sorry,' said Samoya. 'What's the news?'

'First tell me why this person should have an effect upon you?'

'She's my aunt. My father's sister. How did she know I was here?'

'She doesn't,' replied Firmus. 'She's written to tell me that Prince Maaen has killed King Odainat, he's on his

206

way to kill Zenobia and has sent Princess Bernice here with a message for me.'

'Princess Bernice!' and as she said it Samoya felt that *frisson* of danger she had been missing.

'Yes, apparently she's coming to tell me that he intends to be my partner and all my Palmyrene revenues will in future go to him.'

'Oh!'

'She's added something else. She says she has sent a Christian, a Bishop Paul, to Palmyra to warn Zenobia of Maaen's intentions to kill her,' said Firmus.

'Then she'll be all right. Zenobia's good with a dagger,' said Samoya, remembering the night King Hairan was killed. 'Also she can throw a javelin as well as any man.'

'How do you know?'

'Because we trained together in Antioch.'

'You mean you can throw a javelin too?' asked Firmus.

'Yes,' replied Samoya.

'My little darling is full of surprises,' said Firmus, kissing her, then climbing out of the pool. 'Now, what do you propose we do with this Princess?'

'Have an orgy,' said Samoya. 'She's completely sex mad. And . . .'

Samoya stopped. If Maaen was King and Bernice was his emissary and he managed to kill Zenobia and he stayed King, Bernice would know where she was, she would tell Maaen and then she would have to go back to him and be his wife.

'We'll have a masked orgy. I don't want her recognising me. And, Bernice has certain peccadilloes. I think they should be catered for,' she added, but didn't tell Firmus that she would have her revenge on the woman who had led her into sexual slavery and who had stood by and watched her humiliation at the hands of Prince Alif. Samoya blamed Bernice. She hadn't yet learnt that she was responsible for her own actions. She had chosen money, position, sex and Palmyra. She hadn't worked out that it had been her choice. She could have said 'no'. And because of this her desire for revenge was greater. And she was determined that it would be sweet. Very sweet.

'You're being very mysterious,' said Firmus. 'What sort of peccadilloes?'

'She enjoys a little refined punishment. And I think as an honoured guest we should meet her every want and desire, don't you?' said Samoya, wickedly, climbing out of the pool, coming up close to Firmus, kneeling in front of him, taking his cock in her mouth and sucking.

'As always, my dear, I leave everything in your very capable hands,' said Firmus, stroking Samoya's wet head. He loved the touch of her cool hands on his testes, the feel of her lips and tongue on his penis. She worked quickly and expertly and it didn't take long before he had spurted into her mouth.

'When is she due to arrive?' asked Samoya.

'Tomorrow,' he said, clapping his hands for his slaves to come and dress him.

'That doesn't leave me much time, but with money anything is possible,' said Samoya smiling at him, wondering how quickly she could organise the women, find some men and rehearse them in a series of erotic tableaux.

Firmus returned her smile, pleased to see a naughty glint in her eyes. She was up to something and as a result he knew he was going to enjoy himself.

Samoya set to work fast and with great zeal. She called in seamstresses, and carpenters and gave them, respectively, designs and plans to follow. Then she went to Firmus's stables and spent time there picking out various items of equipment, especially whips and crops. Then she chose a magnificent saddle and sent for the saddler. A tall handsome young man came bowing into her presence.

'See this,' she said, handing him a drawing of a large

penis. 'I want this made in leather, stuffed until it's rigid then attached to the centre of this saddle.'

The saddler looked at her in amazement and as he did so she saw his cock bulge under his robe.

'Madam,' he said, 'it's a very odd request.'

'It is isn't it?' she said, smiling. Samoya saw the lust in his eyes. She was reminded that she had not touched another man's cock since she had become Firmus's lover. 'Now I need a model for it,' she said, moving closer to him.

The young man, whose name was Rufus, found Samoya's big lustrous violet-blue eyes staring at him and then dropping to his hips and to his bulge which had appeared suddenly and beyond his control. She was standing in front of him, her full, rounded breasts partially on display, partially covered by the flimsiest fabric, and he ached to touch them. Rufus found himself trembling as she moved even closer to him and he could smell her perfume. His hands holding the drawing began to shake.

'Would you mind if I took hold of your cock to see if it's the right size?' she said to his complete astonishment.

He nodded his head and very slowly she began to lift his robe. His legs were trembling. His hands were shaking but apart from that he stood quite still and allowed Samoya to stroke his thighs and find his naked sex and then ring his cock with her cool hands.

'Hold your robe up,' she commanded. Rufus did as he was told. Samoya stood back and looked at his perfect phallus standing upright, thick, proud and long. 'Oh it's beautiful. I think I would like to put it in my mouth and suck it. Is that all right with you?'

Rufus was incapable of saying anything.

Samoya knelt down and took his glorious manhood in her hands and guided it into her mouth. She ringed its base with one hand, held his sac with another and let her mouth glide up and down along the throbbing ridges of his shaft. When she thought he was close to coming she squeezed him at the base and took away her mouth.

'You do have the most beautiful cock,' she said, openly admiring it. 'I want you to use it as the model for your work. Now, I am having a very special party tomorrow. I would like you to join us. But first I must know if you can perform well.'

Rufus swallowed hard. Her words increased his excitement. He wanted to be taken by Samoya. The whole of his body was screaming, all his nerve endings were screaming, wanting to be calmed down, he wanted to feel her body beneath him. He wanted to be allowed to penetrate her.

'I think the best way to find out is if I bend over and lift my skirt and let you see my bare, and incidentally very wet pussy, and you came up between my legs and perhaps you could be persuaded to let me feel that beautiful prick of yours between my thighs and er . . . well I'll bend over and let's see what happens.'

Samoya turned her back on him, brought her long skirt up around her waist, then bent down with her legs slightly apart giving him the full benefit of her well-rounded buttocks. Rufus put out a hand and slowly began to feel her thighs, then he put his large cock between the outer lips of her labia and started to rub on her soft wetness. Samoya rolled her hips. Rufus took hold of her waist, bent his own legs slightly and before she was expecting it he slid his cock up urgently inside her.

Samoya closed her eyes, delighted by the feel of its pulse, its hardness, its rigidity, pounding away. His hands gripped her hips so that as he thrust in and she was pushed forward so he grabbed her back again and every jab was fractionally harder than the jerk that had gone before. And his balls were rubbing against her between her thighs. The softness of them excited her more as they neatly fitted in exactly where she was longing to be touched. She hadn't had sex in this way for some considerable time. The shape and set of his body, the urgency with which he indulged himself reminded Samoya of Marcus. And suddenly an intense feeling of love and longing poured over Samoya. She was happy with Firmus. Content. But he did not arouse in her the same depth of sexual emotion, love even, that Marcus had managed to inspire. She wondered if she would ever see Marcus again. She kept her eyes closed as Rufus thrust into her, his muscular body shuddering against hers, and she made believe it was Marcus.

Rufus wasted no time on extra niceties. He didn't fondle her breasts or touch her clitoris. He just kept up his furious pace while Samoya's writhing body willingly took every ounce of his thrusting manhood. She wanted to know if he was any good. Now she was finding out. Whilst she was being jerked backwards and forwards another idea came into Samoya's head. She would get him to make a glove for his erect cock. Make it with the seams on the outside with large, heavy stitching. The feel of the ridges would give added pleasure. The thought of it made Samoya's stomach tense. She could feel herself coming. The tingling made her vibrate and shake. Rufus was holding her tighter and tighter, thrusting harder and harder. Then he shuddered and came. And she came too though not with the explosion that she sometimes knew. But she didn't mind. It would leave her open and sexually aroused. She could dream and fantasise more easily when she was wet between her legs. It would help her devise Bernice's 'entertainment' with that much more thoroughness.

'Oh yes, you can perform extremely well,' said Samoya glowing with pleasure and pulling down her robe. 'I definitely want you to come to the villa tomorrow evening. You see, this party I'm giving is for somebody important and she has particular pleasures. She is beautiful, so don't worry, but I will want you to perform on her. I'll want you to do whatever I tell you to do to her. Are you willing to obey me?'

'What's in it for me?'

'Do you need anything more than a good time?'

'I'd like to have sex with you again,' he said.

'Well, I expect that will be possible but I cannot promise anything. However, there's one more thing. I want you not only to make the saddle but also to make a leather glove for your penis with the seams on the outside and heavy stitching. And it must have long ties. Do you think you can do that in time?' Samoya smiled at him, her most lustful smile.

'If I wore it would you screw me with it on?' he asked.

'Without a doubt,' she said, squirming at the thought.

After Rufus had gone Samoya took a group of eunuchs and slaves to the market. She bought bales and bales of black cloth and candles and took them home, ordering all the women in the harem to work. A few of them who were not so good with the needle protested but Samoya told them that they would have endless pleasure as a result of their efforts.

Then she spoke to the carpenters and set aside a room for them to work in. All day long the sound of hammering and banging echoed through the great villa. The entire place was a hive of activity. Each group had their own task. Nobody knew completely what Samoya was planning.

It was late afternoon the following day when Princess Bernice arrived at the villa and Firmus was on the steps to greet her. He helped her down from her litter which was carried by four brawny young soldiers.

Bernice shuddered inwardly the moment she saw her host. He was so fat, gross even, and his grossness was compounded by the flamboyance of his dress. She wondered, with his great girth, when he had last seen his cock. She smiled at the thought of him coupling with anybody. He'd never manage it, she thought maliciously. Well, if he was the master of the house, one thing was for certain: she'd not be having any sex here. He might keep a harem but Bernice decided that must be for prestige and not for use.

Firmus suggested that her escort went to the servants' quarters for refreshment but Bernice said she preferred to keep them by her side. She wanted to deliver the message, retire to her room and have a licentious session with her soldiers. They had managed it on the journey but the thought of sexual indulgence in a luxurious home, in a great big bed, appealed to Bernice enormously. But Firmus insisted the men must be hungry and in need of a rest. He told her they could join her later, after the banquet.

'What banquet?' she asked.

'The one I shall provide for you,' he replied.

Firmus eyed Bernice up and down and found his cock twitching. He saw a pretty woman who looked as she if she had spent days giving herself entirely to pleasure. Her eyes were half-closed and the way she moved her body was immensely sexual. He presumed the four men were responsible, and smiled. He would let Samoya know. They could be added to her entertainment.

Firmus had given Samoya a free hand and she had been most secretive, telling him that everything was a surprise, for him as much as for Bernice and she had barred him from certain sections of his villa. He didn't mind. It excited him to think that Samoya was amusing herself. But she had told him that she did not want to be present when Bernice arrived. She had a fear of being recognised.

Bernice stepped from the litter, her highly sexed body covered in swathes of fabulous material that accentuated the curves of her body. Her black hair was curled and held in place with golden hair-clips and she was adorned with necklaces and jewels. She looked very

213

desirable. Firmus decided that he fancied her and would have her before the night was out.

'We are greatly honoured by your unexpected arrival,' lied Firmus, bowing low.

'I have a message from his Majesty King Maaen,' Bernice announced, as she looked around her admiring the beauty of Firmus's magnificent villa and its well-stocked leafy gardens.

'King Maaen!' exclaimed Firmus.

'Yes. Unfortunately King Odainat met with an accident and my nephew has taken his rightful place,' said Princess Bernice.

'And you have a message for me,' said Firmus. 'Well, now you are here I'm sure that can wait. You must bathe and relax and eat. I have the finest chefs in the world and we can cook anything your heart desires. We have grey mullet, and sardines and sole, goose, duck and lamb served with rice, maize and okra, eggplant and beans, then figs and peaches, apricots and dates, sweet melon and grapes.'

Bernice felt quite overwhelmed by the welcome Firmus had given her and told him that as she had not eaten so well on her journey, everything he suggested made her mouth water.

'In that case tonight we'll have a feast,' he said, leading her into his marble and alabaster villa draped with heavy tapestries and the decoration on the pillars painted in gold. Firmus clapped his hands and a number of his female slaves came running forward. They bowed low to the Princess.

'Take Her Highness to the pool,' he said, doing exactly what Samoya had asked him to do.

In the great pool room the slaves divested Bernice of her clothing. They sponged her body down, lingering over her breasts, her nipples, her belly and between her legs. Then they guided her into the warmed water. Samoya watched the proceedings behind a grille from a window high above. She noticed that Bernice's body had slimmed down. The two women had almost changed places in size. Samoya was now the voluptuous one. Bernice, though still well-rounded, was no longer fat. Samoya had instructed her slaves to begin stroking Bernice's body once she was comfortable in the water. She smiled as, fully clothed, they slipped into the pool and allowed their hands to roam over Bernice's body. And Bernice begin to wallow in their attentions.

'Why are they dressed when they are in the water?' asked Firmus joining Samoya on the hidden balcony, and, standing behind her, began playing with her breasts.

'I have a surprise for her,' said Samoya. 'Just watch.'

Firmus's cock rose and pressed into Samoya's back as the slaves in the water started to close in on Bernice, their hands stroking her nipples then finding her sex. Firmus lifted Samoya's skirts and he began fondling her bare buttocks as the women in the pool below held Bernice's shoulders up and her legs apart whilst one of them came between them and put her tongue to her sex. A great sigh went up from Bernice as the slave parted Bernice's labia and nibbled at her stiff, erect little protuberance. Then other hands began to encircle her breasts. And Bernice's hips were swaying in the water.

Firmus realigned his own position and put his cock between Samoya's legs rubbing at her wet, juicy sex. Samoya leant on the window, jutting out her bottom, giving Firmus great freedom of access.

The slaves gently floated Bernice towards the edge of the pool and stretched out her arms on the side. Then a number of them held her legs open wide. And the slave who had had her head between Bernice's legs made way for another one, taller, broader than the rest.

'Watch now,' said Samoya, wiggling her backside against Firmus's cock, her sex very wet and wanting him to thrust inside her.

The new slave stood up between Bernice's open legs

215

and moved in closer. And suddenly Firmus realised what Samoya had done. The new slave was male. And he had his cock poised at her entrance. But Bernice hadn't yet realised. The other slaves had their heads in the way, their hands roving over her breasts.

Firmus put his arm around Samoya's waist, inched her up and thrust his cock into her wanton pussy. He had anticipated by moments the action of the man below.

Bernice let out a great scream of joy as the totally unexpected happened and she found herself in a pool of water surrounded by women and impaled by a large phallus.

Whilst she was being indulged, some new slaves came into the pool room. They were carrying handcuffs and chains.

Firmus, still watching the scene below whilst pounding into Samoya's sex, was mystified.

'What are they going to do with those?' he asked.

'Don't ask, just watch and stay inside me,' said Samoya, moving back onto him. She was feeling incredibly aroused. She wanted more, much more of everything. And she was going to get it. She was going to give it, too. Samoya felt a real sense of excitement. She knew exactly what she was going to do to Bernice.

'But who is the slave screwing her?' asked Firmus, knowing that all males in his villa were eunuchs.

'He's not a slave. He's your saddler. I went to him yesterday and asked him to make me something special. And then I asked if he would oblige us by coming here and obeying my wishes. He agreed.'

Firmus wondered how Samoya had got him to agree. Had she stroked his cock? Had she taken it out, looked at it? Had she used sexual persuasion? The thought of another man ploughing into her made Firmus jealous and he thrust into her faster. And Samoya, remembering the feel of the saddler's cock, rolled back on Firmus, opening further and further to his pounding member.

216

The unexpectedness of a well-oiled penis suddenly pushing its way up inside her made Bernice come. And left her wanting more and more. She looked up at the face of the man and saw he was extremely handsome. She wondered how he had managed to get into this part of the villa. Or had Firmus supplied him for her? Well, that was a truly hospitable welcome. She closed her eyes and gave herself up to the total enjoyment of sex in the water. She did not feel the fetters being expertly locked around her ankles. The man stayed inside her as hands held her head up and her arms out. Slaves were stroking her arms. She didn't feel the handcuffs fastened on her wrists, she was too busy concentrating on the cock still performing within her. Then the man pulled out and swam away. And Samoya gave a big smile and backed once more onto Firmus's thrusting member as Bernice was left standing in the water, chains around her arms and feet.

'Now what?' asked Firmus, looking at the bemused figure of Princess Bernice.

'I want you to go down and play with her, screw here,' said Samoya. 'She can't move very much or very far. But don't let her come. The women and I are going to change and then I'll come and get her. I've prepared a special room for her.'

Firmus was beginning to enjoy this entertainment. He pulled out, his penis still thick and erect. He quite fancied the Princess, and the fact that she was chained added to his excitement.

By the time Firmus entered the pool room the slaves had departed after silently helping a protesting Bernice out of the pool. They had dried her and oiled her and laid her naked on a great pile of cushions Samoya had ordered to be placed against a wall.

Bernice was confused. Whoever had organised her reception had done it very well. Her handcuffed hands were chained in front of her. She brought them round and down so that she could play with herself. She was lying with her eyes closed, her fingers enjoying the sensations she was getting by rubbing her engorged clitoris, when she felt someone beside her. She hoped it was the handsome young man who had taken her in the pool. She opened her eyes and was shocked to see the mountainous Firmus standing astride her legs, parting his robes and bringing out his tool. Surely he wasn't going to have her? He was too big, too enormous. He'd crush her.

'You enjoyed your aperitif?' he asked, without waiting for a reply. 'The feast will soon be ready but I thought it was time for the first course.'

Firmus knelt down and placed Bernice's handcuffed hands over her own breasts. Then he parted her legs.

'A very nice wet pink pussy,' he said. And there was something in the lustfulness of the man's face, his innate sexiness that made her forget his size and made her want him. His glance beneath his hooded eyes left her needing to feel his prick embedded within her. He jerked her fettered legs up and placed them round his waist so that her sex was level with his cock but her shoulders stayed flat on the cushions. Slowly and deliberately, and with great care, he began to enter her. The very slowness of his rhythm excited her. Every time she wanted to jerk or roll he put a huge hand on her belly and pressed his weight down, forcing her to stop writhing.

Firmus was still slowly screwing Bernice when Samoya and a full entourage of slaves walked into the pool room. Every one of them was clothed, head to toe, in flowing black. They all wore masks and high elaborate head-dresses. There was no way of knowing which was male and which was female. Immediately Firmus saw them he stopped screwing Bernice. A well-rehearsed group came forward, picked up Bernice and began encasing her in wet leather strips. They did it so that her naked breasts were enhanced by the leather above and below, as was her belly by a wider strip fastened tightly around her waist and her sex by thongs between her buttocks and around her thighs. Then she was covered in a swathe of bright red silk, a mask was put over her face and a bigger, more elaborate head-dress attached to her hair. She was carried in procession out of the pool room down some steps and into a secluded part of Firmus's beautiful garden. Here a stallion was waiting for her.

Terrified, Bernice tried to back away. She could not imagine why she had been brought face to face with the horse except . . . Bernice cried out. Somebody pinioned her arms to her side as someone else put a blindfold over her eyes. Unknown hands roamed over her body. Her breasts were fondled. Her sex was opened and caressed. Then she was lifted up into the air and her legs held open whilst she was positioned in the saddle. The saddle that Samoya had had made for her. The saddle with the erect penis thrusting upwards. That was now securely lodged inside Bernice. Then the horse began to move.

Leaving her entourage on the steps, Samoya held the reins and guided the horse around the gardens watching the changing expressions on Bernice's blindfolded face. Bernice sat enjoying the sensations of the leather cock jerking and thrusting inside her, making her wetter and wetter with every step the horse took. And as she rode, the leather strips around her body were tightening, cutting into her flesh. Samoya brought the horse round to the far side of the villa to the room where the carpenters had been working. Her entourage were ready and waiting for her. Bernice was lifted down and carried into the villa.

Inside the room, to her relief Bernice's blindfold was removed. But then she found she was faced with complete darkness. She had no idea what the room was or what it contained. Once more, hands began to roam over her body before they guided her up some steps and lifted her up and over something hard. Her legs were splayed open and chained. Her chained hands spread out taut in front of her and attached to what sounded to her to be metal rings.

Bernice knew her wanton sex was open and intensely vulnerable. Apprehensively she waited for her next moment of pleasure. What would she feel next? A phallus in her sex? In her anus? In her mouth. She allowed herself the smallest wiggle of anticipation. She began to think of her journey here and how she had resented being sent by Maaen to Egypt instead of returning to Palmyra where she could once again continue with her old way of life. Still, the soldiers had provided her with some comfort. But the sight of Firmus had not led her to believe she would be so properly welcomed. Neither had she been introduced to the woman who ran his household. That had given her a moment's anxiety which had vanished when she stepped into the pool and the slaves had started to caress her body. Nevertheless, she was sure there was somebody in charge and she wondered who it was.

Bernice would have been most surprised if she could have seen Samoya. She had let the black cloak slip from her and was now wearing a leather breast-plate with holes for her voluptuous breasts to stick through, around her waist was a thick heavy leather belt, with a variety of whips and rods attached to it. A thin strip of leather was secured to the belt at the back, it wound down through the crease of her buttocks, the pressure exciting her as she moved, and ending at a flat piece of leather in place over her bare sex, but with a carefully shaped hole for a cock to enter the moment she wanted it. This was then attached by further leather thongs to the thick belt via her belly. She had bare feet but leather thongs criss-crossed up her legs and the whole impression was one of a slave-driver.

Bernice's thoughts were interrupted as oiled hands began to snake over her body. They covered her breasts. They paid particular attention to her hard, aroused nipples. Then a tongue was exploring the entrance to her sex. Tethered as she was and with as much movement as she could muster, Bernice began to writhe with pleasure. Then she felt the touch of a feather on her breasts, down her spine, along the crease of her buttocks, and wisping up and down over the outer lips of her sex. Exquisite, thought Bernice, as she revelled in the delirious softness that was slowly driving her beyond endurance.

An erect penis was suddenly presented to her mouth. Her head, held by her hair was jerked backwards, her mouth forced open and the phallus shot into it. Expertly she let her tongue glide over its head, putting extra pressure on the ridge of its cap before taking it fully into her mouth. As she was doing this, unseen hands placed the blindfold over her eyes again. Then the cock was withdrawn from her mouth and without warning, a sharp searing pain lashed her buttocks. Samoya had silently ordered the blindfold to be replaced and all the candles in the room to be lit. She wanted to be able to see her target. Bernice's buttocks. And the moment she did, Samoya wielded the whip with great dexterity and vigour. And Bernice let out a howl of pain. And joy.

Bernice had been excited by the unexpected turn of events: being taken in the pool and having a thick cock stuck in her mouth when she was tied down and helpless. Everything that she had been subjected to had aroused her, made her belly tighten and the sexual tingling in her womb increase. But she had not thought to feel the red-hot blaze of the lash across her well-rounded bare bottom. And whoever was striking her knew what to do. After three carefully placed cuts, someone held her buttocks apart and she felt wet leather trail through her crevice and then a number of short sharp flicks applied to the tender membrane. Samoya could see from Bernice's response that she was enjoying it. She then brought the whip down hard in the same place, cruelly torturing that puckered flesh.

After this, oils and creams were rubbed into the welts and hands began to massage Bernice's flanks, slowly moving down, invading her sex and her burning anus.

A sponge of cold water was then held to her nipples and soon after tiny flicks of the whip heated them before someone took those dark rosy buds into their mouth. And once more her mouth was opened and a cock began to ride inside it. Samoya surveyed her chained adversary with interest. She was enjoying inflicting punishment upon Bernice. She was enjoying watching the changing expressions of pain and ecstasy flit across the woman's face.

Samoya looked around the room. The men and women had now thrown off their black covering. Their leather clothing, which she had designed, enhanced the men's organs, and the women's bare breasts, shaven mounds and bare buttocks and allowed immediate access to anybody who wanted it. And her entourage, now fully aroused, was taking full advantage of this. Women's shoulders were being held back whilst their hips were tipped forward, their legs apart, a man either sucking her sex or penetrating her. There was a great deal of sighing and moaning. Firmus joined them. His cloak was parted and his cock was erect. Samoya thought he should be the one to take Bernice's anus. She stuck the whip into the heavy belt around her waist, went over to him, and stroking his shaft, guided him to where Bernice was chained on a parody of a wooden gym horse.

Samoya trailed her fingers over the livid welts on Bernice's buttocks, let her fingers probe Bernice's sex, briefly touching her clitoris so that the woman let out a great sigh of wanting. Then, with Firmus in position, she aimed his phallus at Bernice's forbidden hole. And he thrust into her, rasping past the welts that Samoya had deposited on Bernice's soft flesh.

Whilst Firmus was occupied screwing Bernice,

Samoya scanned the room for Rufus. She had told him to put on the leather penis glove as soon as he got out of the pool. Samoya roamed amongst the masked and writhing couples until she found him.

He had his head between Soodebeh's fat legs and his tongue was slurping at her sex. Samoya flicked his rump with the tip of her whip.

'I want you,' she said. And Rufus stood up. 'I want to feel that lovely stiff cock of yours deep inside me.' Samoya put out a hand and held his leather covered stalk enjoying the feel of the seams and the ridges.

Samoya lay down, putting a cushion beneath her buttocks and Rufus crawled up between her wide open legs. And slowly he aimed for the hole in her leather pussy-covering and her belly tightened with sweet anticipation as she felt it pushing through, past her outer lips, into the pink, swollen, juicy depths within. She sighed. She raised her hips higher to take him, the ridges of the seams exciting the walls of her vulva. And he moved in and out and she put her hands down so that she could feel her own clitoris. And she began to rub. The more she rubbed, the more he pounded and her legs straightened out going rigid as her womb fluttered and her mouth went dry. She swallowed hard as, with her head moving this way and that, the primeval force within her curled and called to be released and the exquisite agony of climax shook her to her core. Then she moved her hands from herself to the base of Rufus's shaft. He mustn't come. She wanted him to have Bernice. Samoya's body went limp beneath Rufus and she whispered in his ear.

'Now screw that woman on the horse.'

Rufus looked over to where Bernice was sprawled and chained and Firmus was charging into her anus with a force that told Samoya he was about to come.

'As soon as Firmus has finished, take his place. Don't give her time to recover,' said Samoya, enjoying taking her revenge.

Bernice felt her bottom being stretched more and more by someone's penis, then that person withdrew and another entered her sex. She let out a squeal of delight as she felt the seams and ridges of the leather. Whoever had devised her playtime and her punishment had to be admired. Bernice felt certain that someone was directing the performance. Soon after the leather-gloved cock started pounding into her, mouths were clamped over her hard nipples. Bernice began to feel herself coming. She tightened her muscles around the leather-encased phallus, longing at the same time for soneone to touch her clitoris. But this was denied her. She began to jerk as she contracted with the effort of achieving orgasm. Rufus was also satisfying himself.

Satiated on a diet of sensual pain and perverse sexual pleasure, Bernice collapsed and a thought crossed her mind that had never lodged there before. She wondered what it would be like to be made love to. Not violated for someone's pleasure but to have loving hands trailing over her body. And to do the same thing to a beloved. Bernice realised she had always been in lust but had never been in love.

Samoya glanced about the room. Everyone was in a state of surfeit of pleasure. They were lying down leisurely stroking one another. Some had even gone to sleep. And Bernice was lying with her bare, marked bottom uppermost, nipples still hard, mouth still open and wanting. Samoya went over to Bernice, knelt in front of her, parted her sex-lips and very gently began to lick her. She felt the other woman tense and sigh. Samoya took some time before she allowed her tongue to touch the straining, engorged protuberance that she knew was longing to be touched. With great expertise she flicked her tongue backwards and forwards hardening it more, drawing it further out, making the chained woman wince with delicious agony. When she knew Bernice was about to come, Samoya stood up, took the crop from her belt and thrashed her. She ignored her screams and howls and the restricted writhing movements. She relished the pain she was inflicting. And the sight of the livid marks appearing on Bernice's bare bottom and the tears coming from her eyes. Then when she thought she had punished her enough, Samoya bent down once more, opened her sex and sucked at her hard morsel until Bernice came in a great flood of pain and joy.

Some time later, after the banquet for Bernice which Samoya chose not to attend, Firmus joined Samoya in bed. Proprietorially, he snaked his hands down over her body and held her sex.

'You did well,' he said, kissing her softly. 'But you can't stay hidden all the time, sooner or later she will have to know you are mistress of my house.'

'I know,' said Samoya, sadly. 'And that frightens me.'

Firmus kissed her again and she reached down and gently began to play with his genitals.

'Who was that young man you were indulging with such abandon? Was it the saddler?' he asked. Samoya was silent. Firmus continued. 'The one with the leather on his penis,' he added jealously. He loved her so much. He would give her anything and forgive her everything but there was something about her, especially today, that told him she wouldn't always be with him. He hugged her tightly.

'I thought you were too busy taking Bernice's bottom to notice what I was doing,' answered Samoya. 'Didn't you enjoy that?'

'I did, very much,' he said, his cock twitching under her touch and with the memory. Samoya could certainly organise a good entertainment.

'Where is Bernice now?' asked Samoya.

'In bed with the saddler,' replied Firmus.

'That's appropriate,' laughed Samoya.

'How so?' he asked.

'She likes leather. She used to have a couple of leather dildoes on a thong around her waist.'

'By the way,' said Firmus, 'she arrived with some soldiers. I thought you might have asked them to join us. I'm sure they indulged in sex with her from Antioch to Alexandria.'

'I would've done,' said Samoya, laughing sardonically. 'I went to the kitchens to find them. Well they didn't know who I was and the four of them were huddled conspiratorially in a corner with a large, empty pitcher of wine. They had their daggers out and were sharpening them. And as I was only a woman they carried on talking in the mistaken belief I didn't have ears. They were discussing how soon after Bernice had delivered her message to you they should kill her. Apparently Prince Maaen had told them to.'

'I see, so what did you do?' asked Firmus.

'I offered them some more wine.'

'And?'

'I slipped a sleeping potion in it. Then I told the chef that when they were fast asleep they were to be strapped to horses and driven out into the desert.'

Firmus was amazed by her remarks and her actions, especially as he had watched her whip Bernice with considerable pleasure.

'I think she's a silly woman, over-sexed and under loved,' said Samoya, 'but she's not wicked, really wicked and I didn't want her killed.'

'Darling Samoya, you astound me,' said Firmus as she rolled over on top of him, placed his cock at the entrance of her sex and slowly began to ride him.

And that's how they were found when a terrified slave burst in telling them that the Roman garrison had been slaughtered. That the Roman galleys in the harbour, waiting to load the corn crop for Rome, were in flames. And that an unknown army was marching victoriously through the city and towards Firmus's villa.

'Persians!' exclaimed Samoya. 'May the gods protect us because nothing else will.'

'I doubt it's the Persians. They've been well and truly trounced.'

'Well who then? Who else would invade Egypt and destroy the Roman garrison?' said Samoya anxiously.

'Get dressed and we'll find out, and tell Princess Bernice to join us on the villa steps. Whoever it is, we'll give them a welcome. They might be better than the Romans – as conquerors they certainly couldn't be much worse,' said Firmus climbing out of bed and calling for his slaves to dress him.

Firmus didn't let Samoya see his fear or his anxiety. Instinctively he knew something momentous had happened and Firmus had spent his life guided by his instinct. Unlike many men, he listened to it. He frequently acted upon it against his rational judgement and it had paid huge dividends. But now his instinct was telling him that his life and those of the people around him, those he loved and cared for, were never going to be the same again.

Firmus was in a very sombre mood when he stood on his villa steps waiting for the unknown army to appear.

'Do you think it's the barbarians?' asked Samoya.

Chapter Eleven

*D*agmar listened with growing urgency to what the old Bedouin was saying. Then she paid him and ran through the gardens into the palace. She had to see the Queen and quickly. On her way she passed Timogenes sitting in an arbour designing his next uniform.

'No time for that,' said Dagmar, pulling at his arm. 'Come with me.'

'Why?' he asked, trailing after her automatically. But Dagmar didn't give any reply, she just kept running and cursing the fact that Zenobia had extended her villa so that it was now the greatest, and most ostentatious palace on earth. No expense spared, that's what Zenobia had said with considerable glee. And it was true. It was a monument to untold riches.

Dagmar passed Cassius, the philosopher, making notes from his own notes. She didn't stop to speak to him. He was always so cynical and constantly made snide remarks about everyone's intellectual capacity. There was no joy of life in him. To Dagmar it was as if his over-active brain had eroded his emotions. Although she ignored him, he tagged along behind trying to find out why they were running, shouting out to Timogenes to tell him why they were in such a hurry.

Timogenes couldn't tell him and wouldn't if he'd known. He didn't like Cassius. Not only was he the recipient of Cassius's endless intellectual barbs, he also made incessant jokes about his love of uniforms, managing to overlook the fact that since Zenobia had taken him into her army he had won many battles for her and was one of her finest Generals.

When the three of them arrived at the great throne room they found Zenobia in audience. She was sitting on her enormous golden throne, her young son, the King, seated beside her. Both of them were draped in fabulous ceremonial robes but she was wearing the great crown of state. She was reporting to various senators and merchants on her military progress and what laws she wanted passed during the forthcoming year. Dagmar, Timogenes and Cassius could not interrupt her so they sat in silence and waited for her to finish.

They listened to her clear, penetrating and hypnotic voice telling them exactly why she had declared war on Rome.

'They promised my husband, King Odainat the lands north of the Taurus Mountains up to the Black Sea,' she said, 'if he helped them in their campaign against the Goths. And he did. But in my opinion they set up Prince Maaen to kill him so that they didn't have to fulfil that promise. Well, we all know that that traitor was quickly despatched to Hades when he came here to kill me and my son. And ever since I have been trying to get those lands, promised to King Odainat and the people of Palmyra. We also know that Rome has had a continual turnover of weak and ineffectual emperors but they all said they would not honour that promise. So I decided I would take what was mine. You know as well as I do that Rome and its dominions is a place of debauchery, corruption and beggary and that her currency has little or no value. Unlike Palmyra and her provinces which are well run . . .'

Zenobia stopped for applause which came instantly, without hesitation and with genuine enthusiasm. Because it was all true.

'But Egypt was not well run. The Romans were letting the Egyptians starve whilst they took their harvest to feed the Roman army. Well, we put a stop to that. We, the Palmyrenes burnt the ships in Alexandria harbour and we took over the running of that poor benighted country. And look at the difference now. There's enough corn for the Egyptians and for the Palmyrene army. For we must never forget that a successful army marches on its stomach.

'Once I knew Egypt was secure and I could feed my army, I marched north and took what was due to me and to Palmyra. Senators, I have to report that we now rule lands from the Nile through Syria up to the Hellespont.'

A great cry of Long live the Queen, Long live Palmyra rose up from everybody who thronged the vast room.

'However, we do not rest on our laurels. There's more work to be done. The School of Medicine is now finished and operational, what I now want to know is, did we get enough tutors from Athens and how many females has it admitted? Also how is the School of Law and Philosophy? Is it fully attended and what is the ratio of women to men?

'Now, the next item. I have had a petition from the ordinary people of this city. They tell me that they are having difficulty making ends meet. That the various import taxes are too high. Well, I want the water-rates increased.'

There was a general groan and a murmur of amazement from everyone as she said that. But Zenobia carried on regardless.

'The rich caravaneers bringing their oil in on camels in alabaster jars can well afford to pay more for the use of our wells. But I want a decrease for the poorer merchants bringing their produce in on donkeys and in goatskins.

'For the moment senators, that is all. I want you all to go away and work out these new laws and give me the findings I demand within the next few days.'

With that she gave a wave of dismissal and everyone bowed low and backed out of her presence. Dagmar, Timogenes and Cassius stayed where they were until the room was empty. Then Dagmar approached the throne closely followed by Timogenes, which she was pleased about, and Cassius, which did not please her at all.

'Your Majesty,' said Dagmar, bowing low, 'I have a very important message for you. But I think it should be delivered in private.' She glanced at Cassius as she said that.

'Dagmar,' said the Queen patiently looking at her closest female companion still dressed in her Palmyrene soldier's uniform. 'I have no secrets from my friend Cassius. You can speak freely.'

'Your Majesty, Prince Tamoral of the Bedouin sent a messenger to tell you that there has been a change of emperor in Rome.'

'Another one!' exclaimed Zenobia roaring with laughter.

'Yes, ma'am,' said Dagmar, very seriously. 'This one has not been chosen by the Senate but by the soldiers. They killed the old one and made Lucius Aurelian their emperor.'

'Who did you say!' said the Queen with alarm, gripping the side of her throne with sudden consternation. This news was not only totally unexpected, it was also quite appalling. Lucius Aurelian was a brilliant soldier. And he might make a brilliant emperor. But he could be major trouble. Especially for her.

'Lucius Aurelian,' said Dagmar. 'And he's taken over many of your garrisons in the north and Tamoral says he's sent a contingent to Egypt to re-take that country from you.'

'Has he indeed!' said Zenobia. 'Well I'll be ready for him. Timogenes, I order you immediately to Egypt with your men.'

'Shall I go with him?' asked Dagmar.

'No,' said Zenobia. 'I want you with me.'

'But Your Majesty, I know the land. I can help Timogenes. Remember I was with you when you fought along the Nile,' said Dagmar, remembering their campaign and how she was sent back to Palmyra, missing all the victory celebrations, because the High Priest had risen up against Zenobia, because she wouldn't clamp down on the Jews, the Christians and other minor religious sects; and his revolution had had to be put down. She also remembered because of that she had missed meeting up with Samoya whom Zenobia found was mistress of Firmus's household and where Princess Bernice was also staying.

'I remember very well, Dagmar, my dear,' she said. 'But whilst Timogenes goes south to Egypt you and I are going north to Antioch and then on to the Black Sea. No emperor, however fine a General he is, is going to take my hard won lands away from me.'

'And me Your Majesty,' said Cassius in his best, most oily sycophantic voice. 'Would you like me to accompany Timogenes?'

'And what good would you be?' asked Timogenes, sarcastically. 'Would you spout philosophy at the enemy and hope they'd be terrified and run away!'

'You, Cassius, are to stay here in Palmyra and continue teaching our King,' said Zenobia, aware of Timogenes's dislike for her philosopher but choosing to ignore his sarcasm.

The young King made a face at Dagmar. He was not very happy with his mother's decision. He stood up announcing he was tired and left the room. Timogenes kissed the Queen's hands and bade her an emotional farewell. He departed, with Cassius close on his heels, who said he must return to his room to finish the book he was writing on the Art of Rhetoric.

Dagmar and the Queen sat in silence for a moment. Then Zenobia burst into tears. Dagmar put her arms around her and rocked her like a baby.

'I'm frightened,' said Zenobia. 'I wouldn't tell anybody else in the world, but for the first time in my life I'm really frightened.'

'Of what, Your Majesty?' asked Dagmar, dabbing at her tears.

'I don't know,' she said. 'Fear of the unknown. Fear itself. Whatever it is it's deep inside me, like a foreboding.'

'Courage,' said Dagmar. 'Your country is behind you. Nobody will desert you. And I'll always be beside you. Besides, didn't you tell me that the old soothsayer told you that you would reign until the sun went from west to east?'

'Yes, yes that's right, she did. I'll reign for ever and ever. How wise you are to remember, how stupid of me to forget. Well, let's get started, there's so much work to be done.'

Zenobia checked her tears then rose from her throne. She and Dagmar went into an ante-room and there she helped the Queen change from her robes of state into her uniform of a General-in-Chief of the Palmyrene army.

The two of them were ready for war. But Dagmar had no idea that Zenobia would have given half her fortune not to be fighting the one man, the only man left in the world that she cared about and found sexually attractive.

Bernice was sitting in the harem, desultorily stroking one of her slaves' breasts and idly wondering what she should do for the rest of the day. She was bored.

A part of her regretted not returning with Zenobia to

Palmyra. But the woman was such a prude. Listening to her talking, philosophy, art, and warfare, and listing the disgusting debauchery of the Romans and King Hairan et al, Bernice decided she could not have borne the restrictions Zenobia would have placed upon her and her needs in life. However, that was after Zenobia had been in Alexandria for a while. Bernice smiled to herself remembering how Zenobia's arrival in Alexandria had amused her.

Initially, when the army was marching towards the villa, they'd all been frightened. Nobody they knew would kill Romans and take over their garrison. They all thought it had to be the Persians or some barbaric tribe from Africa, even the dreaded Goths. Then, when Zenobia had stormed up to the villa in her great, golden carriage wearing her ceremonial cape of state over her soldier's uniform and announcing she was taking over Egypt, they had realised the soldiers were friendly. And a tremendous wave of relief had surged over them.

There had been a tearful reunion with Samoya. Zenobia forgave her for running away, even told her that she had tried to get her out of the palace before King Odainat had seen her. She had asked Samoya to go back to Palmyra. But she had refused, which was a mystery to Bernice. But then she was mistress of Firmus's household. And he obviously loved her. Bernice sighed. Firmus screwed her and various slaves from time to time but Samoya showed no jealousy. Samoya was affectionate towards Firmus but Bernice detected a distinct lack of passion. She accepted everything Firmus offered with good grace but Bernice came to the conclusion that Samoya was as bored as she was with her present way of life. It was as if total luxury was not enough. Both of them needed something more. A challenge. There were no challenges left in Egypt. Zenobia had everything running extremely well.

Bernice mused on the fun she had had when the Palmyrenes first began to run the country. There was a lot of work to do and she and Samoya and everyone in Firmus's household had participated. But now . . . Now it was different.

Samoya continued to organise 'entertainments' for Firmus. And during these she occasionally punished Bernice. Not as savagely as she had done on her arrival, but just enough to let Bernice know the tables were turned. Samoya was the mistress, Bernice the underling. And Bernice enjoyed it. Samoya knew how to place each stripe to maximum effect. She also knew how to pleasure a woman's intimate parts and exactly when Bernice needed a man. Bernice squirmed at the thought and tweaked the slave-girl's nipples. Perhaps she should remove the girl's clothes and play with her. Go down between her legs, open her labia with her fingers, let her tongue trail over the moistness until she found the girl's hard clitoris. Or should it be the other way round. Tell the girl to go down on her. Bernice opened her legs wide, lifted her robes and began to stroke herself. Perhaps she should send for the saddler. He had proved a consistent and worthwhile playmate, especially when he wore his heavily seamed leather penis-glove. Bernice began to feel more and more aroused.

Bernice was looking her loveliest and most licentious as she lay with her fingers stroking her sex-lips whilst gently sucking on the slave-girl's hard, rosy, pink nipple, when Samoya came into the room.

'Ah Bernice,' she said, 'you look as if you could do with a man.'

'Definitely,' drawled Bernice, parting Samoya's skirt, which instantly revealed her bare shaven pussy, and running a free hand along Samoya's legs.

'We have some unexpected visitors,' said Samoya, moving her hips as Bernice's fingers touched her moist sex. 'They've called to see Firmus but he's in a meeting.'

'Who are they?' asked Bernice.

235

'Never mind who, but I do know them both . . .' said Samoya.

'Know? How know?' asked Bernice.

'Not that well, not yet,' replied Samoya, laughing. 'And I haven't spoken to either of them yet. Just seen them from a distance. But I can tell you both of them look decidedly jaded and in need of cheering up. They told one of the slaves that the Romans are fighting down by the port and are beating the Palmyrenes but I don't believe it. Anyhow, I thought whilst they're waiting for Firmus . . .'

'Who's with him that's so important?' asked Bernice.

'One of Zenobia's Generals. At least he says he is, but he looks more like an actor from one of her plays . . . feathers and baubles everywhere. A caricature of a uniform he's got on. But Firmus knows him and insisted on absolute privacy. Anyhow, I thought perhaps we could give them a game of backgammon with a difference.'

Bernice looked up at Samoya's face and saw the look of sexual hunger. She knew exactly what Samoya meant by backgammon with a difference. And she was just in the mood. She called for a slave to brush her long, black hair and another to bring her one of her fine gossamer robes that accentuated her breasts and nipples and was elegantly slit from belly-button to hem.

In procession, with various female slaves behind them, Samoya and Bernice wandered leisurely into the great hall where they saw two men dressed in severe black and having their dusty feet washed.

'They look like Christians!' exclaimed Bernice.

'They are,' whispered Samoya. 'The slim handsome one is called Anthony, he's mine. The other one is called Paul. He's yours.'

'The big fat one!' said Bernice.

'Yes,' said Samoya, 'and he's not as fat as Firmus.'

'Couldn't we change,' said Bernice.

'No,' said Samoya, firmly.

She was tempted to tell Bernice that she had felt Anthony's cock a long time ago in Antioch, when she had wanted to find out whether men possessed the same equipment as the gods she had seen in the murals. And now some strange force of circumstances had led him to Alexandria and she was going to complete what she had started. She was going to have Anthony. But she resisted the temptation to confide. The choice was hers. She didn't need to offer Bernice any explanation. And she wasn't going to get one. Samoya pushed Bernice forward.

'Go and ask Paul to play with you,' she said. 'See what his reaction is.' If the rumours were true he would react rather well, with an immediate erection. But Samoya kept that to herself. She'd allow Bernice the fun of finding out.

Samoya handed a backgammon board to Bernice. 'I'll wait here for a moment,' she said, stepping back into the shadows of a marbled and mosaic archway. She didn't want Anthony to see her yet. She did want to watch what would happen when Bernice spoke so blatantly to the bishop.

Bernice sauntered over to Paul, but before she got to him she began to feel the force of his personality. There was something about the way the big man sat. Not like Firmus, with the arrogance of immense wealth. There was something else. Something spiritual and wonderfully contained but nevertheless outgoing. She stared at him as she glided across the marble floor. He was large but not flabby. He had strong features and long hair. He was an impressive figure of a man and Bernice was intrigued.

'I'm Princess Bernice,' she said, huskily, in her most sexy voice. 'And I want you to play with me.'

At the sound of her honeyed voice Paul looked up from his thoughts and from the slave washing his feet, saw Bernice, and thought she was magnificently sexual and the best thing that had happened to him since he had arrived in Egypt.

Paul of Samosata, the Bishop of Antioch was tired and weary. He had not had a good day. The temperature was high and so was the humidity; as a result he was hot and sticky. He disliked Alexandria. He had not wanted to come to the city but thought he had better put his own case to the assembled theologians, even though he knew it was a lost cause. They confirmed that they wanted him out of Antioch because of his heresy. And because of his love of women, his harem, and his general licentiousness. Not fit to be a bishop, they'd said. They had issued him with yet another ultimatum. Go or be thrown out by the new emperor. They had told him they had asked Lucius Aurelian for his help in evicting him. Paul had been furious but held his fury in check. If they realised how angry he was they'd send someone to Antioch before he had time to get there. He had pretended to accept their verdict, vowing inwardly to get back to his own city as soon as he could. Then, when he had ventured into the street he had found total mayhem, geese honking, people fleeing hither and thither in panic, mosquitoes biting and obnoxious Roman soldiers everywhere. And his carriage and horses missing.

The Romans, under their new commander and in the name of their new emperor, Lucius Aurelian, had retaken Alexandria from Zenobia and the Palmyrenes and were back manning their garrison. Whether his carriage and horses had been seconded by the Romans or stolen by urchins he didn't know but Bishop Paul knew that without transport he couldn't go anywhere. He was standing looking aimlessly about him when Anthony, his former secretary, suddenly appeared.

'I'm going with you,' Anthony had said.

'But you don't know where I'm going,' Paul had replied.

'It doesn't matter,' said Anthony. 'I'm not staying here. I don't agree with these Alexandrians.'

'Well, we can't go anywhere without my horses,' said Paul.

Then he had remembered Firmus. He had not seen him for some years. But they had been good friends. Perhaps Firmus would be able to help him. He must have horses and camels. He knew he kept elephants but Paul decided that was not the swiftest mode of transportation and he wanted to get to Antioch fast; before his fellow Christians, his enemies, installed their own new bishop.

When they arrived at the villa Paul realised nobody knew that a battle was raging down by the port, or that the Romans were swarming all over the stinking muddy estuary. Everything was beautiful and leisurely. The gardens were in bloom and being watered by slaves who ushered them into the vast marble hall to await Firmus who was in a business meeting. He had issued orders that he must not be disturbed under any circumstances. It was whilst Paul sat there with slaves tending his feet, having vaguely admired the alabaster carvings and the tapestries, the mosaics and the murals, that he heard the alluring voice asking him to play with her. He raised his eyes. Bernice smiled.

Her olive skin glowed, her black hair tumbled in thick curls, her lustrous big brown eyes gazed tantalisingly down into his. He took a deep breath and carried on staring at her, noting how her body was swathed in glorious gossamer that enhanced her rounded, feminine belly, her long thighs and her large breasts with their prominent dark red nipples. He clenched his fists. He wanted to touch them, caress her, ravish her. Whether it was because he was at a low ebb or whether his breath was taken away by her beauty, Paul was never to know. But the Bishop of Antioch fell instantly in love with Princess Bernice. She sank to her knees beside Paul and opened the backgammon set.

'Do you want to be white?' she asked, and felt a tingle of electricity rush through her body as she looked at him and felt the force of his sexuality. Quickly, to cover her confusion, she lowered her eyes back to the board. Paul reached out a hand and touched her face. The contact with him sent a tremor through her and she was unable to move. He put his hand under her chin, turned her face up to his and looked deeply into her large, deep brown eyes.

'Yes,' he said, but he didn't remove his hand. He was saying 'yes' to something more than her question. And Bernice knew it. She twisted away from him and set out the counters. She was shaking. Her hands had gone clammy. Her heart was beating at a rate she'd never known. And the Christian kept gazing at her, making her more aware of herself and her trembling body.

From the far end of the hall Samoya watched fascinated. Paul and Bernice were sitting on cushions on the floor opposite one another but it was as if both of them had gone into slow motion. Everything they did was done with great deliberation. And they stopped from time to time and just stared at one another.

Bernice was winning. She took his counters off the board and their hands touched. It should have been a brief fleeting touch but it seemed as if their fingers were suddenly glued together. Bernice's heart appeared to have left its rightful place and jumped into her throat. She swallowed hard and at that moment Paul's hand reached out for her breast. Bernice found all her coquetry had deserted her. She was unable to play the game. Any game. She was utterly overwhelmed by him. As his large hand held her nipple she stared up into his large, lugubrious, kindly, sensual face, trying to understand the sudden magnetism. But understanding eluded her. All she could do was feel. For the first time in her life Bernice knew passion and the beginnings of love. Real love.

'I want you,' said Paul, in his deep brown voice, that

thrilled her and made her tingle more everywhere, but especially between her legs.

'Yes,' she whispered, hoarsely.

'Forever,' he said, and leant forward and softly touched her lips with his.

'Yes,' she said, without thinking. Samoya saw the sudden soft and gentle kiss and was surprised. She had never seen Bernice kiss a man before she had had sex with him. Something different was happening. And an instinct within her told her not to disturb them. She ordered one of the slaves to bring Anthony to her.

Anthony looked hard at Samoya. Was it her? Was this the girl he had shown the murals to in the bishop's palace in Antioch and who had had the blonde slave, Irene, suck his cock under the table? He scanned her face. She had the same red-gold hair, but she had filled out, was far more voluptuous, and she was wearing make-up. Her lips were painted dark red, emphasising their fullness and her eyes were heavily rimmed with black kohl. She was unbelievably attractive and he got an instant erection.

Samoya glided towards him across the cool marble. As she did so she held her right hand out, palm uppermost. As she met him her palm made immediate contact with his crotch. With her left hand she pulled down the flimsy gauze covering her breasts, letting him see that they were criss-crossed with leather strips, and her large, rosy pink painted nipples stuck through, a silent invitation to feel them.

'Welcome,' she whispered, pressing her body close to his then taking hold of his hand and putting it on her thighs, where the slit in her trousers began, and where he could instantly touch her bare pussy.

'What's your name?' he asked, swallowing hard and shaking.

'What do you think it is?' she asked, squirming as his fingers found her moist sex-lips.

'Samoya,' he said.

'And you're quite correct, Anthony,' she said, rubbing his stiff member through his robe. 'Remember?'

'Yes,' he said.

'So do I,' said Samoya. 'Would you like a game of backgammon, or . . .?'

'Or?' he asked.

'Or would you like to do something else?' she said, wickedly, knowing full well as she rubbed his cock that was exactly what he wanted to do. 'Would you like to feel my breasts, bend me over, part my legs and . . .'

'Yes,' he said.

'Then come with me,' said Samoya, ignoring the waiting slaves and taking him by the hand and leading him into a small ante-room.

Samoya bent over a waist-high padded stool, and parted her legs. Anthony came up between them, raised his robe, exposed her buttocks and the next moment she felt his cock moving along her thighs, his fingers jerking inside her wet pussy. She wiggled her hips backwards and forwards and then, excited by her raised bare bottom, he took off his thick leather belt. He positioned his cock at her entrance, aimed it at her open, moist labia and gradually shoved it in to the depths of her vulva until she was impaled upon his manhood. He held her by her hips and thrust hard again and again, opening her further and further to his thick stiff sex. His testicles were gently knocking against her sex-lips and his shaft filled her up. She was gasping and gasping. The muscles of his hard body rippled against the softness of her bottom. He rode her, then with his hand he smacked her bare buttocks, wanting her to move faster and she responded to the fierceness of his slap. It brought tears to her eyes, but the sudden sharp pain also excited her. He did it again, still lunging his cock hard into her, riding her juiciness, holding her breasts, tweaking her nipples, then, leaving her wet and open, he stepped back. He brought the belt down across her buttocks. Samoya jumped and squealed at the swift, harsh pain.

'You're a wanton bitch,' he said. 'And you must be punished.'

Anthony brought the belt down again, exciting himself as a pink glow appeared on her pale bottom. He came up between her legs rubbing his cock along the soft erogenous zone of her inner thighs, then stepped back and lashed her again. Samoya was sighing and reeling and crying.

But Anthony had no intention of stopping, not yet. He had wanted to possess her for years and he knew she was secretly enjoying the thrashing he was giving her.

When her bottom was tingling, burning with the fresh red stripes, he licked it. Then he parted her sex and inserted his staff inside her again. Samoya rolled and heaved. They slid down to the floor. Without him pulling out, they turned and she was on her back, her legs high in the air, the marble cool against her hot flanks and he pounded surging backwards and forwards until he could feel her belly tighten and she was about to come. They climaxed together and lay side by side, satisfied.

Firmus marched through his villa trying to find Samoya. When he did she was lazing in the pool.

'Samoya,' he said, gazing at her sensuous body, and wondering what she'd been up to to cause her to take a dip in the middle of the day. But he had no time to do more than wonder, other far more important things were on his mind. 'I have some bad news for you. Zenobia's General, Timogenes, has been here. The Romans have taken over the port and there is going to be a battle for the whole of Egypt. I have promised Timogenes every support I can give him. What I want you to do is go to Palmyra and tell the Queen that no matter what happens she can always count on me.'

'You want me to go to Palmyra?' said Samoya, astonished.

'Yes.'

'But why me? Why not Princess Bernice?'

'It has to be you. You're the one person I can trust. Besides, didn't you tell me you can use a javelin?'

'Yes.'

'And you might need to. The journey is not easy, and in fact could be extremely hazardous.' Samoya climbed out of the pool, careful not to show Firmus the marks that Anthony had left on her bottom, and wrapped a towel around herself. Firmus took her into his arms.

'I love you, my darling,' he said, kissing her gently. 'But we all have to make sacrifices.'

Samoya knew trepidation, then fear, followed quickly by excitement. The unknown was reaching out to her. Her days of security were over. She was about to be released, older and wiser and perhaps better able to cope. She nuzzled into Firmus affectionately.

'Very well. But I don't have to travel alone, do I?'

'Of course not. You can take some slaves. The choice is yours.'

'Oh Firmus . . .' she said, remembering the bishop. 'Have you seen Paul?'

'Paul who?' he asked, tetchily.

'The Bishop of Antioch.'

'He's here!' Firmus exclaimed. 'Why didn't anybody tell me?'

'You left orders not to be disturbed. I left him in the great hall playing . . . backgammon . . . with Bernice.'

Firmus left straight away to find his guest and Samoya went off to arrange her belongings for her journey. She knew there were various things she'd need to pack that would not normally be thought of as part of a woman's travelling bag. She went into the kitchen garden and picked a number of herbs.

When Firmus met up with Paul in the great hall he found him holding Bernice's hands telling her about the troubles he was having with his church. And Bernice was gazing adoringly at him with the look of a lovesick young girl. Firmus stared at both of them uncomprehendingly. Paul jumped up at Firmus's approach and the two big men clasped one another in an affectionate embrace. Paul asked Firmus for help, explaining his need to get to Antioch fast. Firmus promised him horses and money and told him how to get out of the city avoiding the Romans. Then he took Paul to one side and whispered that Timogenes had been there and that with the change of emperor things did not look good for Zenobia and her forces. Paul knew that without Zenobia in power his position was extremely precarious. His need to get to Antioch was now doubled.

'I want to go with you,' said Bernice, quietly but firmly. Paul and Firmus looked at her as if she had said the desert was made of green cheese. 'I want to go with you. Please take me,' she said to Paul, pleading with her eyes.

'You want to leave all this!' exclaimed Paul.

'Yes,' she said. 'I want to be with you. I want to be with you always.'

Thrilled and delighted, Paul turned to Firmus and asked him for an extra horse.

'I have money of my own,' said Bernice.

'And you keep it. You'll need it,' said Paul, kissing the top of her head, thinking how strange the world was. Just when his life was at its darkest the most beautiful woman walked into it, prepared to undertake a journey into the unknown, into danger, and, if Zenobia lost the war, possibly into exile with him.

It was dusk. Samoya looked down on Palmyra from the hills above the city. She and her four companions were too exhausted to walk the final miles. Samoya ordered them to rest until morning. They had picked their way through the dead and dying soldiers who had littered most of Syria. They had managed to evade capture by victorious Romans, and rape by bandits. Even fleeing Palmyrenes had attacked them one night when they were sleeping.

As she lay down beside the women, Samoya gave a grim smile. Her herbs had come in handy. She and the girls had joined the soldiers in drinking wine and she had managed to drug them. They had stolen their uniforms whilst they lay in their stupor and put them on. Then, covering themselves again in their black cloaks they had carried on across the desert.

Samoya had wanted adventure. What she had got was a nightmare. War and the ravages of war were everywhere. Zenobia and her army were on the retreat. they had met nothing but hostility but Samoya decided whatever happened they must keep going. They had to get to the Queen and Palmyra. Knowing they were on the perimeter of safety, all of them slept well and deeply.

It was dawn, orange streaks lit up the sky and cast a rosy glow on the war-strewn land when Dagmar found the little group. She had been out trying to make contact with the Bedouin who had not kept their rendezvous. This made her nervous. Made her think of treachery and betrayal. Surely they would not have gone over to the Romans? But she feared they had changed their allegiance. Dagmar knew her duty was now to get back to the palace as quickly as she could and tell the Queen. Not only were her troops dead or deserting but the Bedouin had changed sides. This was a serious blow. They were Zenobia's policemen and her lifeline. They knew what was going on everywhere. If they had joined forces with the Romans then there was no hope for the Queen. Dagmar, dagger in hand, and wearing Bedouin robes was tiptoeing, edging her way past boulders and down the hillside when she saw a mass of black cloth lying beneath an outcrop.

Samoya was awake first. Her keen ears had picked

up the footfalls. Danger. The signal had run through her sleeping brain. Quickly she woke the others.

'Somebody's coming,' she said.

As she turned the corner in the pathway Dagmar was met by five filthy women in dirty, ill-fitting Palmyrene uniforms standing with javelins, poised to throw. Dagmar dropped her dagger and raised her hands high to show she offered them no harm.

'Who are you? Dagmar asked, and Samoya recognised her voice.

'Dagmar!' she said. 'It's me, Samoya, we've come from Egypt, from Firmus . . .'

The two women clasped each other, kissed and cried. They could not believe that finally they were meeting again. Samoya introduced her companions.

'They were slaves,' she said, 'but I've freed them. Now they are soldiers.'

Dagmar gave a slow grin and linked her arm with Samoya's.

'Come on we must get to the palace quickly. I think the worst is about to happen. The Romans are closing in on us.'

'We've passed nothing but dead and dying on our way here,' said Samoya, starting down the hill towards the city.

'I don't know what we do now,' said Dagmar, sadly. 'Neither do I know what the Queen does now.'

They entered Palmyra easily. There was no one at the gates. No customs man to take a toll of what they had or didn't have with them. The city was like a ghost town. Very little noise, no hustle and bustle.

'Where's everyone gone?' asked Samoya.

'Into the hills I suppose or to the Euphrates, anywhere where they'll be safe and well away from the fighting.'

'But,' said Samoya looking at the buildings which were all intact, 'there doesn't seem to have been any fighting here.'

'No, there hasn't been, and they're hoping if there isn't, if they offer no resistance to the Romans, they can come back and pick up their lives as if Zenobia had never existed,' said Dagmar.

The palace still had guards on the gates. They recognised Dagmar and let her through. She told them to allow Samoya and her troop to pass as well, which they did.

Zenobia was in her throne room. She had some loyal senators and Cassius the philosopher with her and was discussing what her next move should be when Dagmar, Samoya and her companions entered.

'I think you should go to Persia,' Cassius was saying. 'You signed a treaty with Shapur, the Persian emperor, he should honour it and come to your rescue.'

'But he doesn't answer my calls. How many messengers have you sent to him, Cassius?'

'Many, Your Majesty,' Cassius said.

'And not a single reply. I should have heard by now.'

'You will have to go, you yourself,' said Cassius. 'It's the only way.'

Dagmar looked at the Queen's face and felt deeply sorry for her. Retreat was not in her blood. But she was surrounded. The only roads free of Romans were the ones to the east, to the Euphrates, to Persia. Then the Queen saw Dagmar and her bedraggled companions.

'Dagmar, what news from the Bedouin?' she asked.

'They didn't keep their appointment, Your Majesty,' replied Dagmar, 'I think they've changed sides.'

'Then you must go to Persia,' said Cassius.

'Who is that with you?' asked Zenobia ignoring Cassius's remark.

'Samoya,' said Samoya, stepping forward. The Queen left her throne and came down to greet Samoya. She threw her arms around her and hugged and cried.

'Samoya, Samoya,' she said through her tears, then held her at arm's length. 'You look dreadful, quite dreadful.'

'We've had a terrible journey,' said Samoya simply.

Zenobia clapped her hands. Faithful slaves appeared.

'Food, we all need food,' she said. The slaves bowed and departed.

'I've a message for you from Firmus,' said Samoya. 'It's this: no matter what happens you can always count on him. He will give you whatever help and support he can. He couldn't come as he's helping Timogenes.'

'And what was the position in Alexandria when you left?' asked Zenobia.

'Very bad, the Romans had retaken the port and there was fierce fighting all over Egypt.'

'And I've lost everything,' said Zenobia. 'All my lands in the north; Antioch is Roman again. And that terrible Lucius Aurelian has banished Paul the Bishop. Sent him into exile. That's what his Christians wanted and that's what he did. Poor Paul.'

'Did he go alone?' asked Samoya.

'I don't know,' replied Zenobia.

'Tell me, is it the same Lucius Aurelian we met outside Antioch?' asked Samoya.

'It is,' said Zenobia, with fury.

'Oh!' exclaimed Samoya, but the rest of her thoughts were forgotten as food arrived, was laid out on the tables in front of them and they began to eat.

It was whilst they were eating that Zenobia remembered the day she had met Lucius Aurelian. It had also been the day she had met the old crone who had told her she would be loved by two emperors. And wasn't Shapur an emperor? The Emperor of the Persians. So that was the answer. She must go to Persia, Shapur would fall in love with her and give her anything she wanted. She and Palmyra would rise again.

'Cassius is quite right,' said Zenobia, seemingly apropos of nothing. With food in various stages from a plate to their mouths everybody looked at her quite blankly. 'I shall go to Persia.'

'How?' asked Samoya.

'What do you mean, how? I shall ride across the desert to the Euphrates River and then I'll take a boat . . .' said Zenobia.

'You can't ride across the desert as Queen Zenobia of Palmyra, the Romans or their allies would kill you,' said Samoya.

'Mmm,' Zenobia saw the sense in that. 'In that case I shall go as an ordinary citizen. We'll all go as ordinary citizens,' said Zenobia.

'How ordinary?' asked Samoya.

'I shall go dressed as a washerwoman, and you can go as whatever you like,' announced Zenobia, then a thought struck her. 'Or, perhaps you prefer not to go at all?'

'No, no, we'll go with you,' said Samoya. 'Won't we?'

And Dagmar agreed and so did Samoya's warriors. The senators said they thought it best if they stayed in Palmyra and carried on running the city. But to everyone's surprise Cassius agreed to accompany Zenobia and her party.

'Oh no, Cassius,' said Zenobia, 'that's not necessary.'

'Oh but it is, Your Majesty,' he said, bowing very low so she couldn't see the look of smirking triumph on his treacherous face. 'You see, you'll need protection. I've heard Aurelian's troops are everywhere. He's going from west to east – with his sun god.'

Blind panic gripped Zenobia when she heard that. The old crone's voice echoed in her head. 'Only when the sun goes from west to east will your reign end.'

Chapter Twelve

*S*amoya stood on the balcony of her villa and looked across at the hills, then down to the Tiber making its dark brown and desultory progress through the city of Rome below. She was wearing the most fashionable and elegantly draped robe made from the finest soft grey silk. It emphasised the curves of her womanly body, outlining her well-shaped breasts and picking up on the violet-blue colour of her eyes. Her lovely red-gold hair was hanging loose. The house was, for once, pleasantly quiet and she was happily waiting for her husband to come home.

As she stood there she saw two figures making their way along the winding footpath to her home. The sun glinted on the taller one of the two. Samoya recognised a familiar stride. She smiled a smile of pure delight and rang the bell for her slaves, told them visitors were arriving and they were to be made extra welcome. The best wines were to be brought from the cellar and the best cheeses delivered to the table. Samoya turned back and stood staring out at Rome thinking the view she had now was not the view she'd had when she had first arrived.

Then, she had seen Rome as a stinking, heaving,

rotting mass of narrow alleyways, shrieking people, grand buildings, thievery, skulduggery, whores, gladiators, and the occasional triumphant procession. She had been a prisoner, fettered and abused, displayed and used.

Samoya remembered how she had been shackled to the wall in a grim cell, the cries of street traders coming up through the open window mingling with the stench of the Tiber. She was filthy, so were the scrappits of hay she'd been lying on. She had looked across at Dagmar who was in no better a state. They had been paraded. The crowd had thrown things at them, jeered at them, pelted them with rotten food and the smell inside and outside the cell had overwhelmed them. They had no idea how long they were going to stay prisoners. What would happen to them if they were released? Would they be sold as slaves? Would they be executed?

'Well, anyway, that Cassius got his just deserts for betraying us,' said Samoya, remembering how the Emperor Lucius Aurelian had ordered his execution. That had surprised everyone. They all thought they would be the ones who would meet an untimely end, especially Zenobia. But no. After he had won the bitter war between himself and the Palmyrene Queen he had put Cassius on trial for treason, had him executed and had taken Zenobia and her followers as his prize prisoners to Rome.

'She looked magnificent, didn't she?' said Dagmar, referring to Zenobia, who had been draped in golden chains and displayed in Aurelian's triumphant march along with all his other captives. 'The crowd were almost too scared to throw things at her.'

'But where is she now?' asked Samoya, anxiously. 'Two weeks and not a word about her.'

Zenobia had been held in the cell with them but after the procession she had disappeared.

The two women had felt acutely alone. They were

chained too far apart to touch one another, have a cuddle, cry on each other's shoulder, share their grief at the death of Timogenes in battle in Egypt and for Firmus who had gone missing after raising an army in favour of Zenobia and against Rome – fighting for Palmyra to be Palmyrene again. But Aurelian had heard. He'd force-marched his men back to Syria and had razed Palmyra to the ground. Only a few pillars of the Temple of the Sun God were left standing.

Suddenly the doors of their prison were clanked open and a soldier stepped inside, unlocked Samoya and Dagmar from their fetters and told them both to follow him.

They were taken along narrow winding corridors then into a large room and told to sit on a chair and wait. Then the soldier had departed. Samoya and Dagmar looked at one another in amazement. They were past fear. Some moments later an old woman appeared with fresh clothing over her arm.

'You're to come with me,' she said. And they followed the old crone down some more corridors until she opened a huge door and they found they were in a communal bath-house.

'What's happening?' Samoya asked.

'You'll find out,' said the old woman, with a toothless grin. 'Now get in the water and wash yourselves.'

The joy of floating in fresh clear water, the filth of days of journeying and the dirty cells slowly washed away from their bodies and their spirits had revived. They began to splash around and play. After a while the old woman called them out and dressed them in fine, bleached white linen shifts and delicate leather sandals. Then a couple more soldiers came, handcuffed them and ordered them to march behind them.

They were taken out into the sunlight and through a part of the city they had not seen when they'd been paraded as Lucius Aurelian's prisoners. It was an area of elegant and wealthy villas. They climbed the hill in neat formation behind the soldiers. When they arrived at the top they were faced with the biggest, most elegant villa of them all. And the soldiers pulled on the bell at the gates.

Another soldier came out to greet them. The soldiers escorting Samoya and Dagmar saluted, pushed the two women through the open gates and departed back down the hill.

A female slave met them on the steps and ushered them into the main hall, which was stylishly but not ostentatiously designed. She told Dagmar to sit on a silk and gold couch and left her handcuffs on. She asked Samoya to follow her. As she did so, both women looked at each other helplessly. Were they now to be parted? Was this a slave merchant's house? Were they about to be sold?

The female slave then indicated she wanted Samoya to cross the courtyard filled with potted orange and lemon trees, and bay trees and pots of sweet smelling rosemary and thyme and basil. Then they entered under an archway into the inner sanctum of the huge villa. Once there, the slave opened two enormous doors and bowed Samoya into the room.

Full of trepidation, Samoya walked in and found to her great surprise Zenobia sitting on the floor playing backgammon with her son. They both jumped up when they saw her, rushed to greet her, and held her tightly. Then the slave told Zenobia's son he had to leave his mother. She collected up the backgammon board and promised him a game whilst his mother was busy on state business.

'I don't understand,' said Samoya, looking and feeling completely perplexed.

'The Emperor's orders,' said Zenobia.

'What is?' asked Samoya.

'Everything is. Me being here, you and Dagmar being released,' said Zenobia. 'Come, sit here beside me and I will tell you. Remember how that old woman we met outside Antioch said I would be loved by two emperors . . .?'

'Yes, and she told Dagmar she'd be a soldier and me a widow twice before I was a mother,' said Samoya.

'Well,' said Zenobia, 'I thought the second emperor had to be Shapur. That's why I agreed to go to Persia. But it wasn't. The second emperor is Lucius Aurelian.'

Zenobia looked at Samoya, her eyes shining bright.

'Lucius Aurelian loves me,' said Zenobia simply.

'But that's terrible,' said Samoya.

'Of course it's not, don't be ridiculous. How else do you think I managed to get you and Dagmar released,' said Zenobia sharply.

'It is, because he's married,' said Samoya.

'And that's why he gave me this beautiful villa,' explained Zenobia.

'This is your villa?'

'Yes.'

'But what are you going to do all day? You'll be bored.'

'No I won't,' said Zenobia, firmly. 'There's work to be done here. Look at the place. It's so . . . so ordinary, so classical. Such good taste. It needs some life, some exuberance. I'll have gold there and there and murals and tapestries everywhere and cushions, instead of these ridiculous chairs. Of course the Roman matrons will scoff, "typically Palmyrene, no breeding my dear" that's what they'll say behind my back. But they'll come to gawp. And they'll eat my food and drink my wine. No Samoya, I won't be bored; besides, the Emperor comes to see me every day.'

'You'll get tired of making love,' said Samoya, pragmatically.

'He doesn't come to see me just to make love!' exclaimed Zenobia. 'Although that is wonderful.'

Zenobia gazed into the middle distance dreamily thinking how wonderful it really was. The most power-ful man in the world who for her was also the most sexually exciting, was her lover. But then in Zenobia's mind the two were always combined. Sex without power held no aphrodisia for Zenobia.

When they had finally come face to face, she the captive, he the General – the Emperor, they had looked at one another and remembered that day outside Antioch when he had helped her onto a stretcher. And the memory had made both of them tremble. Their eyes had locked into each other's as it had done before; with a deep longing. Lucius Aurelian had treated the deposed queen well. He had kept his distance from her but made sure she was comfortable on the marches and on the boat that took them to Rome. Once there he'd had no option but to throw her in with the rest of the prisoners and parade her for his greater glory, the greatest trophy of his Palmyrene campaign. But after his victory parade he'd had her brought to him.

'Well, what else does the Emperor come to see you for?' enquired Samoya.

'Work,' replied Zenobia.

'Work!' exclaimed Samoya.

'Yes. He said I ran Palmyra and her dominions exceptionally well and that Rome needs somebody to organise it. He's been away on too many campaigns and so I'm mapping out new laws and . . .'

'What new laws?' asked Samoya interrupting and mystified.

'Corn laws for the poor, stabilising the monetary system, building a new wall around the city, like mine around Palmyra . . .'

'Oh I see!' said Samoya. 'And of course he'll get the credit for it.'

'Yes, unfortunately he will. But does it matter? Life will be better for everyone.'

'And you're going to do this all on your own!' said Samoya, a touch of disbelief in her voice.

'No, he's sending a scribe to help me.'

'And do you know what's going to happen to me and to Dagmar?'

'No, that depends on you,' said Zenobia.

'Depends on us!' exclaimed Samoya annoyed. How could anything depend on them? They were prisoners. They couldn't get back to their own country. 'You mean it depends on us whether we are sold into slavery or executed?'

Zenobia's reply was stopped by the sound of trumpets and the doors flung open. His Imperial Majesty, Lucius Aurelian, the Emperor of Rome strode in with his escort. Zenobia and Samoya bowed.

Briefly acknowledging Samoya, Lucius Aurelian took hold of Zenobia's hand, kissed it then led her to a chair.

'Has anything been mentioned?' he whispered in Zenobia's ear.

'No. She's completely bemused. Doesn't know if she and Dagmar are to be sold or executed.'

Whilst the Emperor and Zenobia talked in whispers, Samoya glanced about the room and then looked at Lucius's escort. Fine figures of men all of them, in their uniforms, their short tunics, their breast-plates and their helmets. Well trained, good fighting men with rippling muscles. She looked at their arms and legs, sun-tanned and scarred from the battles they had fought. But one of them wasn't sun-tanned. He was black. Coal-black, and his skin had a silky, glistening blue sheen. She gave a sigh. She had only ever known one man with skin like that. Marcus. Marcus whom she'd loved and longed for. Marcus, whom she'd dreamed about in Palmyra and in Alexandria, on marches, crossing deserts, on the storm-tossed boat that brought her to Rome. Marcus, whom she had imagined touching her, caressing her when she was at her lowest ebb. Marcus. Why had she been so foolish as to let him think she wanted to be married to Prince Alif? Had it been her arrogance? Her temper? All that was another world away. She put it out of her mind.

The Emperor was looking at her. So was Zenobia, but the black soldier wasn't. His eyes stared straight ahead. He stayed rigid and to attention, his eyes never leaving the figure of the Emperor. Samoya straightened her back, stood more erect. Nobody must realise what she was thinking. The Emperor turned back to whisper again to Zenobia. Samoya tried her hardest to decipher the face under the heavy Roman helmet. Then her heart gave a massive leap. It was Marcus. Samoya's heart started pounding. Her mouth went dry. She felt her face flush. Her whole body began to shake. She could not believe her eyes. Marcus was in the same room as her and as gloriously handsome as ever. She eyed his muscular thighs beneath his tunic, his broad chest, and what she could of his handsome face – it seemed a little older, and more interesting because of it. Samoya longed to run to him, to feel his skin, to touch him, to kiss his lips. So near and yet so far, she thought. And then the Emperor kissed Zenobia's hands, nodded his head in her direction and departed, taking his escort with him.

Samoya was left with a deep feeling of anti-climax. She couldn't think what to do or what to say. Suddenly she felt deeply sleepy.

'You have had a very busy day,' said Zenobia, looking at Samoya with interest, noticing how the colour had drained from her face when the escort departed. 'Would you like to lie down?'

'Yes,' she said. 'But what did the Emperor say? Did he tell you what was to become of me, and Dagmar?'

'No, but my new scribe will arrive shortly,' said Zenobia, clapping her hands for her slaves. 'But you must rest now. I expect the Emperor will tell me later of his decisions .'

The slave came in and Zenobia ordered her to take Samoya to the guest bedroom. The great doors were opened to let her pass, then closed behind her. And Samoya was face to face with Marcus. Neither of them could move. It was as if both were transfixed to the spot. But the accompanying slave wasn't and she silently withdrew, leaving the two of them alone.

'Marcus!' Samoya gulped, tears of joy springing to her eyes.

'Samoya!' he said and held out his arms. He took two steps towards her and engulfed her in a passionate embrace. 'Samoya, I thought I'd lost you forever. I've never stopped thinking of you, wondering what had become of you. And I've never stopped loving you.'

'Marcus,' was all she could say before his lips came down on hers, gently at first, then deeper, searching her mouth with his tongue, wanting to take all of her in one movement. He slid his hands down her body, holding her buttocks, pulling her closer to him so that she could feel the strength and length of his arousal. The moment he touched her Marcus's stomach had tightened into an excited knot. One of his hands left her bottom and travelled upwards, to her breast, to her nipples.

Samoya gasped. She was shaking as if she had never had a man touch her before. The excitement within her was running riot. Her nerve endings were on edge, wanted to be soothed down, wanting to be stroked.

Marcus picked her up in his arms and ran with her along the wide corridor.

'Marcus, Marcus, where are you taking me?' she half-squealed, half-laughed.

'To bed,' he said, his honey-coloured voice exciting her.

He kicked open a door that was ajar and ran with her to a great, high bed.

'I'm supposed to be lying down in the guest-room,' she said.

'This is the guest-room and you are lying down,' he replied, flinging himself on top of her, pulling up her robe so that her thighs, her belly, her sex were exposed to his gaze. 'Marcus . . .' she began.

259

'Ssshh,' he said, closing her mouth with his lips and stroking her open legs, letting his fingers wander softly to the top of her thighs. 'I want you.'

Samoya could feel the hardness of his member against her body, she twisted slightly under him so that her hand could search for his manhood. She had to feel it, encompass it, play with it, suck it. His fingers started to penetrate her willingness. Her sex opened beneath his soft, exploring fingers. She squirmed and gasped as he dived deeper into her loving wantonness. Then she wriggled away from him so that he could remove his clothing and she could take off her robe.

Naked, they lay beside each other, stroking and feeling, a whirl of anticipation flowing between them. Slowly she snaked her way down his body and took his manhood into her mouth. He lifted and turned her so that her pink, juicy sex was hovering against his lips. He trailed his tongue along her wetness and then nibbled at her hard small protuberance, making her muscles contract and her body squirm. Together they floated on a sea of sensuality, their bodies entwined like dancers and moving on eath other's moisture. Her hard nipples pressed against his muscular chest, his hard penis pressing between her thighs. Then he took her hands, clasped them together above her head and let his cock push between her thighs where his fingers had been. She opened her legs further, wider. She had to take him. There was a great need inside her to feel him conquering her. Slowly, with great deliberation, his cock pushed through her wet sex-lips. She gasped again and again as she felt his magnificent member take control of her. Her hips rose upwards to meet each thrust. His lips came down on hers at the moment his cock found the centre of her being. Then, as his tongue moved fast and furiously inside her mouth so his prick imitated that movement, pounding into her sex.

'Take me. Keep taking me,' her brain, her body, her

mind was saying, every ounce of her responding to every ounce of him.

They were tingling, throbbing with pent up emotion and both of them felt, at the same time, the same primeval curl of essential being within the depths of their stomachs, and also felt it crying out to be released.

Samoya raised her hips higher to take more of him and he pushed harder into her, possessing more of her. And then the rush hit them. Love and energy came pouring down through their bodies and in one gigantic explosion of tensed muscles the two of them climaxed simultaneously. Marcus held her tightly, showing no inclination to leave. She began to speak. She wanted to tell him things. She also wanted to ask him questions but he put a finger over her mouth.

'Marry me,' he said.

Samoya cuddled into the well of his arm.

'Yes,' she said. 'But what will the Emperor say?'

'I think that's the news the Emperor wants to hear,' he replied.

'You mean . . . the Emperor set us up? Arranged for you to come here as his escort?' she said in amazement.

'I mean exactly that,' said Marcus. 'You see, I told him I wanted you. But I wanted to be sure you wanted me. The Emperor understood that. He doesn't like coercion. I'm not really part of his escort. I am a commander of the legions.'

'Where were you then when he was in Syria?'

'I was in the Ukraine fighting the Goths,' he said. 'But now they're beaten . . .'

'And so are we,' said Samoya.

'Yes, but you are in Rome and I have a beautiful villa up in the hills and I want you to be my wife and . . . Will you marry me?'

'Yes Marcus. I will because I love you. I've always loved you. I wanted to run away and marry you when I first met you.'

'And I did too,' he replied, kissing her cheek then

261

rolling off the bed. 'Come, I want to tell the Emperor that you've agreed to marry me.'

Dagmar had been left sitting alone for a long time. She had watched the Emperor and his escort come and go. A slave brought her peppermint tea to drink and a selection of delicious small cakes to eat. She asked why she was being kept waiting. The slave told her that soon she would understand but she was not at liberty to give her any reasons.

Then a young man arrived. He told the slave he was the scribe sent by the Emperor. Dagmar and the young man sat side by side silently waiting to be called.

Dagmar took a number of furtive glances at him. She was sure she had seen him somewhere before. But she couldn't remember where. She started to look at him more carefully. He was shortish but handsome, he had hazel eyes and light brown hair. He had long tapering, almost feminine fingers and Dagmar found them curiously erotic. She looked at his sandalled feet. They were long and tapering too. To Dagmar's complete surprise she began to wonder what other parts of him were like. Did he have a long tapering penis? As she thought that her brain did a somersault. She remembered. He was Anthony, Bishop Paul's secretary in Antioch, the one whose cock she had sucked when he should have been playing backgammon with Samoya. Dagmar remembered that she had found him desperately attractive then, but as a slave she could do very little about it. She looked down at her handcuffed wrists. She was no more, no less than a slave now. Perhaps because of her restraints she allowed her imagination to go wild. She imagined finishing the job that Samoya had started so long ago. She thought of her hands going up under Anthony's robe and finding, then feeling his shaft.

Anthony was sitting beside the blonde woman feeling puzzled. She was pale-skinned and blonde. She looked as if she should be a slave. She wasn't dressed like one

262

but she was handcuffed. Anthony found that erotic. He started thinking of having sex with a woman who not only had her hands bound but her feet as well. Mentally he stripped the blonde woman beside him. Imagined her breasts, her luscious bare bottom. What was she? Who was she? He was convinced her face was familiar. But he could not recall where he could have seen her before. There was something thrilling about her. Anthony found his penis twitching, growing of its own accord. He shifted uncomfortably in his seat and as he did their eyes met.

'Is your name Anthony?' Dagmar asked.

'Yes,' he replied, more mystified than ever.

'Are you a Christian?' she asked.

'Mmm, yes,' he said, with some hesitancy. It wasn't always a good idea to admit to being one.

'My mother was too,' said Dagmar.

'Then you should be,' he said.

'Possibly,' she said, but from what she'd seen so far of the behaviour of Christians she wasn't convinced that they were any better than anyone else.

Dagmar moved her gaze from Anthony's face to his lap. That was when she noticed his bulge. She found herself with an almost uncontrollable desire to touch it. Well, she could. She would do what Samoya had done before. She would fall on the floor. Of course the handcuffs were a problem, but not an insurmountable one. But did she want to do that?

'Were you employed as the Bishop of Antioch's secretary?' Dagmar asked, bringing her hands up to her head as if she had a blinding headache.

'Yes,' he replied, swallowing hard. Her bringing up her bound wrists was infernally erotic. 'How did you know?'

'I pleasured you at the merchant Pernel's house. And I'd like to do the same thing now.'

'Would you!' Anthony exclaimed, shifting in his seat,

opening his legs, and even more excited than he was before.

'Yes, I would,' said Dagmar, and she slipped down and knelt in front of him.

Anthony stayed as if glued to his chair and watched her handcuffed hands disappear under his robe and then the coldness of them touch the warmth of his stiff member. Then her head disappeared under his robe as well. He let out a great sigh as her mouth clamped over his cock and she began to suck. Up and down went her head under his clothing, up and down went her mouth over the tip of his penis, up and down went her hands along his shaft.

Anthony's legs shot out, he braced himself against the back of the chair as he could feel his sap rising. She was working him up into a frenzy. Infernal handcuffed woman, he thought. And wanted desperately to have her. Have her bound and lying naked in front of him. Touch her buttocks. Even, the thought crossed his inflamed mind, chastise her a little for turning him on to such a degree. With those thoughts falling over one another in his mind, with the idea of smacking Dagmar's bare bottom he lost control and released himself into her mouth.

Anthony and Dagmar were back sitting quietly side by side when the slave came to collect Dagmar. She still had no idea who she was going to see, why she had been brought to the villa, or where Samoya had disappeared to.

She followed the slave who opened the high doors into the chamber where Zenobia was sitting with Samoya and a man. They both turned round as she entered. Dagmar got a shock when she recognised Marcus. She got a shock but nothing more, no leftovers of desire. She had decided she wanted Anthony. There was a strange mixture of the dominant and wanting to be dominated in him that appealed to her.

264

Zenobia stood up and held out her arms to Dagmar. They embraced.

'I am sorry that you had to wait so long,' said Zenobia.

'Oh, I managed to amuse myself,' said Dagmar.

'I have some news to tell you. Samoya, and Marcus the handsome young man beside her . . .'

'Hello, Marcus,' said Dagmar, shaking his hand as if they'd never met. Their episode on the banks of the Orontes would be their secret. There was no need to tell anyone about it. It was over and done with.

'. . . have decided to marry,' finished Zenobia.

'I'm so very happy for you both,' said Dagmar kissing Samoya and nodding her head in Marcus's direction.

'I didn't want to part you and Samoya so I had to know what she wanted to do before I could ask you to come here and live with me,' said Zenobia.

'As what?' asked Dagmar warily.

'My son mustn't forget his roots,' said Zenobia. 'I want you to tell him the tales and teach him the way of the desert. Will you do that?'

Dagmar didn't have to think about it for too long. She knew Zenobia and all her ways, both generous and irritating.

'Yes,' she said.

'Tell the scribe to come here,' said Zenobia, clapping her hands, imperiously. One of her slaves left the room to return some moments later with Anthony.

'Anthony!' exclaimed Samoya. 'Anthony! You! What are you doing in Rome?'

'I'm a Roman,' he said. 'A Christian Roman. That's why I went to Antioch, to learn from Bishop Paul. And Aurelian sent me back to Rome.'

It was Zenobia's turn to be amazed. 'You knew Bishop Paul?' she exclaimed.

'I was his secretary,' he replied.

'Anthony, please, tell us if you know,' said Samoya, 'when the bishop was exiled did anybody go with him?'

'Yes,' he replied. 'A woman called Bernice. She refused to leave his side. Said she loved and adored him, he was her life, without him she was nothing. So she was ordered into exile with him.'

And whatever hardships everyone in the room had gone through they all found that piece of information completely uplifting. Samoya and Zenobia smiled at one another. With happiness and relief.

'And now you are to be my scribe, my secretary,' said Zenobia.

'Yes, ma'am,' he said.

And Dagmar allowed herself a quiet inward smile. If they were both working at Zenobia's villa there would be plenty of time for them to play together.

Samoya heard the clanking of the bell in front of her gates. Her visitors had arrived. She passed the dining room noticing the bread, cheeses and cold meats, olives and other snack delicacies laid out ready for an *al fresco* meal. And the different types of wine opened with large silver goblets beside them. Then Samoya went out to the main steps to greet Dagmar and her husband, Anthony and their new baby.

'We've just come from the Queen,' said Dagmar, who couldn't get used to calling her anything else. 'She suggests we call the baby Luke. It's Christian but has a hint of Lucius about it.'

Samoya laughed and was reaching for the wine when Marcus walked in.

'My wife's at the bottle again, is she?' he said, kissing Samoya.

'For the first time in ages,' replied Samoya as the nurse came in carrying two babies and the peace of the house was shattered as they began to howl.

'My twins,' said Marcus proudly. 'Let's drink to everyone, and especially the babies, to Luke and Theodosius and Zainab. May they all have a long life and a good one.'

'Theodosius I know is Greek meaning gift of God, but I've never heard the name Zainab before. What does it mean?' asked Anthony.

'It means life from Zeus,' said Samoya with a completely straight face. Wild horses would not drag from her the fact that it was Zenobia's Syrian name. What the Romans didn't know they couldn't fight and argue about.

Marcus poured the wine. Samoya looked at everyone in turn. Each of them had travelled a long way but in the end all their roads had led to Rome.

Queen Zenobia ruled Palmyra and her dominions from 267 AD–272 AD when Lucius Aurelian beat her in war and took her to Rome. He surprised everyone by not putting her to death but gave her a mansion overlooking the Tiber, and she outlived him.

Paul of Samosata, the heretical Bishop of Antioch, was banished by the Emperor Lucius Aurelian who was the first Roman Emperor to make a ruling for the Christians in a dispute within their community.

Firmus the incredibly wealthy Egyptian, originally from Selucia, vanished after organising an uprising in favour of Zenobia against the Romans. Some say Aurelian had him put to death.

Timogenes was a famous and extremely brave Palmyrene warrior. He was killed in Egypt.

King Odainat was a brilliant General who married Zenobia and was murdered by his nephew Prince Maaen.

King Hairan was a particularly nasty, debauched man and it is rumoured he was murdered by Odainat, possibly with Zenobia's help.

Prince Maaen killed his uncle King Odainat and would have killed Zenobia but it is thought she was alerted and killed him instead.

Cassius Longinus was a Neo-Platonist philosopher who was hanged by Lucius Aurelian for treason and treachery.

Lucius Aurelian, a peasant from Pannonia, rose through the ranks to become Emperor of Rome. He ruled from 270 AD–275 AD.

Visit the Black Lace website at
www.blacklace-books.co.uk

FIND OUT THE LATEST INFORMATION AND TAKE
ADVANTAGE OF OUR FANTASTIC FREE BOOK OFFER!
ALSO VISIT THE SITE FOR . . .

- All Black Lace titles currently available
  and how to order online

- Great new offers

- Writers' guidelines

- Author interviews

- An erotica newsletter

- Features

- Cool links

BLACK LACE – THE LEADING IMPRINT
OF WOMEN'S SEXY FICTION

TAKING YOUR EROTIC READING
PLEASURE TO NEW HORIZONS

LOOK OUT FOR THE ALL-NEW BLACK LACE BOOKS – AVAILABLE NOW!

All books priced £6.99 in the UK. Please note publication dates apply to the UK only. For other territories, please contact your retailer.

NOBLE VICES
Monica Belle
ISBN 0 352 33738 9

Annabelle doesn't want to work. She wants to spend her time riding, attending exotic dinner parties and indulging herself in even more exotic sex, at her father's expense. Unfortunately, Daddy has other ideas, and when she writes off his new Jaguar, it is the final straw. Sent to work in the City, Annabelle quickly finds that it is not easy to fit in, especially when what she thinks of as harmless, playful sex turns out to leave most of her new acquaintances in shock. **Naughty, fresh and kinky, this is a very funny tale of a spoilt rich English girl's fall from grace.**

A MULTITUDE OF SINS
Kit Mason
ISBN 0 352 33737 0

This is a collection of short stories from a fresh and talented new writer. Ms Mason explores settings and periods that haven't previously been covered in Black Lace fiction, and her exquisite attention to detail makes for an unusual and highly arousing collection. Female Japanese pearl divers tangle erotically with tentacled creatures of the deep; an Eastern European puppeteer sexually manipulates everyone around her; the English seaside town of Brighton in the 1950s hides a thrilling network of forbidden lusts. **Kit Mason brings a wonderfully imaginative dimension to her writing and this collection of her erotic short stories will dazzle and delight.**

Coming in December

THE HEAT OF THE MOMENT
Tesni Morgan
ISBN O 352 33742 7

Amber, Sue and Diane – three women from an English market town –
are successful in their businesses, but all want more from their private
lives. When they become involved in The Silver Banner – an English Civil
War re-enactment society – there's plenty of opportunity for them to
fraternise with handsome muscular men in historical uniforms. Thing is,
the fun-loving Cavaliers are much sexier than the Puritan Roundheads,
and tensions and rivalries are played out on the village green and the
bedroom. **Great characterisation and oodles of sexy fun in this story of
three English friends who love dressing up.**

WICKED WORDS 7
Various
ISBN O352 33743 5

Hugely popular and immensely entertaining, the *Wicked Words*
collections are the freshest and most cutting-edge volumes of women's
erotic stories to be found anywhere in the world. The diversity of themes
and styles reflects the multi-faceted nature of the female sexual
imagination. Combining humour, warmth and attitude with fun, filthy,
imaginative writing, these stories sizzle with horny action. Only the most
arousing fiction makes it into a *Wicked Words* volume. This is the best in
fun, sassy erotica from the UK and USA. **Another sizzling collection of
wild fantasies from wicked women!**

OPAL DARKNESS
Cleo Cordell
ISBN O 352 33033 3

It's the latter part of the nineteenth century and beautiful twins Sidonie and Francis are yearning for adventure. Their newly awakened sexuality needs an outlet. Sent by their father on the Grand Tour of Europe, they swiftly turn cultural exploration into something illicit. When they meet Count Constantin and his decadent friends and are invited to stay at his snow-bound Romanian castle, there is no turning back on the path of depravity. **Another wonderfully decadent piece of historical fiction from a pioneer of female erotica.**

Coming in January 2003

STICKY FINGERS
Alison Tyler
ISBN O 352 33756 7

Jodie Silver doesn't have to steal. As the main buyer for a reputable import and export business in the heart of San Francisco, she has plenty of money and prestige. But she gets a rush from pocketing things that don't belong to her. It's a potent feeling, almost as gratifying as the excitement she receives from engaging in kinky, exhibitionist sex – but not quite. Skilled at concealing her double life, Jodie thinks she's unstoppable, but with detective Nick Hudson on her tail, it's only a matter of time before the pussycat burglar meets her comeuppance. **A thrilling piece of West Coast noir erotica from Ms Tyler.**

STORMY HAVEN
Savannah Smythe
ISBN O 352 33757 5

Daisy Lovell has had enough of her over-protective Texan millionaire
father, Felix, and is determined to get away from his interfering ways.
The last straw is when Felix forbids her to date a Puerto Rican boy.
Determined to see some of the world, Daisy goes storm chasing across
the American Midwest for some sexual adventure. She certainly finds it
among truckers and bikers and a state trooper. What Daisy doesn't know
is that Felix has sent personal bodyguard Max Decker to join the storm
tour and watch over her. However, no one can foresee that hardman
Decker will fall for Daisy is a big way. **Fantastic characterization and lots
of really hot sex scenes across the American desert.**

SILKEN CHAINS
Jodi Nicol
ISBN O 352 33143 7

Fleeing from her scheming guardians at the prospect of an arranged
marriage, the beautiful young Abbie is thrown from her horse. On
regaining consciousness she finds herself in a lavish house modelled on
the palaces of Indian princes – and the virtual prisoner of the extremely
wealthy and attractive Leon Villiers, the Master. Eastern philosophy and
eroticism form the basis of the Master's opulent lifestyle and he
introduces Abbie to sensual pleasures beyond the bounds of her
imagination. **By popular demand, another of the list's bestselling
historical novels is reprinted.**

Black Lace Booklist

Information is correct at time of printing. To avoid disappointment
check availability before ordering. Go to www.blacklace-books.co.uk.
All books are priced £6.99 unless another price is given.

BLACK LACE BOOKS WITH A CONTEMPORARY SETTING

☐ THE TOP OF HER GAME Emma Holly	ISBN 0 352 33337 5	£5.99
☐ IN THE FLESH Emma Holly	ISBN 0 352 33498 3	£5.99
☐ A PRIVATE VIEW Crystalle Valentino	ISBN 0 352 33308 1	£5.99
☐ SHAMELESS Stella Black	ISBN 0 352 33485 1	£5.99
☐ INTENSE BLUE Lyn Wood	ISBN 0 352 33496 7	£5.99
☐ THE NAKED TRUTH Natasha Rostova	ISBN 0 352 33497 5	£5.99
☐ ANIMAL PASSIONS Martine Marquand	ISBN 0 352 33499 1	£5.99
☐ A SPORTING CHANCE Susie Raymond	ISBN 0 352 33501 7	£5.99
☐ TAKING LIBERTIES Susie Raymond	ISBN 0 352 33357 X	£5.99
☐ A SCANDALOUS AFFAIR Holly Graham	ISBN 0 352 33523 8	£5.99
☐ THE NAKED FLAME Crystalle Valentino	ISBN 0 352 33528 9	£5.99
☐ ON THE EDGE Laura Hamilton	ISBN 0 352 33534 3	£5.99
☐ LURED BY LUST Tania Picarda	ISBN 0 352 33533 5	£5.99
☐ THE HOTTEST PLACE Tabitha Flyte	ISBN 0 352 33536 X	£5.99
☐ THE NINETY DAYS OF GENEVIEVE Lucinda Carrington	ISBN 0 352 33070 8	£5.99
☐ EARTHY DELIGHTS Tesni Morgan	ISBN 0 352 33548 3	£5.99
☐ MAN HUNT Cathleen Ross	ISBN 0 352 33583 1	
☐ MÉNAGE Emma Holly	ISBN 0 352 33231 X	
☐ DREAMING SPIRES Juliet Hastings	ISBN 0 352 33584 X	
☐ THE TRANSFORMATION Natasha Rostova	ISBN 0 352 33311 1	
☐ STELLA DOES HOLLYWOOD Stella Black	ISBN 0 352 33588 2	
☐ SIN.NET Helena Ravenscroft	ISBN 0 352 33598 X	
☐ HOTBED Portia Da Costa	ISBN 0 352 33614 5	
☐ TWO WEEKS IN TANGIER Annabel Lee	ISBN 0 352 33599 8	
☐ HIGHLAND FLING Jane Justine	ISBN 0 352 33616 1	
☐ PLAYING HARD Tina Troy	ISBN 0 352 33617 X	

To find out the latest information about Black Lace titles, check out the website: www.blacklace-books.co.uk or send for a booklist with complete synopses by writing to:

Black Lace Booklist, Virgin Books Ltd
Thames Wharf Studios
Rainville Road
London W6 9HA

Please include an SAE of decent size. Please note only British stamps are valid.

Our privacy policy
We will not disclose information you supply us to any other parties. We will not disclose any information which identifies you personally to any person without your express consent.

From time to time we may send out information about Black Lace books and special offers. Please tick here if you do not wish to receive Black Lace information. ❑

Please send me the books I have ticked above.

Name ....

Address ....

....

....

....

Post Code ....

Send to: Cash Sales, Black Lace Books, Thames Wharf Studios, Rainville Road, London W6 9HA.

US customers: for prices and details of how to order books for delivery by mail, call 1-800-343-4499.

Please enclose a cheque or postal order, made payable to Virgin Books Ltd, to the value of the books you have ordered plus postage and packing costs as follows:

UK and BFPO – £1.00 for the first book, 50p for each subsequent book.

Overseas (including Republic of Ireland) – £2.00 for the first book, £1.00 for each subsequent book.

If you would prefer to pay by VISA, ACCESS/MASTERCARD, DINERS CLUB, AMEX or SWITCH, please write your card number and expiry date here:

....

Signature ....

Please allow up to 28 days for delivery.